About the Author

Rachel Moore has been writing since before she could write (her poor mother had to put pen to paper as young Rachel expertly dictated stories). She is surrounded by a wonderful family and friends and her amazing boyfriend, Matt. She also owns as many pets as her landlord will allow her to have at one time. Rachel lives in Saint Louis, Missouri. This is her first novel. Your comments are welcome at rachelmoorewrites@gmail.com

The Space Between

Rachel Moore

The Space Between

Olympia Publishers
London

www.olympiapublishers.com
OLYMPIA PAPERBACK EDITION

A CIP catalogue record for this title is
available from the British Library.

ISBN: 978-1-78830-381-1

First Published in 2019

Olympia Publishers
60 Cannon Street
London
EC4N 6NP
Printed in Great Britain

Dedication

For my mom, who always knew I could. Love you mostest.

Acknowledgements

I would like to extend my deepest thanks to my family (Mom, Dad, and my brother, Brad) for your continuous support over the years. You've been my foundation and I love you all! I could never have made it this far without each of you.

I would like to thank my boyfriend, Matt, the love of my life. You've been so patient with me during this process, even when I made you read the book with specific instructions to tell me if I did okay writing as a boy (ha ha). Your suggestions for book design were invaluable. I used to think that getting a book published would be the best thing that ever happened to me, but then I met you. Turns out the book was the second best thing in my life.

I would like to thank my cousin, Sarah Ranney, for taking the photo of me used in the book during what she called "remembering to bring my camera when we were going to hang out together anyway", but what I refer to as "The Epic Photo Shoot".

I would like to thank you, the reader, for giving this book a chance! (Especially if you are NOT related to me, because I expect all my family and friends to buy this book just because they are so faithful to me). Every book purchased is deeply appreciated, as you are believing in me as a writer ... and helping to pay for my shopping addiction. Hello, Amazon Prime.

Lastly, I would like to thank the staff at Olympia, for believing in me and my work. I appreciate all your help with my manuscript. Your staff have been excellent to work with thus far. (And, if this acknowledgment has earned me any brownie points, I look forward to working with you in future endeavors as well ... hint hint).

Enjoy!
Rachel Moore

CHAPTER ONE

Nick and Sam were brothers. Well, not biologically speaking, but they may as well have been. The summer when they were both eight years old Nick swiped his father's pocket knife and the two of them hurriedly climbed the ladder which led up to his tree house. There they each carefully pricked the palms of their hands until a tiny speck of blood bubbled to the surface, bright and dark red. Then they spat on their palms and shook hands, as men do, which made them blood brothers and therefore sealed the strongest bond possible that two boys who are not *technically* related could have. Each boy knew that the other's blood and saliva coursed through their veins, circulated through their hearts, and that therefore every beat of life that took place in their bodies was a part of the other boy as well.

The ritual that had taken place three summers ago was not the only thing that bonded the boys. They practically shared a birthday, which surely meant that they were predestined to be the very best of friends, as they were born only three days apart from one another, and in the same hospital at that! Surely they were supposed to have been twins, but somewhere, in the great scheme of things, something had gotten mixed up and each boy had ended up in the womb of a separate woman.

Nick and Sam didn't let this small error of the universe bother them too much, as they were aware that the way things are and the way things should have been don't always match up. Both boys had agreed, after discussing the situation at length, that Sam should have been born to Nick's parents. It had been declared that Nick's parents were decidedly the better of the two sets.

Nick's father was an actual *dad*, as opposed to Sam's, who was definitely a *father*. Mr. Lynch allowed Sam to call him Pete, as grown-ups hardly ever did, and he was superb at all things sports related. Both boys were thrilled when Pete got out whatever ball, puck, or racket the situation or season required, and taught them the correct way to catch a fly ball or tackle an opponent. Pete always had time for the boys, and he had a deep jolly laugh that started in his belly and worked its way up through his throat until it exploded out of his mouth, causing his whole body to shake.

As wonderful as Nick's dad was, his mother was even better. May Lynch (who actually allowed Sam to call her 'Mom', as if she also understood that the two boys were meant to be part of the same family, although Sam had felt too strange to do that and had stuck with her using her first name instead) was always baking fabulous desserts and telling stories. According to May, her mother had always wanted to have a daughter and she had always wanted to name that daughter 'May'. When she got married, May's mother insisted that she and her husband only practice the art of making love during the month when conception would produce a child in May. Her husband, however, apparently had other ideas, and as the story goes, there was a lot of love-making going on throughout every month of the year. When she did give birth to her daughter it was during the cold month of December, about as far away from May as one can get. However, May said that her mother was nothing if not stubborn, and insisted that the infant was to carry the namesake of the month of which she should have come into the world.

Nick and Sam enjoyed this story very much. Although Nick's grandmother had passed away before he was born, the boys agreed that they would have liked her. Obviously she, too, understood that the great plans of God or anybody else could go awry. She knew she was supposed to have that baby in the summer, but something caused something else to change, and little May popped out on Christmas Eve instead.

Despite the obvious discrepancies between the calendar and the name, May's name actually suited her quite well. May Lynch was very much like the month she was named for; her very presence was like a burst of fresh spring air after a cold, bleak winter. She also tended to smell like honeysuckle, no matter what the season. The boys imagined the scent came from her shampoo or soap or perfume, but a thorough investigation of the bathroom one afternoon left them wondering. Perhaps if the smell didn't come from some man-made source, it came from May herself, somehow seeping out of the pores of her skin as if she, herself, was the very essence of spring.

Sam would never admit it to Nick, but he was very much in love with May. He had actually mentioned it once. It was sometime during the last winter, and it was too cold to play outside so the boys had taken to Nick's room to play a boring game of checkers, which neither of them was very interested in.

Nick had been going on and on about some girl at school that he had the hots for, and Sam felt that he needed to add something to the conversation, so he said shyly, "I really love your mom."

He had been worried about his friend's reaction, but Nick simply shrugged and said, "Of course you do, everyone does."

Now that the words had been spoken out loud, Sam felt that they needed to be understood. Nick had to realize that he wasn't speaking of her in terms of simply being his friend's mother. "No, no, I mean, I love not just your mom, but *May!*"

Sam then bit his lower lip, as he often did when he was nervous, and wondered if Nick would be happy or sad that one day after Sam was just a bit older, and made his affections known, he would become Nick's step-father. It did make Sam sad that Pete Lynch would somehow have be out of the picture at this point, but Sam figured that the feelings he carried for May were so strong that obviously they were meant to be together; nature had simply messed up again by getting the timing all wrong, and once everyone understood the situation then Pete would happily bow out. He would shed a single tear and say stoically, "You're right, Sam. I shall give you my wife, with no hard feelings. The better man has won." But since Pete was a great guy, Sam would continue to invite him over for the lunches that his new wife would make, because she was a great cook, and there was no reason to deny that to Pete. He could come once a week for dinner even, on Sundays perhaps.

Nick wasn't even looking at his friend, he was musing over the checker board, contemplating where to move his piece. He haphazardly slid a black chip over by one square. Nick was always black, and Sam was always red.

"Oh, you mean like the month of May?" he asked, peering over at Sam's pieces. "Yeah, I can't wait till it gets warmer out too. Winter sucks."

Sam realized that his friend was maybe unable to absorb the depth of the information that he was being given, and therefore, rather consciously or subconsciously, had decided to misunderstand the information.

Sam nodded, allowing his friend to think that he had been talking of the seasons, and took his turn in the game. Maybe it was easier this way, to allow Nick to become a bit more mature, before throwing this new life upon him.

Everyone always thought that Nick was the 'leader' of the two of them, that he was wiser and more knowledgeable in general. In some ways that was true. Nick definitely knew things that other boys their age didn't know, a fact that made him very popular in school. Sam was smart too, but he understood things like science and history. Nick knew things that were actually important, like how girls got pregnant, and what a blow job was, and how you should steal one of your mom's bras to practice how to unhook it, 'cause real women appreciated things like that. His information was not always accurate, but his peers were ignorant to that fact and therefore accepted everything he said as truth. Nick was also older by three days, four hours, and two minutes, so he had obviously seen more of the world than Sam had, a fact which couldn't be argued.

Sam fell into his role as 'follower', only because he was happy enough to allow Nick to take the lead. What people didn't realize, however, was that Sam knew a lot more than he let on, and in fact was the actual leader in many ways. He often steered Nick to figuring something out on his own, allowing him to believe that he had come up with a solution to a problem by himself.

It was like that now, when Sam knew that Nick simply wasn't ready to hear the full truth, so he softened the blow, figuring there would be plenty of time to get into all of those things in the years ahead.

The Lynch's were also wonderful because they practically let Sam live with them, as the boys knew that nature had always intended anyway. Occasionally Sam would worry that he was overstaying his welcome, but anytime he mentioned it Pete or May, they would simply smile fondly at him, ruffle his hair, and say that he was such a polite young man and that he was always a pleasure to have around, plus that they understood his home 'situation'. That was all it was ever referred to as, the 'situation', and it seemed enough of a reason for Sam to be welcome at any hour of any day at their home. Eventually, Sam stopped bringing it up altogether, finally confident that he was truly welcome and was in fact the nearest thing to a family member that he could be, what with only sharing a single drop of the Lynch blood.

On this day the heat was unusually stifling, even for mid-July. The boys were up in the tree house attempting to fan themselves with pieces of cardboard. The makeshift fans did no good, they just forced more of the sticky hot air into their faces, and rather than providing any relief they only served in making the boys' arms tired.

Nick stopped fanning himself as a sudden tingling pain shot up his arm, making it feel numb and fiery. He gave his arm a fast shake, watching his skin jiggle but without actually feeling it.

Sam inhaled deeply and was certain that he caught a whiff of a fresh apple pie just coming out of the oven. This was probably not so, since the tree house was pretty far back from the actual house, but Sam believed that he had some kind of sixth sense where May was involved, and perhaps if she was currently smelling the sweet scent of sugary apples and doughy crust than he was, too.

"Man, this heat is killer!" Nick moaned, rolling onto his stomach and propping his head up in his hands.

Sam nodded his agreement. It was the kind of heat that made your whole body immediately be covered in a sheen of sweat as soon as you walked outdoors. You always felt wet and sticky, and dark stains formed in the armpits of your shirt that never seemed to go away.

Sam glanced at Nick's shirt and didn't notice any similar stains. He knew that his friend had been using deodorant for some time now, and he was intensely jealous. Sam could smell the ripeness of his own body, and he was sure that others could smell it as well. It seemed a very grown-up thing for Nick to be doing, and Sam longed for a stick of deodorant of his own. Yet he was far too embarrassed to ask Nick to borrow his. That didn't seem right, and he knew that his own parents would probably not buy him any. He hoped that May wouldn't think he smelled bad, that would be especially humiliating, and Sam could feel his face flushing as he thought of it. May was far too polite to say so, but Sam knew that she would want her future husband to be a real man, a user of deodorant, or no doubt she would be embarrassed to introduce him to her friends, who may be asking themselves when he drew near, "My, what *is* that smell?"

"Wow, look at the tits on this one. I wouldn't kick her out of bed."

Sam's attention was jerked back to his friend, who was now leafing through a magazine full of naked women. The magazine, and a few others like it, had been taken from Sam's father. Sam had once mentioned seeing such a magazine peeking out from under the couch in his father's study, and Nick had been extremely excited and demanded that the boys sneak in at the earliest possible time to ransack the place. They had found three magazines in all, although there must have been many more, as the thievery had to be done quickly, and since, Mr. Mavers had never mentioned anything being missing. He would have mentioned it too; he would have beat Sam to within an inch of his life if he had had any clue.

Because of this, and because he was a little embarrassed about the women in the pictures, Sam had been reluctant to go on the stealing expedition. Yet Nick had been persistent, as he always was, and won out in the end, as he always did, by insisting that it was worth the risk and that they would surely become the most popular boys in school. Sam neglected to point out that of course it was worth the risk to Nick, as he would not be the one punished, but Nick didn't seem to think about things like that.

Sam wondered now if his father had noticed the missing items, but had simply been too embarrassed about their contents to mention anything to his son. Either way, Sam believed that it was a small miracle that he had gotten out unscathed, and with something to show for it besides.

That had been last summer, and a year later the magazines were all dog-eared and wrinkled, but were altogether not in too bad a condition because Nick insisted that they be treated with such care.

"Which one, lemme see," Sam said, laying down on his stomach next to his friend.

Although they had looked at every picture so many times that both boys had each one virtually memorized, it was still fun to occasionally pull the magazines out and pretend to look at them anew, noticing this or that that hadn't been noticed before.

"This chick, here," Nick said, tapping his finger on the page. "Man, what I wouldn't do to be able to squeeze a set of tits like that."

Sam nodded but said nothing. He was sure that if Nick had ever been presented with such a situation, he would giggle uncontrollably and run away. Nick liked to talk a big game. He liked to use curse words and sex words and words that he probably had no idea of what they actually meant. This always impressed the other boys at school, but it didn't impress Sam. Nick was such a child in so many ways, whereas Sam was wise beyond his years in a way that he couldn't explain, and because he couldn't explain it, he didn't bother to try. He simply let Nick and the Lynch's and the teachers and everyone else go on thinking that he was just an eleven-year-old, with an eleven-year-olds' thoughts, although Sam knew that he was different from everyone else his own age. From everyone else of any age, for that matter.

Looking at the pictures in the magazines was more to satisfy a scientific curiosity for Sam. He did long to know things about the fairer sex, not in a sexual way exactly, but just to *know*. Sam understood that when the time came he would be with his beautiful, mature, loving May, the woman that had always been there for him since practically the day he was born. Therefore, he felt no need to waste time thinking of the girls in his school or the women in these pictures as other boys seemed to do all the time.

"Yep," Nick continued, not seeming to notice or care if Sam was paying any attention to him. "Those are definitely some of the best tits I've ever seen."

Sam knew that the images in the magazines were in fact the only tits that Nick had ever seen, or was likely ever to see anytime soon. Nick liked to tell the other boys that Melissa McMeyers, who was thirteen and a well-known whore, had pulled up her shirt and let him grab her boobs, but Sam didn't believe that for a moment. He had pretended to be impressed like the other boys had been, asking questions about what they felt like and if her nipples got hard or not, and giggling and pounding one another on the back. In truth though, Sam thought the chances of Melissa McMeyers allowing Nick to do that, he was a mere child compared to her, were very slim indeed. Most of the boys had a crush on Melissa, primarily because she suddenly seemed to sprout boobs out of nowhere. One day she was as flat-chested as all the other girls, and then suddenly, bam! She had two beautiful mounds of womanhood under her soft pink sweater. Around her, the boys either became slack-jawed, practically drooling, or they became rambunctious, accidently-on-purpose bumping into her, and high-fiving one another on their success.

The only breasts that interested Sam were those belonging to a real woman, his May, and he would never belittle her by calling them *boobs* or *tits* or any other raunchy name that Nick could come up with. Occasionally he would use such words around his friends, although it was uncomfortable for him to do so, but Sam understood the need for putting up a front around his peers, or around anyone. He had to seem like the other boys, he had to appear to be normal, although Sam was about as far from normal as a person could be. Even around his best friend/brother, although so much was shared between them, Sam knew that Nick wouldn't understand some things about his life; he simply wasn't capable of it, so Sam had to act the part.

Sam's life required him to do a lot of acting, and he often played a different role depending on who he was with. When he was with the Lynch family, he was polite and helpful. Around his teachers, Sam was studious and well-spoken. When in the company of his classmates, he mostly copied their raucous behavior so that he would fit in better, or at least stand out less. Being in his own home required the most acting of all, because this was the role that wasn't even human. It was here that Sam had to play the part of the mouse, trying to stir as little as possible, make the smallest amount of noise, and attract the least amount of attention, all while avoiding the traps that waited for him around every corner.

It was only when he was alone with Nick that Sam felt the most like himself, although after so many years of playing parts, Sam wasn't entirely sure he knew who that was anymore. Maybe at some point you just became the character that you were pretending to be? No, Sam didn't think so. Some truths were just too obvious, no matter how much you wished they weren't. They would come bubbling up to the surface at just the most inopportune moment, and Sam would have to use his acting skills to push them back down and keep them at bay.

"It's too hot in here," Nick stated suddenly, closing the magazine and carefully putting it back in its hiding place, in the crate under the old blanket that smelled like mold.

"Do you want to ride bikes?" Sam asked, knowing it would probably fall to him to come up with a new, more fun idea.

"Eh." Nick shrugged as he brought himself up into a sitting position, crossing his legs and drumming his fingers on his knees.

"C'mon, if we pedal really fast the breeze will help to cool us off," Sam urged, sitting up as well.

Nick sighed loudly and replied, "Sure, why not. It's not like there's anything else more exciting to do in this shitty town." He stood up and stretched awkwardly, since he had had a growth spurt recently and didn't fit into the tree house as well as he used to.

Sam followed suit, although when he stood up he was able to stretch his arms to their full length above his head. He wondered if his own growth spurt would be coming soon. He hoped that when it did, his mother might decide it was time for him to have deodorant. It was very difficult to ask his mother for things, and unless the situation was particularly urgent he normally just hoped that she would recognize his need on her own. Sam wondered how long it would take before the smell of his body would force him to raise this need to the category of 'urgent'.

As the boys climbed out of the tree house a quick breeze sent the smell from Sam's sweaty underarms straight to his nostrils, and he decided that it probably wouldn't be that long after all.

Nick led the way to the rusty yellow shed that sat in the corner of the Lynch's backyard. He gave the door a swift kick, which always helped it to move more promptly, and pulled it open. The door hesitated, then opened with a stiff groan.

The boys squinted as they walked into the sudden shadow. As the sunlight found its way into the darkened shed, its contents became recognizable. The riding lawnmower took up the bulk of the space. It had been purchased only two years prior and therefore wasn't as rusty and dirty as many of the other objects. Nick said that he had heard his father telling his mother that it was high time for a rider, that his knees would give out before he was forty, and that the local hardware store was having a huge sale. Pete must be as persuasive as his son could be.

There were several red plastic gasoline jugs, and although they were empty the containers still gave off a strong smell of gas. There were two gallons of Sea Green paint, though neither boy could find anything in the home or yard that had ever or would ever be needed to be painted such a color. There was a giant chest that appeared to be made out of some type of strong plastic, similar to the Tupperware that May put her leftover baked goods in. The boys had long since gone through the chest, but it only held some boring looking papers and a pair of roller skates with one wheel missing off the right skate which had apparently belonged to May in her youth (oh, how Sam had fantasized about watching his love careening through a park, the wind whipping her hair behind her!).

Stored more prominently in the shed, right in the front, were two bikes. The first was brand new and a brilliant red, so bright that it seemed to be emitting light all on its own, even when being ridden on a cloudy day. There were old baseball cards placed securely in the spokes of its wheels, and the seat was made of a rich black leather and embroidered with white. A sparkling brass bell was fastened to the handlebars and made a delightful chiming sound when rung.

The second bike was smaller than the first, and a person couldn't be certain upon first glance exactly what color the bike was. At first it appeared to be grey, but in a different light it would take on more of a light blue luster, as the bike had been painted more than once during its lifetime and now retained colors of both coats of paint. The boys had discussed the possibility of painting the entire thing sea green, but it was decided that a fresh coat of paint in such an atrocious color would hurt the bike more than help it. The seat had a gaping hole where some of the stuffing tried to ooze out. A piece of duct tape held back a spring that was always threatening to poke its way though, much to the surprise of its rider. The spokes of the wheels had been bent so that they stuck out at a weird angle. When the bike had been purchased for five dollars at a garage sale, its one redeeming quality had seemed to be the fact that it, too, had come with a bell. It wasn't until later, however, that the rider realized that the bell had been broken many years earlier, and now refused to make a sound.

Each boy grabbed the bike to which he claimed ownership of, and they were on their way.

"C'mon, Sam, catch up!" Nick hollered as he pedaled through the uneven terrain of his backyard, then out onto the street, ringing his bell all the while, signaling to the neighborhood that he was out and about.

Sam struggled momentarily as his front wheel came into contact with a small branch. He swerved too far to the left, but he was able to quickly correct for it and regain his balance.

Sam pedaled hard to make up for lost time, finally pulling up alongside his friend, and the two found an even pace, sailing easily along the street.

The subdivision of Stony Meadows had neither stones nor meadows, but it was a quiet street with few houses which sat on relatively large yards. The Lynch's owned one of the houses towards the end of road where the street veered into a cul-de-sac. This was an excellent area for bike riding because it was nice and flat with extra surface area. There were hardly any cars to contend with, and everyone in the neighborhood knew the Lynch boy and his Little Friend, so drivers were gracious in letting them pass.

If the boys were to head in the opposite direction, the street sloped gradually downward which gave the bikes just enough momentum to get going very fast. The street then went back uphill, but just a little, and if you had gained enough speed on the way down then you could actually coast up the brief hill without having to pedal at all. It was like defying gravity.

Today, Nick decided that they should start by biking toward the cul-de-sac, and the boys kept an easy pace as they rode around and around. Apparently, however, this was just a warm-up, because suddenly Nick grinned, dinged his bell, and shot off in the other direction, down the hill.

Sam hooted and shoved off after him, watching with a near morbid fascination as his friend picked up speed and then raised his hands into the air above his head, cheering "Wooo!" as he rode.

Sam never rode with his hands raised, especially not when going down a hill. Riding at a few paces behind Nick, Sam tried to enjoy the breeze that was now flowing over his body, cooling the sweat from his forehead and his armpits. As the bike gained energy, Sam clutched the handlebars more tightly. He watched as Nick reached the bottom of the hill and felt a wisp of envy. Sam wondered if, when a person rode their bike with their hands up like that, they indeed felt as though they were flying.

The boys biked for nearly an hour before hunger sent them back to Nick's house.

After stowing their bikes back in the shed, they trotted inside, still high off their ride.

"Mo-om, we're hungry!" Nick shouted as he kicked off his shoes and padded through the living room and into the kitchen. Sam scurried along behind him.

"Hey there, you two, did you have a good ride? I saw you pedaling back and forth out the window," May answered with a smile. The kitchen was in the front of the house and faced the street, where a window above the sink looked out onto the road.

"It was very nice, thank you," Sam answered, pulling out a chair from the kitchen table and sinking onto it.

"Is there anything to eat?" Nick asked, opening the refrigerator and peering in.

Sam wondered if, whenever his own growth spurt hit, he would be as hungry as Nick always seemed to be.

"Well, dinner will be ready in only an hour or so, and I wouldn't want you to spoil your appetites," May began, but smiled indulgently as her son made an exasperated face. "Oh, all right, there are still some cookies left over. Just don't eat too many."

Nick leapt up and raced to the cookie jar, grabbing two cookies and tossing one to Sam. As his mother turned her back back toward the oven, he quickly grabbed three more.

"Sam," she asked without turning around, still busy at the stove, "will you be joining us for dinner this evening? I have pot roast and carrots, and I'm mashing up some potatoes now. Plus there's fresh apple pie for dessert!"

So, Sam thought, *I was right about the pie after all*. It pleased him to know that they were in fact so connected with one another.

"Sure, May, that would be great!" he answered with enthusiasm, and May turned around and gave him a quick wink, which sent his heart quivering.

The asking and answering to dinner was a mere formality. Sam ate dinner at the Lynch home nearly every night; it was really just assumed at this point. He wondered why they even bothered with the dialogue at all. Perhaps to keep up some form of normalcy? After all, most boys would have to ask permission to stay later at a friends' house. But the Lynch's knew, as did Sam, that he wasn't like most kids, because of the 'situation' and all. No, the Mavers would just assume that their son stayed in the Lynch household as long as possible.

"Can I help you get anything ready, May?" he asked hopefully.

"Suck-up!" Nick whispered, but it wasn't in a mean way. Nick was used to his friend being a little peculiar around adults, his mother especially. It didn't bother him any, and often Nick actually benefitted from the never-ending politeness of his friend.

"You're so sweet to offer, Sam, but no, everything is under control. Why don't the two of you go find something to do in Nick's room, and I'll call you when it's ready?"

"Okay, May," Sam answered.

"Okay-May, Okay-May!" Nick parroted, dancing around and shoving another cookie into his mouth. "Have a nice day, May. In the kitchen, we shall not stay."

Sam grinned and quipped, "In Nick's bedroom, we will play."

Nick hooted and yelled, "How 'bout another cookie, whatdaya say?"

May grinned and chased them out of the kitchen, calling, "You two get out of my way!"

Laughing, the boys ran out of the kitchen, the smells of roast and potatoes and apples lingering in their noses. And, as always, it was mixed with a brief hint of honeysuckle.

CHAPTER TWO

Dylan Murphy's dog, Shelia, had puppies. It was by far the most interesting thing to happen in Stony Meadows in quite some time.

Dylan lived nearby, only a three minute and twenty-two second bike ride away, and Nick and Sam made it a point to visit often.

They were very disappointed to have missed the birth itself, as both had been looking forward to watching a bunch of blood and goo come out of a dog's butt. Dylan claimed that he had watched the whole thing, but then he slipped up by admitting that the birth had happened overnight while he was sound asleep. Sheila slept in a dog bed in the garage, so he hadn't heard any commotion.

There were five puppies in all. Sheila wasn't a big dog, she was a mutt of some sort, and the puppies were unbelievable tiny. They didn't even look like real dogs; they were just squirming little masses, their eyes squeezed shut.

Nick would scoop one up at random and turn it over in his hands, inspecting it to see if it was a boy or a girl (three boys, two girls). He once tried to throw a tennis ball, but soon realized that neither Sheila nor the day-old puppies were interested in playing fetch.

Sam was more gentle with them, holding them close to his chest to keep them warm and stroking their soft fur, cooing to them when Nick wasn't close enough to notice. He always made sure never to hold a single puppy for too long, being careful to return it to its mother. Sam knew that the mother dog could offer a comfort to her young that he could not.

Obviously, they would have to be named immediately. Dylan made the argument that since they were his dogs, he should be allowed to name three of them, but he generously allowed Nick and Sam to each name one also, assuming that Nick would bring one of his magazines for him to look at during their next visit.

It was a fair deal and the boys readily agreed. The puppies were various shades of white to light brown, some with blotches of darker brown in various locations on their bodies. Dylan choose his puppies first, picking the three darkest ones. Nick got to choose next, since it was his magazine that had sealed the deal, and he chose the light brown one, mostly because it was the only remaining male. That left Sam with the white puppy that was unfortunate enough to have a large brown spot on the top-left center of her head, as well as being the runt of the litter. Dylan and Nick thought this dog was funny looking, but actually Sam was very pleased because the dog had actually been his first pick. More than anyone else, Sam knew what it was like to be different, and he believed that he and this puppy shared a kinship.

Dylan named his puppies Larry, Moe, and Curly, not caring that one of them was a girl. He would often forget which puppy he had assigned which name to, and took to calling all three of them 'The Three Stooges', often not using their individual names at all.

Although they dared not mention it, Nick and Sam agreed that Dylan was completely unoriginal and obviously lacked all matter of creativity. They vowed to give their puppies fabulous, unique, well-thought-out names. It was necessary to consider the naming process overnight, as they didn't want to rush anything.

On the second day they visited, the boys expected that the puppies would have their eyes open and be more active. They were surprised to see that the situation was basically the exact same as it had been the day before.

Nick scooped up his puppy and said, "I christen thee 'Raphael' after the best Teenage Mutant Ninja Turtle. When you get older I will put a bandana over your head with little holes cut out for your eyes so that you can see. You will be a crime-fighting dog and all your brothers and sisters will be jealous."

Sam approved of the name that his friend had chosen, but he was especially proud of the name he had come up with. He picked up the tiny white puppy and spoke softly to her. "Hello, little puppy, I'm in charge of naming you so I'm gonna call you Charlotte, after the spider in Charlotte's Web. She was very helpful to that poor little pig that no one liked. I wanted to name you Wilbur, after him, but then I remembered that you're a little girl dog but I thought Charlotte was a pretty good name. What do you think?"

The puppy squirmed in his hands and let out a soft whine, which Sam took as a sign of approval. He nuzzled his cheek against Charlotte, feeling her soft warm body against his skin, and whispered, "I'm gonna do everything I can to make my parents let me keep you when you get bigger. They will probably say no, but I'm gonna try real hard."

Gingerly, Sam placed the puppy back down between her siblings, where she immediately began to search out her mother's teat and began suckling.

"You know, human babies do that too," Nick said, watching the puppies drink.

"Duh, everyone knows that," Dylan answered, his nose buried in the magazine Nick had brought. "Do you think that Melissa McMeyers squirts milk out of her boobs too?"

Nick scrunched up his forehead as he pondered the question. He didn't like to admit when he didn't know an answer, so he normally just made one up. "Yeah, of course she does."

"But my sister has little boobs and I never see anything coming out of those," Dylan pointed out, glancing up from the magazine.

"Well, how old is Katie?"

She's twelve, one year older than us."

"Well, that explains it then," Nick scoffed. "The milk doesn't start shooting out 'till the girl turns thirteen. Then it just goes all over the place, and the girl has to wear little containers taped to each of her tits to keep the milk from making a mess."

"That's not true."

"Sure it is," Nick answered, getting warmed up to his story. "When your sister has her birthday, look out. If she hasn't attached those little cups yet, that milk is gonna come squirting out and it will get all over you. Then you'll be covered with your sister's boob juice."

"You're lying! That's not the way it works," Dylan cried, although he didn't look entirely convinced with his own argument.

"Wait and see for yourself then, but I'd wear a raincoat on that day if I were you."

All of the boys threw their heads back and laughed loudly. They knew that the story Nick had told wasn't completely true, but it was probably at least partly true, and besides, they didn't have any better ideas.

"So how long until these puppies are ready to start playing?" Nick asked, picking up the tennis ball from yesterday and throwing it in the air.

"I don't know. Maybe by tomorrow? Or in a month?"

"You don't know anything, Dylan," Nick said, sighing. He laid down on his back and threw the ball up and down, wiggling as he tried to get comfortable on the hard cement floor.

"Do so. I know lots of stuff. You probably don't even know who the president is."

"What in the hell are you talking about? That smartass Sarah Connelly is our class president."

"I meant the President of the United States, dumbass."

"It's Ronald Reagan, *dumbass*."

Before the boys could continue their squabble, the door to the garage opened and Dylan's mother stuck her head out.

"Did I just hear you use a curse word, Nick?" she asked accusingly.

"Yes, he did," Dylan answered. "Nick is a very bad influence on me."

"Bad influence or not, I think it's time that your guests went home for the day. You boys are more than welcome to come back tomorrow to visit, but it's getting late and Dylan needs to come get cleaned up for dinner."

"Okay, Mrs. Murphy," Nick and Sam chorused in unison. They said a quick goodbye to the puppies and patted Sheila on the head, which made her wag her tail. She was probably jealous that her kids were getting all the attention lately. Then they sauntered out of the open garage door to where Nick's bike was held up by its kickstand and Sam's bike, lacking a kickstand, lay in the grass.

"So, do you think your mom will let you keep Charlotte?" Nick asked as they pedaled back toward his house. Nick's dad was allergic to dogs, so it was already assumed that Raphael would be given to another family, unless Dylan could convince his mother to let him keep all the puppies, which he was trying hard to do.

"I don't know, but I really hope so. It would be so nice to have a pet, especially one as cool as Charlotte."

"Yeah, that would be cool."

The boys rode in silence for a while, each contemplating what it would be like to have a dog of their very own.

When they arrived back at the Lynch's house the boys carefully stowed their bikes in the shed. Pete was a super nice guy, but he was strict on a few things, one of which was that his yard didn't look too cluttered up with the boys' toys.

May walked out the backdoor and smiled. "Welcome back. I was just about to give Mrs. Murphy a call to send you boys home. Dinner is almost ready. I made spaghetti with meatballs, and there's enough to feed an army. Sam, would you be willing to join us for dinner to help us eat all this food?"

"Sure, May, that sounds great. Thank you."

"Is there Parmesan cheese?" Nick asked. "And garlic bread?"

"I wouldn't have it any other way," May promised him, winking at Sam.

Sam liked when May winked at him. It was like she was acknowledging the special bond they shared. He hoped that when he grew older and became her husband, she would continue the habit. He noticed as he followed her inside that May was wearing a light blue T-shirt that fit just tightly enough across the chest to show off her round breasts. Sam wondered if she still had milk in them, and made a mental note to look in it up in the encyclopedia set in the school library when the summer was over. What would he look under, though? Milk? Breasts? Never mind, he had plenty of time to figure it out.

***

Nick and Sam took great pleasure in watching the puppies as they developed. Within weeks their eyes opened and they began walking clumsily away from their mother, although never *too* far away, to explore the world around them. Soon, Dylan's mom had told them, it would be time to find homes for them all.

Sam had been putting it off, practicing his speech over and over, but he decided that the time had come to approach his parents about keeping Charlotte.

Sam waited until his father was away at work and his mother seemed to be in a relatively cheerful mood.

"Mom?" he asked, walking into the living room where his mother was watching television. "Can I ask you about something?"

"What is it?"

"Well, the thing is, that since I don't have any brothers or sisters, and since my friends aren't really allowed to come and visit me here, and since I always do my homework and my chores and-"

"For God's sake, Sam, just spit it out already."

"I was wondering if I could get a puppy," he said in a rush. "And not just any puppy, but a special one named Charlotte. I've know her since she was just one day old, and she is a very good dog, and we could have her for free. Plus I would completely promise to take care of her; you and Dad wouldn't have to do a thing."

"Absolutely not," his mother answered in a monotone, not bothering to avert her eyes from the TV.

Sam wasn't ready to admit defeat. "But she would keep me company, and it would make me so happy, and I hardly ask for anything."

"Sam," his mother said, finally turning to look at him. "Do you have any clue how much trouble a puppy is? They are messy, they chew everything up, they shit all over the house, and you have to take them to the vet, plus they're expensive."

"I would take care of her; I would take her for walks and feed her and train her not to go to the bathroom or chew things up. I would clean up after her and cut grass for the neighbors to earn the money to keep her."

"Sorry, but the answer is no." His mother turned her attention back to the TV.

Sam lowered his head and squeezed his eyes shut, hot tears welling up behind his eyelids and threatening to spill over. Although he cried often, he hated to do so in front of his parents, so he quickly ran to his room.

He could hear his mother's voice calling after him, "You didn't *really* think your dad would let you have a puppy, did you?"

Sam closed the door to his bedroom and wished for the millionth time that his dad hadn't removed the lock on the door. He threw himself down on his bed and allowed the tears to fall, sobbing over the dog that he knew the universe had meant to belong to him, and scared for both her future and his.

It was a Friday, which was never a good day in the Maver household. If at all possible, Sam tried especially hard to spend the weekend nights at Nick's house, but the Lynch family was on vacation for the week. Friday was payday for his father, which meant that as soon as he got off work at the steel factory, he would head to the bar. The later he got back, the worse it would be.

That was why when Sam finally woke up after crying himself to sleep, looked at the clock on his nightstand and saw that it was past midnight, he got worried.

He heard his father's car pull into the driveway and saw the shadows disappear from his bedroom wall as the lights from the car were shut off. He heard the front door open followed by heavy footsteps, getting louder by the minute.

It was warm in his bedroom but Sam shivered and scurried down into the blanket that was resting on the foot of his bed, pulling it around him until his entire body was covered. He could hear himself breathing, and his breath felt hot as it bounced off the blanket and came back into his face.

Suddenly, his door was flung open, the light switched on, and the cover was pulled back and thrown on the floor. The sudden light made Sam blink.

"Sweetheart, it's the middle of the night, why don't you just let him sleep?" Sam's mother was asking as she followed her husband into the bedroom.

"Are you kidding me?" his father boomed. His breath stank of cheap scotch. "I work all day to provide for this family, and I get home, and there are dirty dishes piled up in the sink!"

Sam shrunk down into his bed, trying to make himself appear smaller. He realized that he had been so upset over the dog that he had fallen asleep without doing his evening chores.

"That's my fault, actually," his mom was stammering. "Sam was really upset earlier, and when I came to check on him he was sound asleep, so I just let him be."

"Unbelievable. You're just as useless as he is!" His hand suddenly lurched out and smacked his wife hard across the cheek. Unprepared for the blow, Patricia Maver was knocked off balance and fell to the floor, holding one hand against her face and crying.

"Get up." Sam's father turned to him, his face red with anger, his eyes wide. He grabbed one of Sam's legs roughly and tugged, until Sam fell off the bed and landed on the floor with a thud.

"I said, *get up.*"

Sam quickly sprang to his feet, his head bowed, bracing himself for what he knew was coming.

"You like to act like a little kid. You're never going to become a man unless someone hardens you up."

Sam let out a quick breath of air as his father's fist landed directly in the center of his stomach. He cowered down.

"Mark, leave him alone!" his mother cried meekly from her spot on the floor.

Ignoring her, Sam's father sneered, "My God, you can't even take a hit like a man. You're weak. You're a weak little shit who can't do one thing to earn his keep around this house."

Without meaning to, Sam let out a scream as his father balled up his fists again and hit him hard in the face.

A spurt of blood erupted from his nose and shot across his bed. Sam felt a stinging pain so strong that it was almost blinding.

"No!" he heard his mother sobbing, but the voice seemed to come from very far away.

Sam staggered and struggled to remain upright, but his father gave him a mighty push and he fell back onto his bed, the wind knocked out of him.

"Fucking pussy," he heard his father say, as he thankfully left the room, slamming the door behind him.

Sam fought for air, his breathing coming in tight gasps, barely aware as his mother held an old shirt of his up to his nose, tilting his head back towards the sky.

"I'm sorry, baby," she cooed, holding him.

Sam knew she was sorry. She was always sorry. But she never did anything to stop it.

Patricia disappeared for a moment and came back with a package of gauze, which she ripped into thin strips and shoved up Sam's nose. She held a bag of frozen peas up to his right eye, which was already getting swollen.

She held him and rocked him, just like he was in fact still the little, helpless boy that his father despised. Sam felt a pounding in his head, like he could feel the blood as it rushed through. He wondered idly if any of Nick's blood, which he knew coursed through his veins, had ended up on his bed.

Sam didn't remember much about the rest of the night. All he knew was that when he woke up the next morning his father was gone, probably off to hang out with his brother, Sam's Uncle Ned. His mother was quiet, parked in front of the television. She looked up when Sam came in and started crying quietly at the sight of him, saying that perhaps they should go to see Dr. Smith today.

"No," Sam mumbled, "Dad always says that doctors ask too many questions."

"I know, but I think we need to do something about that nose of yours. It's all crooked."

"Really?" Interested, Sam padded into the bathroom and looked into the mirror. Indeed, his nose was pointing in a slightly different direction than it normally did. There was dark, crusty dried blood around the entire lower half of his face, and the skin under both of his eyes was sunken and turning a deep shade of purple.

He walked back into the living room and found his mother rooting around for her purse. Sam pretended not to notice the bruise that was forming across her cheek. If you looked closely enough, you could see the shadow of different fingers in it, almost like his father still had her in his grasp.

Sam allowed his mother to help him into the car and buckle his seatbelt, which he found ironic considering that she normally didn't care much about his personal safety.

Neither of them spoke on the way to the doctor's office until they reached the parking lot.

"Just tell Dr. Smith that you were playing ball with your friends, and that a baseball hit you right in the nose. It's easier that way. There's no use getting your father involved now, is there? We wouldn't want Dad to get in trouble now, would we?"

Sam shook his head. They only went to the doctor if the injuries were really bad, like when he was six years old and his father had broken his arm after he had forgotten to take his cereal bowl from the table, and the milk had curdled and stunk up the whole kitchen.

Sam repeated the story his mother had told to the kindly old doctor, who looked as though he either didn't believe what Sam was saying or didn't believe that a person could possibly be that bad at baseball. But he simply grunted and nodded, adding, "That nose is broken, we need to set it." Then he wrote out a prescription for a pain killer of some sort and handed it to Patricia, who tucked it into her purse.

During the drive home, Sam sat staring at his reflection in the side mirror, trying to make sense of the face which looked back at him.

Without looking at him, Sam's mother said, "So I was thinking, maybe we could get your dad to agree to letting you have that puppy after all."

CHAPTER THREE

"C'mon Charlotte, c'mon girl!" Sam cried, urging the dog to run along behind him. The dog trotted happily, following him as he ran back and forth along the sidewalk.

"That dog of yours follows you everywhere," Nick observed as he watched.

The boys were in the front yard of the Lynch house, because Charlotte wasn't allowed to go in the house or Pete would start sneezing up a storm. It was true, he wasn't just faking it. The boys had discovered that when they snuck the dog in one day and hid her in the hallway, waiting to see if Pete would start one of his sneezing fits. He had.

"I know, isn't it great?" Sam replied, sitting down on the grass next to Nick.

"Here girl, go get it!" Nick cried as he grabbed a small stick and tossed it down the sidewalk. Charlotte raced after the stick, scooping it up in her mouth and dropping it between the two boys.

"Good girl," Sam said, ruffling the hair on her head and tossing the stick again.

"She sure is good at fetch," Nick mused. "We should enter her in a dog show or something."

"Yeah, I bet she would win first place. She's super smart."

"And then we would get our picture in the newspaper, and probably get about a thousand dollars or so in prize money."

"What would you do if you had that much money?" Sam asked, picking a blade of grass and weaving it between his fingers.

Charlotte returned the stick and Nick threw it for her again. "I don't know, lots of stuff. Like, first I would buy a remote control airplane, that would be radical. Then I would probably buy the neon green high top sneakers that mom says are too expensive. And I would get a boat. And take a trip to Hawaii. And with that kind of money, I could probably take Melissa McMeyers and her giant tits out on a date."

Nick leaned back, propping himself up on his elbows, thinking. "Heck, I might even take her to Hawaii with me. Then she would probably have a lot of sex with me. I mean like, all the time."

"I know what I would do with a thousand dollars," Sam mused. "I would move to Maine, where my mom's cousin is supposed to be, and see if I could live with her."

Nick looked inquisitively at his friend. "If you had a thousand dollars you'd be rich. Why wouldn't you want to buy something cool? Plus, if you moved, we couldn't hang out anymore."

"That's true," Sam admitted. "I guess maybe I would just move in with you at your house, and pay for my parents to move to Maine."

"That's more like it."

The boys laughed noisily, picturing the surprised look that would come over the Mavers' faces as they were suddenly shipped off to the other side of the country.

"Say, I'm hungry. Want to see if Mom has anything to eat inside?"

"You're always hungry, but sure. Let me just tie Charlotte up in the backyard."

The boys wandered around to the back of the house and Sam knelt down to attach the rope to the dog's collar. The Lynch's had been nice enough to allow the boys to tie a rope around the base of the tree that held the tree house. This way, if Sam wanted to run inside for lunch, Charlotte could stay outside and enjoy the autumn air. If Sam were planning to spend the night, it had been decided that Charlotte would be allowed to sleep in the garage. She had a blanket out there and everything.

The Lynch's seemed to be very understanding as to why Sam didn't want to leave the dog unattended at his house, and they didn't ask any questions about it. They just said that since Charlotte was now house broken and well trained, she could have the garage all to herself, having to share it only with their old station wagon.

"I'll be back in a little while, girl," Sam said, stroking Charlotte's hair affectionately. She seemed to understand what he was saying, and she laid down and rested her head on her paws, happy to relax outside and await the return of her owner.

"Mo-om, what's to eat?" Nick asked, walking into the kitchen and rummaging through the pantry.

May walked into the kitchen and Sam felt his breath catch in his throat. She was wearing a towel. A *towel*. It was wrapped around her entire body and knotted at her chest, and her hair was wound up into the turban of a smaller towel.

"Excuse me, I didn't realize you were here, Sam, although I guess I could have guessed." She winked at him, and Sam swore that his heart missed a beat.

"Geez, Mom, you're so embarrassing!" Nick cried, his face getting red. "No one wants to see that!"

May grinned and replied, "Sorry about that. I got all sweaty from dragging all the winter clothes up from the basement, so I decided to take a quick shower. I'll go change now, before I embarrass my son any further. Oh, and there are lemon squares sitting on the counter."

As May disappeared Sam felt his breathing slow down to a normal pace, and he tried to relax his shaking hands.

"Shit, sorry about that," Nick mumbled. "Parents are so damn oblivious."

Sam nodded, still not trusting himself to speak.

Nick found the lemon squares; they smelled delicious, and were covered in a thin coating of powdered sugar, which would make them even better.

Sam helped himself to one and took a large bite, liking the way the lemony goo filled up his mouth and mashed up against his teeth. His future wife really was the best cook. By the time he was married to her and was really old, like thirty or so, he imagined he would be a very fat man indeed.

"So what do you want to do now?" Nick asked, his mouth full. Little crumbs flew out of his mouth and landed on the counter.

"I don't know. We rode bikes all day after school yesterday, so we should find something else to do."

May came back out, dressed in a pair of jeans and a long-sleeved purple shirt. Her feet were bare, and her damp hair was making wet spots on the shoulders of her shirt. "If you boys are looking for something to do, why don't you rake the leaves out of the back yard?"

"Seriously, Mom?" Nick said in anguish. "We're not *that* bored."

"Tell you what, if you do both the back yard and the front yard, and you bag up all the leaves and you do a really good job at it, I will give you each five dollars."

The boys looked at each other, grins spreading across their faces. Verbal communication wasn't necessary between them in this situation.

"Sure!" Nick yelled, while Sam cried, "Definitely!" They high-fived one another.

"Great, there should be a couple of rakes in the shed. Look behind the lawn mower. Thanks, guys."

Wow, Sam thought, *only a truly nice mother would not only offer to pay them for doing normal chores, but would* thank *them besides!*

Shoving the rest of their snacks into their mouths, Nick and Sam hurried to the backyard. Sam unhooked Charlotte's leash; he wasn't worried about her getting into the street or somewhere else she shouldn't be if he was out there with her.

The boys went to the shed; Nick gave it a swift kick, and they pulled the door open.

"Yep, here they are!" Nick said, venturing into the garage and coming back out with two rickety looking rakes. He looked around the yard, saying, "This probably won't take very long. Maybe fifteen, twenty minutes?"

As it turned out, Nick's calculations were way off. The boys had been working for over a half an hour, and the backyard was only about halfway done. Charlotte thought they were all having great fun; she kept running around and jumping into the piles of leaves. It was a little annoying but pretty funny to watch, and since it was more funny than annoying, they let the dog have her fun, even though it meant straightening up all the piles again before they could be bagged up.

Although the day was brisk, Sam could feel beads of sweat forming on his brow from all the hard work. His arms were getting stiff and feeling like Jell-O. At least his underarms weren't sweating, as his mother had finally decided that Sam did in fact stink, and had added deodorant for him to her regular shopping list.

"Man, this is taking forever!" Nick groaned, half-heartedly dragging his rake through the grass. "Let's take a break."

"Okay."

The boys let the rakes fall to the ground and walked over to the tree house, climbing slowly up the ladder. Nick settled himself onto the floor and stretched, yawning.

"Charlotte, you stay down there, okay?" Sam called, poking his head out of the door and looking down at the dog.

She barked and wagged her tail, then walked in a slow circle and laid down to take a nap. Sam knew she understood.

"So, what do you think of that project Mrs. Elliot assigned to us?" Sam asked, sitting in a cross-legged position across from his friend.

"I think Mrs. Elliot is a real bitch," Nick commented. "That project is stupid. So we each have to pick a state and write a whole freaking report on it? And we can't even pick Missouri, 'cause we live here? What a load of crap."

"Yeah, it's gonna take a long time," Sam agreed. "What state are you going to pick?"

"Hell, I don't know, somewhere awesome at least. I wish I could pick Hawaii, but that's in a different country."

"No it isn't; Hawaii is one of the states."

"What? It is? No kidding!" Nick smiled and said, "Okay then, I call Hawaii. What are you gonna pick?"

"I'm not sure, maybe Maine where my relative lives. I've never been outside of Missouri, so there isn't a place that I've visited that I could choose."

"That's stupid, never leaving Missouri," Nick scoffed. "I've been to... let's see - Illinois, Tennessee, Texas, and Florida." He was ticking each name off on his fingers. "Wow, you've never even seen the ocean, huh?"

Sam shook his head, and Nick sat back, looking at him in wonder. "That sucks, dude. I wish your parents would let you go on vacation with us some year."

"Yeah, I wish."

"Hey, maybe next summer? I mean, they let you keep Charlotte and all. I never thought they would go for that, so maybe they're getting nicer?"

"Yeah, maybe." Sam fiddled with his shoelace, not meeting Nick's eyes. By the time Nick had gotten back from vacation over the summer Sam's face had healed quite a bit, and he had simply told his friend that he took an elbow to the nose. Nick knew from experience not to pry, and Sam hadn't offered any more details from the events of that night.

"So, our birthdays are coming up," Sam said, to change the subject.

"I know, I can't wait!" Nick's voice often got higher when he was excited. "We'll finally be twelve, and that's almost a teenager, and that's practically being an adult."

"It will be really cool. What are your parents gonna give you for a gift?"

"I asked for a remote control plane, but Dad says those are pretty expensive, and he thinks I'll just crash it and wreck it anyway. So I don't really know what I'm getting. What are your parents getting you?"

Sam shrugged, and turned the attention back to his friend. "Is it true that you get to have a party?"

"Yep," Nick answered proudly. "Actually, I've been meaning to tell you about that. They said that you and I can have a joint birthday! They're going to make it a party for both of us, with two different cakes and everything! Mom said she will make us each whatever kind of cake we want. Plus, we're allowed to invite Dylan and Ryan and the Reevis brothers and they can all spend the night."

"Far out!" Sam cried, suddenly ecstatic. He didn't want to tell Nick, but he had never gotten to have a real birthday cake before. Normally on his birthday his mom would present him with some new shirt or a toy that he was much too old for, not even wrapped or anything. Usually they would order out for pizza, and one year his mom bought cupcakes from the store. They were marked down to half off, because they were stale. Occasionally, his birthday wasn't even remembered.

"Yeah, it's gonna be awesome. We are going to rent movies and stay up all night prank calling the girls to piss them all off."

"Sounds cool." Sam was mostly just thinking about what kind of cake he was going to ask for. May was going to bake him his very own cake?! Sam could hardly believe his good luck.

Suddenly Sam was full of energy. "Let's go finish raking the yard now!" he exclaimed, moving towards the ladder. "And we can talk about what movies we're going to rent!"

"Okay, okay," Nick said gruffly, following his friend out of the tree house.

Charlotte heard them moving and stood up immediately, wagging her tail, thrilled to be reunited with her owner once again.

***

There were helium balloons floating against the ceiling, moving back and forth with the invisible currents of air so that they seemed to have a life of their own. A huge banner exclaiming in bright letters 'Happy Birthday!' was tacked on one of the walls of the living room. And as promised, not one but *two* cakes sat on the kitchen table. One was chocolate with chocolate frosting, and written in red icing were the words, 'Happy birthday Nick'. The second cake was vanilla with strawberry frosting, and this one said, 'Happy birthday Sam'. Each cake had twelve candles stuck around its perimeter, which Pete was currently trying to light.

As the group of boys cheesily shouted the words to the birthday song, each trying to be louder than the rest, Sam felt himself smiling. Not just on the outside, he knew there was a huge grin across his face. But it felt like he was smiling on the inside as well, as if that made any sense. But he couldn't help it, he felt so warm and happy and loved in this home away from home.

Today was October the 19th, Nick's actual birthday. Because it fell on a Saturday it was decided that this would be the best day for a party. It was a beautiful day for it, too, warmer than it normally was at this time of year.

The boys had spent the day playing football in the backyard with Pete, then were allowed to open presents. Sam had never received so many gifts before at one time, not even on Christmas when his aunts and uncles and his grandmother would sent gifts through the mail.

From Dylan he received a glow-in-the dark dog collar for Charlotte. "It's really more of a present for your dog than for you, but I thought you would like it," he had said. Dylan still felt no small amount of pride at having introduced Sam to his pet.

Ryan Harding had given each of the boys a hand-held video game, which was unbelievably cool. Then the Reevis brothers had produced their gifts of Nerf guns, which shot out rubber arrows and were quickly introduced into the football game as a new sort of opponent to be dealt with.

Nick and Sam had already agreed to give each other tiny little remote control robots, which they were hoping to use to send messages back and forth to one another while sitting at their desks during school, certain that their teacher would never catch on. Sam had been saving his money for months, constantly offering to clean out his mother's closet or wash his father's car. Mostly, he had done chores and odd jobs for the neighbors. It had been difficult to earn the money, but he was proud of himself for being able to do it. He was pretty sure that Nick had simply asked his parents for the money to buy Sam's gift.

The boys were thrilled when Pete and May brought out their gifts... pogo sticks! *Two* of them! Sam could hardly believe that the Lynch's had been willing to get him such a fabulous gift, especially since he wasn't even a member of the family. Well, not a real member anyway. One drop of blood's worth.

Each of the boys tried out the pogo sticks, which were more difficult to master than you would expect. Even Pete tried, and managed to fall over, much to the delight of everyone. He grinned, got up and dramatically wiped off his rear end, saying, "Now that everyone has had a turn and I'm the only person that has been injured, maybe it's time to put the pogo sticks away."

When the sun started to set and the evening got cooler, they went inside and had make-your-own-tacos for dinner, and were now about to cut into their own personal cakes. It had been the greatest of days, and it wasn't even over yet. There were still scary movies to watch (Pete said that since the boys were twelve, they could rent *sort* of scary movies; nothing too graphic though.) and an entire night of snacking and hanging out.

"Okay, blow out the candles!" May shouted, clapping her hands.

"Mom, this is *so* lame," Nick said, but he was smiling.

Sam made his wish, as he had heard you were supposed to do.

Both boys bent over their respective cakes and heaved great puffs of air, watching as the tiny flames flickered and went out. Sam watched as the tiny wisps of smoke danced into the air. It was the first time he had ever blown out candles on his birthday before.

May was cutting pieces of both cakes and putting the slices on paper plates, which the other boys were quickly grabbing. Sam took a piece of his vanilla and strawberry cake, and lifted a bite to his mouth. It was probably the best cake he had ever eaten. Maybe because it was his.

***

"Good morning!" Sam said to his parents. It was three days later, and they were both sitting at the kitchen table, his father reading a newspaper and drinking his coffee before getting ready to leave for work, his mother staring intently at thin air.

His mother nodded at him, his father said nothing.

"So it sure looks like a nice day outside," Sam continued, hoping to prolong the conversation. No one spoke.

Sam walked over to the refrigerator and poured himself a glass of milk. He noticed an unidentifiable package of frozen meat of some kind thawing on the counter. "What's this?" he asked, pointing at it.

His mother jerked out of her trance and said, "It's what we're having for dinner."

Sam took a deep breath. "I was hoping maybe we could order out for pizza for dinner tonight."

"I already have hamburger thawing. You'll eat what we have. If you don't like it, go to your friend's house for dinner."

Sam sighed, picked up his book bag, and went outside to wait for the school bus. It looked like this would be one of the years where his birthday was forgotten entirely.

CHAPTER FOUR

The weather should have been colder for early November in Missouri, but Mother Nature must have been smiling that day.

Sam and Nick ran along ahead of Pete, both of them full of pent-up energy caused by having to spend so much of their time playing indoors.

"C'mon, Dad!" Nick called back to his father. "There's gonna be a line if you don't move faster!"

"Then I suppose we will just have to wait in a line then, won't we?" Pete answered pleasantly, not bothering to quicken his pace.

The boys ran around, kicking loose rocks towards one another and scuffing their shoes along the pavement, laughing.

As Nick had predicted, a small line had formed at the mini-golf course by the time the trio had crossed the parking lot. It seemed that the Indian summer had called out to many other families in the area as well.

"I'm so gonna beat you in golf!" Nick whispered loudly, playfully shoving his friend.

"No way, I'm awesome at golf!"

"I call the red ball," Nick stated.

"Fine, then I call the blue ball. Blue balls are the best anyway."

For some reason Pete began chuckling loudly. The boys turned to look at him, but he didn't explain the joke, so they continued jostling one another as the line moved forward.

The family in front of them moved out of the way and Pete leaned up against the counter, saying, "Three for miniature golf, please."

"Sure," answered the teenage boy. He tossed his head back so his long hair moved out of his eyes while they exchanged money, then handed over three putters, three golf balls, and a score card with the tiniest pencil that Sam had ever seen.

"Actually, can we trade in this orange ball for a red one?" Pete asked.

"No problem-o," the boy answered, taking the ball back and turning to rummage around for one in the requested color, handing it to Pete.

Sam smiled to himself. Of course Pete had been paying attention to their special requests and would make sure that they were fulfilled. That or he simply knew it was easier to ask for a different ball rather than to hear the boys bicker over them later.

"Here you go," Pete said, handing each boy a putter and the ball of their choosing. He kept the taller putter and a yellow golf ball for himself.

Sam loved mini-golf and was thrilled when Pete had suggested it earlier. He had only played twice before, once for a cousin's birthday party, and once with the entire Lynch family. May hadn't wanted to come this time, and that was probably for the best. Sam required all of his concentration to be on the game, as opposed to on his friend's mother. Nick had beaten him by several holes the last time, and Sam was excited to finally have a chance to even the score. Plus when she was there, May just walked around saying things like, "This is such a *cute* alligator stature!" or "Oh, what a *precious* little windmill!" and paying very little attention to the game itself. May was good at many things. Baking was one of them. Miniature golf was not.

Pete might have been remembering the same thing, because he said, "Ah, just us men here this time, fellas."

Nick and Sam exchanged a grin and took practice swings with their putters while Pete wrote their names on the score card.

"I'm going first!" Nick announced.

"Nick, Sam is our guest, let's let him go first. You can go second."

Nick scrunched up his face but must have decided that the point wasn't worth an argument, and he conceded the first green to his friend.

Sam smiled, rolling his blue golf ball between his fingers. He liked the way the pockmarks felt against his skin.

"All right, Sammy, let's see what you've got!" Pete called. "You're up!"

Sam set his ball down on the black rubber mat, carefully positioning it over the little cut-out hole so that it couldn't roll away. Then he stood up and scrutinized the green, trying to figure out his shot. He had two options. The first path was a clear shot to the hole, but there was a large plastic gorilla in the way, with moving parts. The gorilla's hand moved back and forth, which could easily knock his ball in the opposite direction that he wanted. The second route held no obstacles, but it was full of dips and hills that would be difficult to steer the ball through.

"Oh man, c'mon Sam! Why do you have to take so long?" Nick whined. "Just take a swing, already!"

Pete shot a warning look at his son before saying, "That's all right, Sam. Take your time, there isn't a group behind us yet."

Making up his mind, Sam spread his feet a bit to widen his stance. He reached the putter around his body, then sent it forward, aimed perfectly at the ball. Because he had timed his swing just right, the ball whipped past the gorilla while it's hand was out of the way. It sailed down the green and came to a stop just a foot or so away from the hole.

"Wow, nice shot!" Pete said, thumping Sam on the back appreciatively.

"Yeah, yeah, but watch this, I'm gonna get a hole in one!" Nick set his ball down and immediately took a swing. The ball surged forward and smacked against the gorilla's hand as it came down, blocking the shot. Because it had hit with such force, the ball actually sailed backwards past Nick and landed on the sidewalk behind him, bouncing once before rolling to rest in the grass.

Pete and Sam started laughing hysterically. Nick looked a little angry, but then he joined in the laughter as he went to fetch his ball.

"Go ahead and take another turn," Pete said. "Maybe use a little less force this time."

"Okay, that was just my practice swing anyway. This time is for real."

"I'm totally gonna beat you," Sam quipped, watching as Nick took a second shot, this time aiming for the hills and valleys. Nick had used a lighter touch, and this time the ball didn't have enough gumption to make it up the hill. Once again, it rolled back to him.

Nick was starting to lose his patience as he lined up the ball for a third time, saying, "That last shot was also practice." He combined the best of both his shots, using a harder swing but aiming for the side which was sans-gorilla. This time the ball had enough energy behind it to roll across all the hills, and came to rest directly in the hole. There was a satisfying little 'pop' sound as the ball plopped inside.

"YES!" Nick cried, putting both his hands on either end of his putter. He kissed it, then brought it up high into the air above his head like it was a trophy. Sam rolled his eyes.

"You know, son, being a sore winner is just as bad as being a sore loser," Pete offered.

"Sorry. I mean, you did a good job also, Sam. Just not as good as me." This time Pete rolled his eyes.

Nick ran to the hole and scooped out his ball, then the boys watched as Pete took his turn. He went the route of the gorilla also, timing his shot well but failing to get his ball as close to the hole as Sam had.

Sam took another shot, gently knocking his ball into the hole, then Pete did the same. Pete took the score card and pencil out of his pocket and starting making notations.

"That's a hole in one for me!" Nick shouted. "And you two are tied for last place, ha ha. Write that down, Dad."

Sam could see Pete hesitate. Technically, it had taken Nick three swings to sink his putt, while he and Sam had only taken two. But Nick was dancing around, looking very pleased with himself after the failure of his first two 'practice' swings.

"Maybe we shouldn't keep score at all," Pete said, frowning.

"No way, Dad, we have to keep score! What's the point in playing otherwise?" Nick asked, confused.

"Because it's fun. It's father-son-friend-bonding time."

"Okay, whatever, it's *bonding* time. But it's bonding time *with* a score card."

Pete laughed, coming to a decision. "All right, but if we're keeping score than we are going to do it fairly. I'm counting all three of your swings, buddy."

"*Da*-ad, those were *prac*-tice!"

"I will leave the choice up to you, Nick. Either we can say that this first hole was a practice round for all three of us and we will start keeping score at the second hole, or we will mark you down for a three, or we won't keep score at all."

Nick pondered this for a moment as they walked on to the next green, allowing the very patient family that had come along behind them to take their turn on the first hole.

"Okay, then. Go ahead and put me for a three. I will make that up anyway, now that I'm warmed up." Nick grinned and Pete gave a small sigh of relief that this wasn't going to turn into a debate.

The sun beat down, warming people enough that the lightweight jackets they had on over their sweatshirts and sweaters started to get peeled away. It was a quick reminder of the autumn temperatures, and the promise that spring would come once again. Winters could be surprisingly brutal in Missouri, snowy and frigidly cold. When springtime chose to reappear it was always regarded with relief, as sufferers of the cold made cries of, "That was the longest winter we've ever had!" and "That was the coldest winter I can remember!" Of course, the winter was always just as long and just as cold as the one before it, but the heat of the summer made it easy to forget those days. Thus, the cycle continued.

Pete unzipped his jacked and shook himself out of it, tossing it over his arm as he watched the boys. They had come to a hole that was obstructed by a sandpit. Nick was tapping at his ball, chasing it around with the putter since he kept putting too much force on it to slide gently into the hole. Sam, who was ignoring his friend, was diligently writing his name in the sand with his finger.

Pete smiled, watching them for a moment. He was always amazed at the differences between the two boys, which were becoming more apparent as they grew older. Sam seemed to be very intuitive, retrospective, and was always gentle and kind. By contrast, his own son could be impatient and stubborn, and was far more talkative. By the same token, however, each boy was remarkably the same in all the ways that really seemed to matter. They were virtually attached at the hip, a package deal in that you could rarely find one without the other. Probably without realizing it, the boys were also fiercely protective of one another, something that Pete knew would serve them well as they grew older and life tossed more difficult problems their way.

"Da-ad, you're up!" Nick called. "Pay attention!"

"Sorry," Pete answered, laughing as he lined up his putt. At least the boys had each other as playmates. Not only did it ease some of the parental burden, but Pete had secretly always hoped for more children. Due to complications during Nick's birth, that wasn't an option for the family, and Pete felt especially fond of the other youngster which had somehow become such a constant fixture in their lives.

Pete arched back and took his shot, and the three watched as his ball got stuck in the sand pit, right in the middle of the letter 'M' that Sam had so carefully drawn.

The boys started giggling and Pete laughed also, raising his hands in surrender and muttering, "Yeah, yeah," as he walked into the pit to go after his ball.

By the twelfth hole it seemed that the boys were growing weary of the game. Nick was paying even less attention to his shots, and on one hole Sam had spent most of his time picking up bugs he found and gently placing them on the wheels of the windmill, watching as he gave them 'rides' as it spun around.

They hurried through the last holes until they reached the final one, the 'Hippo Hole'. This hole involved a narrow ramp with a steep drop off on both sides. If a person could get their ball all the way up the ramp, it would fall into the giant hippo's mouth, a red light would flash and a bell would sound, and that person would win a coupon for a free game on a future visit. It was a sight that Nick and Sam had only seen happen once before. During their last mini-golf adventure, they had begged to watch other families try their luck with the hippo, hoping to see that celebration once again. The Lynch's had agreed for a while, watching with amusement as the two boys had cheered for complete strangers, heaping words of encouragement and advice on the hippo-hole hopefuls. The boys could only dream of achieving such an accomplishment themselves.

Sam placed his ball onto the rubber mat and eyed the hippo. Unlike the carefree attitude of the last several holes, this was all business.

"Good luck, Sam," Nick whispered, not wanting to disrupt his friend's concentration.

Sam sent up a tiny prayer, although he wasn't sure if God would be angry over being bothered by such a thing as mini-golf, but he figured it was worth a shot. Sam was thinking that if he won the free game, perhaps Pete would feel that he would have to invite Sam back again. Today had been so much fun, for both Sam and the many lucky bugs he had found.

He tapped his ball and watched, his own mouth as wide-opened as the hippo's. Miraculously, the ball went up the ramp and straight into the hole.

Just as they had seen it do before, the red light started blinking and the bell went off. Sam dropped his putter to the ground, shocked.

At the sound of the bell, the teenage boy from before emerged from the little cashier's office. He walked up to Sam, held out a card, and said in a monotone, "Congratulations, you have managed to feed Harvey, the Hungry Hippo. Enjoy your coupon for a free game on us." Then he turned on his heel and walked back into the building.

"Wow, that's awesome!" Nick cried, craning his neck to read Sam's coupon. "It's my turn next, and I'm going to do the same thing."

When the bell quieted, Nick set his ball down and looked up at the ramp, squinting as if trying to measure it. He then gave his ball a lofty whack, and they watched as it got about three quarters of the way up, then fell off into the abyss.

"That was really close, good job," Sam said, concerned that his friend would be angry.

Nick muttered something in reply and said, "You're up, Dad."

Pete stepped up and pretended to eye his shot, then gave the ball a clumsy whack so it would fall off the ramp early. Pete didn't believe in losing on purpose to the boys, he felt that they needed to learn how to let others win as well (his own son was especially in need of this lesson). But in this case, if he were to achieve a free game also, no one would want to be around Nick for the rest of the day.

"Dad, that was an awful putt," Nick said, laughing, his good humor quickly returned.

"Oh well, I guess only Sam has this Harvey Hippo character figured out. He seems a little shady to me. I mean, why is he always so hungry?" The boys laughed and followed Pete to turn in their putters. Enjoying their laughter, he continued, "Why doesn't he save all the balls that fall off the ramp? Then he would never be hungry!"

"He would be so full he would probably start throwing balls back at all the annoying people!" Nick cried, squealing with delight at the idea of an inanimate hippo hurling golf balls at unsuspecting people.

"Yeah," Sam giggled, joining in. "And people would have to wear hard hats so they wouldn't get hurt, 'cause of all the golf balls flying around."

"Speaking of golf balls flying around, would you two like to take a few swings out on the driving range? That's where all the adults practice." Pete smiled at the boys.

"Wow, really! That would be radical!" Nick was prancing around, thrilled with the offer. Sam joined him, running in little circles and jumping at random. They had never been on a driving range before, and this new territory felt like a stepping stone to becoming the grown-ups that they practically were already.

Barely able to contain their excitement, the boys seemed to get a second wind of energy as they trotted along next to Pete while he purchased a bucket of balls. They carefully selected their clubs and found an open practice area.

The golfing complex was set up like a triangle. The miniature golf course, the driving range, and the small club house made up each of the points. A short distance away was a large golf course and a more prominent club house.

The driving range area was crowded as well, people of all ages were in the practice slots, and the air was filled with a cacophony of whacking sounds as countless clubs and balls connected.

The boys were trying to take it all in, transfixed by the motion of so many golf balls sailing through the air at once and landing at different points on the green.

"Dad, can I be the driver first?" Nick asked, looking hopefully at his father.

Pete frowned, asking, "What do you mean?"

"You know, the golf carts. Can I drive one first?"

"Oh," Pete said, suddenly understanding. "Sorry buddy, you're thinking of the golf course itself. Here, there are no carts. We're just going to practice our swings."

Nick looked infinitely disappointed, and Pete quickly amended, "I tell you what, if you boys get some good practice in hitting the long ball, maybe one day next summer we will play a few holes on a real golf course. Does that sound like fun?"

"Totally!" they answered in unison, and the earlier disappointment was quickly forgotten.

"You can go first this time, Nick," Pete said, letting his son select a ball.

For the next half hour the three took turns hitting golf balls. After some practice and instruction from Pete, Nick turned out to be pretty good at getting distance behind his ball. Sam, meanwhile, kept struggling, often exerting a lot of energy on swings that simply whooshed through the air, never even connecting with the ball.

"Don't worry, Sam. You get an 'A' for effort, that's for sure!" Pete came to stand behind Sam, gently moving the boy's hands so they were in a better position to hold the driver. Pete held his hands over Sam's and together, working as one, they arched the club back and swung forward. They hit the ball with a mighty thump.

Sam watched with awe as the ball went sailing far in front of him, coming to rest near the placard that read '200 yards'.

"Wow," Sam breathed, amazed that the tiny little white ball which was so recently right in front of him now occupied a space so very far away.

"Great job, Sam," Pete said, giving his arm a squeeze.

"That went even farther than most of my balls," Nick mused, then quickly added, "Of course, you did it with Dad's help."

"Sometimes asking for help can be a good thing," Pete responded as he lined up a shot for himself. "And lending a hand is always a good thing."

Pete carefully took a few practice swings to be sure his shot was lined up correctly, then grinned at the boys and said, "Watch this, I'm going to aim for that sign that says 500 yards."

"Dad, you'll never hit the ball that far. Instead you should aim for that guy driving around collecting balls, in the golf cart with the little cage protecting him. That's where I've been aiming."

Pete laughed, shaking his head, and took his swing. The three watched as the ball rose high into the air, coming to rest less than halfway to the goal that Pete had set.

"So much for that idea, huh Dad?"

"Nick, the important thing isn't that I hit the ball far, the important thing is that I tried."

Sam picked up the empty ball bucket and announced sadly, "That was the last one."

"All righty, I guess that means it's time to head home," Pete answered, stretching. "I'm getting hungry. Maybe I'll pick up some pizza on the way. Do you two know anyone who would like to share some pizza with me?"

"Dad, stop being goofy, you know we love pizza!"

"Oh, thank goodness, I won't have to eat it all myself, then."

Sam laughed, his spirits lifted again. He was amazed that a day could possibly contain so much fun... and for *no particular reason*. Miniature golf? The driving range? Pizza? And it wasn't even anyone's birthday.

Sam lagged behind Pete and Nick as they headed back to the car, his attention straying.

The days grew shorter at this time of year, and even though it was still early the sun was already starting to set. The air was getting cooler, and Sam could see other families grudgingly packing up their things as they headed for home. The warm spring-like day had come to an end, and everyone's good mood seemed to have ended with it as people remembered that the forecast for tomorrow would be much cooler.

Parents were forcing the arms of their children into the coats they had taken off earlier. A youngster was crying; probably he was getting hungry, or cold... or his arms were getting tired.

"C'mon, Sam, we need to have a discussion about pizza toppings!" Nick shouted happily, trying to hurry his friend along. Sam could do that sometimes, just get lost in his thoughts, which often made him move at an annoyingly slow pace.

"Coming!" Sam hollered back, hurrying to catch up to where Nick and Pete were patiently waiting by the car.

Sam and Nick hopped into the back seat, carefully fastening their seatbelts around their waists.

Sam half-listened as Nick debated the merits of pepperoni versus bacon, and instead watched as the sun quickly made its downward descent. It seemed that once it started to set, the sun was pulled by its own momentum. The sheer weight propelled it downward, until its eventual disappearance behind the shadow of the Earth. Once it started to fall, there simply was no stopping it.

CHAPTER FIVE

Sam and Charlotte were walking to Nick's house. The walk took well over ten minutes, and much longer if it had to be done when it was snowing or raining. He had come this way so many times that Sam was certain he could find his way to the Lynch home in his sleep.

For the umpteenth time, Sam wished he could ride his bike between the houses, letting the dog trot along behind him. It would save so much time. It was an impossibility though, and he considered himself lucky that he was able to keep his bike at Nick's home, or he wouldn't be able to ride at all.

Sam thought back to when he had first received the bike. It was a few years ago, he couldn't remember exactly when. Nick had had a bike for what seemed like a lifetime by then; he had been riding a tricycle then a bicycle with training wheels before finally graduated to a regular bike. Sam had learned to ride by borrowing Nick's bikes. Pete had spent hours showing both of them how to keep their balance, and May had delved out many Band-aids during that time. Sam had been incredibly jealous of the freedom that having a bike of his very own offered his friend.

When he was small, May used to pick Sam up from his house to babysit him for the day. As soon as he was old enough, Sam starting making the journey on his own, for fear that one day May would get sick of making the drive and would stop allowing him to come over. It wasn't even babysitting, not really, when you considered the fact that Patricia Maver didn't work. She fancied herself a 'stay-at-home' mom, but as the story went, she claimed to May that she simply didn't have it in her to care for a baby, and could May just help her out one or two days a week? That turned into four or five days a week. Then Patricia couldn't handle having a toddler, and soon a little boy was just too much for her, and so on.

May never even asked for money, as the Maver's had little, since Mark tended to drink most of what he made. Instead, feeling sorry for the innocent little boy who was so close to her own son in age, May simply took it upon herself to basically raise two children instead of just the one.

One day when his mother was in a particularly good mood, Sam had brought up that having a bicycle of his own would certainly help him to be more efficient. Not only could he get back and forth from the Lynch's home to his own quicker, but he would be able to reach neighbors that lived even farther away, which meant more jobs which meant more money that he could contribute to the home. (Sam and his mother had a deal; whatever money Sam made, half went to the household, and half he could keep. It was only fair, since they provided his food and clothing and a roof over his head.)

This argument seemed to sway his mother, who somehow got her husband to agree as well, and the following Saturday mother and son went canvassing neighborhood garage sales. On their third stop of the morning, they found Sam's future bike. It was the most beautiful thing he had ever laid eyes on, and he was so excited that he insisted on pedaling it home while his mother drove the car on ahead. If Patricia wondered when or how her son had learned to ride a bike, she didn't mention it.

For three weeks Sam had ridden that bike all over the neighborhood. Finally, he was able to keep up with his friend, and they didn't have to take turns using Nick's bicycle. Nick was always gracious about lending his bike, but things were *so* much better when each boy could ride at the same time.

One day Sam was returning from Nick's home and for some reason that he couldn't now remember, he had been in a hurry. He took the turn into his driveway too quickly, causing the bike to skid out from underneath him. Sam had fallen onto the hard pavement, badly skinning his knee and elbow.

Upon feeling the searing pain and seeing the blood, he had quickly made his way into the house, running past his mother, and gone into the bathroom where he used an old washcloth to remove the blood and gravel from the wounds.

Unfortunately, at that moment his father had gotten home from work, and he stormed into the house.

"Where is he?" Sam could hear the booming voice of his father, and he worked faster at cleaning his skin.

"I don't know," his mother said, her voice barely audible over the sound of the television.

Footsteps through the living room. Footsteps in the hallway. A pounding fist on the door of the bathroom. "Get your ass out of there, right now!" he bellowed.

Slowly, Sam opened the door of the bathroom and peeked out.

"You're coming with me," Mark said gruffly, grabbing his son by the arm and jerking him down the hallway, not noticing the blood that was seeping from his elbow.

Sam was dragged through the living room, where his mother didn't look up from the show she was watching, and out the front door.

"There!" his father yelled, pointing.

Sam followed his gesture and saw with dread that in his effort to tend to his wounds, he had left his bicycle in the middle of the driveway.

"What in the *hell* is this doing here?" Mark's voice boomed. Probably the entire neighborhood could hear, and were tittering to themselves over what a bad son Sam was.

"I'm sorry, I fell off and hurt myself and -"

"I don't give a rat's ass what you did. I care about what you *didn't* do, which is put this damn bike away! I almost ran over it with the fucking car! Now, how would you like to explain that?"

"Sir, I -"

"Shut up!" his father hissed. "Just shut your fucking mouth. We let you have a bike, and this is how you treat it. Obviously, you don't care what happens to it." Mark ran over and held the bike by its handlebars, then proceeded to kick at the wheel.

"No, please don't!" Sam squealed, but that seemed to only infuriate his father further. He shoved his boot into the spokes of the wheel, bending them outward.

Sam clenched his hands into tight fists, until he could feel his fingernails digging into his palms so hard that they hurt. He tried not to scream, or cry, both of which would make the situation worse.

Suddenly they heard the engine of a car being started up, and they both turned to look as their neighbor's car backed out of their driveway. The neighbor glanced at them and gave a hesitant little wave.

Mark glared at the man, but the interruption had been enough to stop him. Sam supposed his father didn't want to be seen beating the crap out of an inanimate object.

"Fuck this," he said, giving the bike one more swift kick so that it went sailing across the driveway. "If I ever see that bike out here again, I will purposely run over it with the car, got it?"

Sam nodded, his face red with pent-up emotions, the pain from his elbow and knee forgotten. He watched his father storm back into the house, then quickly ran over to the bike, propping it upright. He climbed on and gingerly tested it out. It still worked; even though the spokes were bent it didn't appear to be enough damage to alter the bike too badly.

Without telling his parents he was leaving, they probably wouldn't notice anyway, Sam slowly rode to Nick's house, hoping the Lynch's would allow him to store the bike there. He knew that if his father destroyed it, he would never receive another.

Sam shook the memories from his thoughts, trying to enjoy the walk. Charlotte trotted along at his side, happy to be heading to Nick's. She liked spending time over there. It was better than being cooped up in Sam's room all day, which is where she had to be if she was in the Maver household.

"Hey there, Sam," Nick said when they arrived. He bent down to pat the dog on the head. "Heya, Char. Good girl." The dog licked his cheek, and Nick laughed.

"So, what do you want to do? Do you want to go up into the tree house?" Sam asked.

"Nah, I was thinking that since we're twelve now, we're probably getting too old for that thing."

"Oh, right," Sam answered, trying not to let his disappointment show. He loved the tree house, it was a place that belonged solely to him and Nick. It was a place where secrets were shared and kept, since no one could possibly overhear them. It was where they had become true brothers.

"Yeah," Sam continued. "I had been thinking the same thing."

"So, what else is there to do? I'm super bored. There's not even anything on television on a stupid Thursday night."

"I know."

"And soon, it will be too cold to hang out outside much anymore." Nick wrapped his denim jacket tighter around him for good measure.

"Yeah."

"Man, I'm hungry."

"Want to go see if your mom has any snacks?" Sam asked, knowing that his May always had a fresh baked goods of some sort lying around for them.

"Whatever."

The boys trudged into the garage where they left Charlotte, then entered the kitchen.

"Mo-om, what's to eat?" Nick called.

May was in the kitchen, closing the oven. "Hey there, you two, I'm just putting dinner in the oven. Lasagna tonight! Sam, would you care to join us?"

"Sure, May, I'd like that. Thank you."

"Screw the lasagna, I'm hungry right now," Nick moaned.

"Watch your language, young man," May warned. "I still have some brownies if you didn't eat them all yesterday. And I was just getting ready to bake some chocolate chip cookies. Would you boys like to help me?"

Nick picked up a brownie and took a giant bite. "Mo-om, no one wants to help you make stupid cookies. That's boring." His teeth had brownie goo stuck to the front of them.

"If you help me, I'll let you eat some of the cookie dough," his mother promised, smiling at him.

"Wow, that sounds great! I'd love to help!" Sam said with true enthusiasm. He wasn't sure which sounded better, eating raw cookie dough or creating something with May.

"I guess it sounds okay," Nick conceded, grumbling and glaring at his friend.

"Excellent! Nick, could you please grab me that glass bowl from the top shelf of the cabinet? And Sam, there is a large spoon and a set of beaters in the drawer to your left."

The boys gathered the equipment and added it to where May had set a cooking tray out on the counter.

"Great. Nick, could you please measure out the butter, flour and sugar? Sam, I'll need you to crack two eggs for me into this bowl."

"Okay." Sam retrieved two eggs from the carton in the refrigerator and gently carried them back to the counter. His hands were shaking a little and he realized how nervous he was to be working in such a close proximity to May for an extended period of time. He prayed that he wouldn't drop the eggs or spill pieces of shell into the bowl or in some other way make a fool of himself. Carefully, he cracked the eggs against the side of the bowl and sighed with relief as the yolks and the gooey white stuff fell perfectly into the bowl.

"Nice job, Sam," May said, nodding her approval, and he felt himself flush with pleasure.

"Now, let's add the best part! Here Sam, measure out the chocolate chips!" She handed him a bag and Sam cautiously tore it open, pouring the chips into the measuring cup she gave him.

"We need more chips than that!" Nick cried.

"All right, put another handful in there," May agreed, smiling as she tilted a bottle of vanilla extract into a measuring spoon. "I suppose you can never have too much chocolate."

"Isn't that the truth?" Nick said, mixing the ingredients as each person added something to the bowl.

"Alrighty, I think we're ready to mix this batter up." May picked up the beaters and put them into the bowl. "Sam, would you do the honors?"

"Let's turn the beaters on before we put the mixer in the bowl!" Nick suggested wickedly, grinning.

"And that is exactly why I didn't put you in charge of the mixing," May replied, smiling at him and winking at Sam. "Sam, would you be so kind?"

"Sure!" Sam said, proud to take the control that May offered him. He pressed the 'on' switch and they all watched as the mixer hummed to life, churning through the ingredients until a sticky paste formed.

"Okay, I think that's good." May reached for the beaters, and as she did so her hand brushed against Sam's. He caught his breath.

She unhooked each of the silver mixing tools from the machine and handed one to each of the boys, saying with a grin, "As promised. Enjoy!"

Eagerly, Sam and Nick grabbed the beaters and began licking the sugary substance from them.

Meanwhile, May greased the cookie sheet and got out a teaspoon, using it to ball up little mounds of batter. She then used her finger to slide the balls onto the tray.

"Let's make one giant cookie instead!" Nick suggested, his words muffled through all the batter that was sticking to his tongue.

"I don't think that would cook all the way through," May answered.

Sam slowly licked the dough, wanting to savor every morsel of it, and watched as May's fingers deftly made a dozen or more little balls of batter, placing them on the sheet. He thought it odd that if a little heat was added, these gooey mounds would turn into actual cookies.

"Okay, the oven is all ready, so I'm going to slide these in now. Thanks so much for your help, boys."

"No problem, we were happy to help. Anytime, May."

"Stop sucking up," Nick said and playfully thumped Sam on the head. "C'mon, let's go to my room, unless you want to volunteer us to help with the vacuuming."

"That would be nice," May grinned.

Sam laughed and followed his friend.

As they walked down the hallway, Sam did what he always did, and gazed at each of the photographs that lined the walls. In the living room hung the professionally done family portraits and school pictures of Nick, but it was the hallway pictures that Sam liked the best. These were the silly, unplanned, candid pictures that hadn't been posed.

There was Nick when he was a baby, with cake smeared all over his face and wearing a 'First Birthday' hat tilted at an angle on his head. There was one of May and Pete holding hands in front of an ocean. There was a picture of Pete playing frisbee with Nick in the middle of a park on a spring day, when the leaves were just beginning to bud.

Then there was Sam's favorite shot, a picture which included him as well. A few years back the Lynch's had invited him to accompany them on a picnic, and Sam had happily obliged. The closest thing he had ever done that resembled a picnic was the time that his father had screamed so loudly and so long during lunch one day that Sam had simply taken his food and eaten it on the back porch.

The picture was of all four of them, taken by some friendly passer-by. Sam and Nick were sitting next to each other in the foreground with Bugle chips stuck on all their fingers. They were pretending to claw at one another with their extra-long fingernails. Pete and May were sitting behind them, smiling not at the camera but at the boys' antics. The picture reminded Sam of how the universe had originally intended that things should be, with him a true part of the Lynch family.

There were no family pictures hanging in the Maver household. Just an old wedding photo of his parents that was displayed rather haphazardly in the living room, on an end table leaning up against the wall. There were normally magazines covering the bottom half of it, so that it looked like two heads were floating in marital bliss.

"Sam, what the hell are you starring at?" Nick's voice was impatient.

"Sorry, I'm coming." Sam realized he had been daydreaming about the past quite a lot today, and he gave his head a tiny shake and forced himself to focus on the present.

Sam entered Nick's room and Nick closed the door behind them, twisting the little brass knob to make sure the door was securely locked behind them. Sam sighed wistfully.

"So, I was thinking about asking out Lizzie Shaper," Nick was saying as he threw himself dramatically on his bed.

Sam sat in the bright red bean bag chair that was resting on the floor. "Really? Like, on a date?"

"No dummy, I don't want to actually *go* anywhere with her. I just want to see if she would say yes, then be willing to make out with me after school or something."

"Huh."

"So, do you think she would say yes?"

"Probably, most of the girls at school seem to like you."

"Yeah, that's true." Nick laid back and smiled, thinking of the general good view the opposite sex tended to have towards him. "I think I'll ask her out tomorrow."

As it turned out, Nick needn't have worried about the reaction that Lizzie Shaper would have upon being asked out by him.

At lunch the following day she simply squealed an ecstatic "yes!" then ran off to tell her friends that one of the cutest and most popular boys in school had just asked her out. This was followed by much squealing and giggling. Nick watched the hoopla from the other side of the lunchroom and took another bite of his sandwich.

That afternoon, he offered to walk Lizzie to the bus, and *carried her book bag*. This was simply to seal the deal. He then managed to convince her so sneak off around the side of the building, *just for a minute*, and there he experienced his first kiss. It was simple, quick, just a brief peck on the lips, but he knew that soon there would be tongue, and the grabbing of boobs.

Lizzie lived in the opposite direction of the boys and therefore took a different bus, which meant that there was no chance of her overhearing as Nick shared all the details with his best friend.

"So, it happened," he said in a hushed voice.

"What happened?" Sam asked, leaning into his friend, his tone equally conspiratorial.

"I just made out with Lizzie Shaper," Nick answered proudly.

"Really?" Sam wasn't sure how to respond; did the situation require a 'congratulations'?

"Sure did."

"So… what was it like?" Sam asked, knowing that Nick would tell him whether he showed interest or not. But the truth was, Sam *was* interested.

"It probably lasted for at least two minutes or so, with lots of tongue. I'm talking tons. She was obviously into it, I practically had to push her off of me. She took my hand and held it over one of her boobs, but since I'm a gentleman I put my hand down and said, "No, sweetheart, we need to take things slow."

"I doubt that," Sam said wryly.

As if his friend hadn't spoken, Nick continued, "I was thinking that if I carry her lunch tray for her or something tomorrow, she'll probably let me have sex with her by the end of the week."

"Uh-huh."

"It's pretty cool having a girlfriend," Nick decided, folding his hands behind his head. "You should get one."

"It's not like I can just go pick one up at Walmart," Sam countered.

"I could ask Lizzie if any of her friends are interested in you."

"Thanks, but I don't think so. There's no girl that I want to go out with." Well, Sam thought, that was true. It wasn't a *girl* that held his interest. Idly, he wondered how Nick would feel if Sam asked him and Lizzie to go on a double date with him and his own mother.

The bus stopped at the entrance of Stony Meadows and both boys hopped out. It was simply assumed that Sam would be going to Nick's house, but only briefly today since he had to go home and let Charlotte outside. He knew that even if his mother had been willing to help with the dog (which she wasn't), she would forget anyway.

"So why don't you want a girlfriend?" Nick pestered, kicking at a rock with the toe of his shoe.

Sam had been hoping his friend would be willing to let this conversation go, but it appeared that luck was not on his side today. "I dunno, just not interested, I guess."

Nick turned to look at his friend with a gleam in his eye. "You're full of shit, Sam. I know that the other day when you were at my house you got a boner. That's why you had to run to the bathroom, isn't it?"

"What?" Sam stammered, completely taken aback. He could feel his face growing bright red as he cried, "What are you talking about?"

"Oh, come on, you know. The other day you had been in the kitchen talking to my mom about something, then you got a weird look on your face and made a run for it. You weren't just taking a dump either, I know 'cause I listened at the door for a second, and no one can take a dump that quietly."

Sam was staring open-mouthed at his friend. Unfortunately, he knew exactly what day Nick was referring to. Sam had been sitting at the kitchen table watching as May was working in the kitchen and chatting to him. Suddenly a bit of the sauce she had been stirring sloshed out and ended up on her apron.

"Silly me, that was clumsy!" she had commented, wiping off her hands and pulling the apron off over her head. But what May didn't realize was that when she took off that apron, it caught a bit on her sweater. As she pulled it up over her head, the corner of her sweater came up too, just for a moment, but long enough to give Sam an unforgettable image of her cleavage, which was tucked into an angelic looking white bra. Other than the pictures in his father's magazines, Sam had never seen a real live girl's breasts before, and he had certainly never seen the breasts of the woman whom he dreamt about at night.

The sweater had fallen back into place almost immediately, but it had been long enough to burn a searing image into Sam's mind, one that he couldn't stop starring at. Immediately he had felt himself get hard, and his entire body flushed. Mortified, he had wiggled around, thanking God that he had been sitting with his legs under the table when it happened. Quickly, he had mumbled some excuse and made a run for the bathroom.

Once inside he threw the door shut behind him and locked it tight. Then, as though his hands didn't belong to his body anymore but rather had taken on a life of their own, he unzipped his fly and took out his penis. He cupped it in his right hand and stroked it back and forth, using his left hand to lean against the sink for support.

Within seconds, a white sticky goo had shot out of the tip and he felt his body shudder violently, then relax. Taking a moment to catch his breath, Sam had looked around him in dismay, then used several long pieces of toilet paper to clean up the tile floor.

Sam zipped his fly, washed his hands, and splashed cold water on his face. He gave the toilet a flush just for effect. Sam then looked at himself for quite a while in the mirror, turning his head this way and that, until he was satisfied that no one would be able to tell what he had just been doing.

He had nonchalantly wandered out of the bathroom and down the hall, past baby Nick in a birthday hat and the day of the picnic, and entered Nick's room. At the time, Nick hadn't looked as though he suspected anything. Apparently, however, he knew far more than he had let on.

Sam now looked at his friend, his face hot.

"Hey, don't worry about it, man, I do that all the time," Nick was saying breezily. "You know the other day at school when we had that pretty substitute teacher? Why do you think I had that textbook in my lap until she excused me to go to the bathroom?"

Sam was staring incredulously at Nick. Nothing seemed to embarrass him, nothing was off-limits. He wondered what it must be like to feel so comfortable in your own skin.

"Anyway, I just figured that while you were being all polite listening to my mom talking your ear off, you probably started daydreaming about those chicks in the magazines."

"Um, yeah, that's what happened."

Nick peered more closely at his friend, who looked as though he were getting close to tears. "Hey man, it's nothing to be embarrassed about. My dad told me that this stuff is perfectly normal."

"You mean your dad actually *talks* to you about this stuff?"

"Sure. I mean, doesn't your dad?"

The boys looked at each other as each realized the slim chances of Mr. Maver talking to his son about anything, much less the birds and the bees.

"So wait," Nick said, "Do you, like, not know *anything* about this stuff?"

"Of course I do!" Sam said huffily, suddenly defensive. "I've read about all kinds of stuff in the encyclopedias at school."

"Oh, please, that's so lame!"

Sam averted his eyes, ashamed.

Nick sensed the change and softened his voice. "Hey, listen, if you ever have any, like, questions or anything, you can ask me, okay?"

Sam turned to his friend and smiled gratefully, nodding his head. Nick was a fine brother indeed.

CHAPTER SIX

"So listen, I was talking to Dylan at school, and I have an idea."

"Oh, boy."

"Yeah, we were talking about those nudey magazines, and of how old they are, and how we need to see some new chicks."

"Okay..." Sam looked at Nick warily.

"We need you to steal some more from your dad."

"Uh-uh, no way; he'd kill me!" Sam moaned. "I'm still amazed that I got those other ones. I don't want to push my luck."

"Oh, come on, Sam. Look, I'll go with you and we'll do it together, okay?" Nick said pleadingly. "It will be okay, I promise. Please? Sa-am, please?"

Sam sighed, then nodded his agreement. He knew that once his friend had an idea in his head, there was no getting away from it.

"Great!" Nick exclaimed, clapping his hands together. "What time does your dad get home from work?"

"You mean you want to go *today*?" Somehow, Sam thought he would have more time to mentally prepare for the heist.

"Sure, why not? You have to go home soon to let out Charlotte anyway, right? I'll just walk over there with you, we'll swipe the magazines, then I'll hide them under my coat and walk back home. C'mon Sam, he won't even be home for a couple hours, right?"

Sam gathered his thoughts and answered, "Yeah, okay, let's do that. We better leave now, though."

"Sure thing." Nick walked to the front door and opened it a crack, hollering, "Mo-om, I'm going for a walk with Sam, I'll be back soon."

Sam understood why Nick had said they were going on a walk as opposed to Sam's house. May would never have believed that.

They walked quickly, as two people on an important and dangerous mission tend to do.

Within minutes they were at the Maver household, and Sam whispered to Nick, "My mom will be in the living room watching television. If you're quiet she won't even know you're here."

"What if she turns around to talk to you?"

"She won't," Sam answered, his voice certain. Nick didn't question him.

Sam opened the front door and walked in, saying casually, "Hi mom, I'm home from school."

His mother didn't answer, much less turn around.

"I'm going to let Charlotte out of my room now," Sam continued, walking down the hall. It was bleak and empty, painted a dingy beige.

Tiptoeing, Nick followed his friend and watched Sam open the door to his bedroom. Immediately Charlotte came bounding out, thrilled to see them both, and started jumping and licking them.

Sam laughed, petting her. "Down girl, you know better than that." He turned to Nick and whispered, "I'm going to take her outside; you go in there and see what you can find. Just be quiet!"

Nick gave a mock salute and went in the direction that Sam pointed, quietly opening the door to the study.

"Okay Char, let's go outside!" Sam said in his regular voice, leading the dog back through the living room. He grabbed her leash from where it was hanging on the hook and bent down to attach it to the dog's glow-in-the-dark collar.

Then Sam heard a noise that made him freeze, dread coursing through his veins and causing his throat to constrict. *It was his father's car.*

But no, it couldn't be. According to the clock hanging above the couch his father wasn't due home for nearly two hours.

And yet, here he was.

"Mom?" Sam asked in a tiny voice. "Do you know why Dad is home early?"

If Patricia heard her son speak, she gave no sign of it. Her eyes never left the television screen.

Sam's thoughts were racing as he contemplated what to do. The leash dropped to his side as he stood up.

Charlotte circled him, confused.

The front door was pushed open and Mark Maver walked inside, kicking some dirt off the soles of his boots and leaving it to rest on the floor.

"Get this dog out of my way," he said by way of a greeting.

"What are you doing home already?" Sam asked meekly.

"Apparently some fuck-up at work fucked something up. There was a problem with one of the machines on the line, and rather than pay us to stand around, they sent us all home early. Hopefully the damn thing will be up and running by tomorrow." Mark took off his heavy coat and tossed it, watching as it landed squarely on the couch next to his wife. She didn't look up.

Sam was thinking about Nick, and wondering if he had heard his father arriving home. There must be some way to get a message to him, to tell him to hide until Sam could get his father out of the way long enough for Nick to sneak out. If there was ever a time for Nick to receive a subliminal message from Sam, this was it. For a moment, Sam squeezed his eyes shut and tried to send his thoughts through the living room, down the hallway, and into the study where Nick was.

"Well, at least you get some extra time off," Sam said loudly, hoping that Nick would hear him speaking.

His father looked at him guardedly. Normally their conversations didn't last this long. "Yeah, whatever, I'm gonna go take a shower."

Sam breathed a sigh of relief. This was perfect, Nick would have plenty of time to get out of the house while his father was in the bathroom. They were saved.

Mark headed down the hallway towards the bathroom... and bumped right into Nick, who was walking out of his study.

"What the hell?" Mark's voice was confused, but quickly turned angry. "What in the hell is your friend doing over here, Sam? And why in the fuck was he in my study?"

Nick's face went white and he quickly put his hand behind his back.

"What are you holding?"

"Nothing."

Mark laughed haughtily. "Don't give me that shit. Let me see what you have."

Sam felt himself growing weak, and he offered up a tiny prayer. He wasn't sure that there was a God, in fact he tended to doubt it based on past experience. But if there was a powerful deity of some sort looking down on him, now was the time to make His presence known.

Slowly, Nick brought his hand around and showed Mark what he was holding.

Mark didn't say anything for a moment. Then he hissed quietly, almost calmly, "Give me those, and get out of my house."

"I'm sorry." Nick's voice was wavering and he shot a pathetic look in the direction of his friend before walking slowly down the hall.

Surprisingly, Mark didn't even wait for Nick to leave, his rage was so great.

"You fucking little bitch!" he yelled, grabbing Sam roughly by the shoulders and shoving him into the wall, pinning him there.

"Hey!" Nick yelled, out of instinct. As soon as he heard himself speak, Nick clamped his mouth shut, horrified.

Mark turned to him and said vehemently, "Get out of my fucking house. I'd better never see you over here again."

Nick's eyes were wide and he slowly backed up, bumping into an end table as he went.

Mark shifted his attention back to his son. "And just what the hell do you think you're doing? You invite your useless nosy friend over, who breaks into my study and tries to steal my private things?"

"I'm very sorry, sir, we only -"

"Shut up!" Mark yelled, his eyes dark. Sam had rarely seen him so upset before, and wondered if he was embarrassed about the magazines, and if that was adding to his anger.

Sam watched as different looks passed across his father's face, finally ending in disgust.

"You little *shit*!" Mark smacked him across the cheek and Sam tried to duck down, freeing his other arm from where his father was holding it.

He was in an awkward kneeling position when Mark kicked him hard in the chest. There was a snapping sound, and Sam howled in pain.

Charlotte, who had been whimpering nearby, suddenly leapt up and rushed toward Mark, growling, her teeth bared. Just as Mark was arching his arm back, his hand in a fist, the dog grabbed his hand and dug her teeth into his skin.

Mark screamed, equally in surprise and in pain. He stood up and screamed, "Get this fucking dog out of my house!" He then kicked Charlotte in the side. She was pushed back by the force but didn't slow down, she barked and stood guard, slowly circling him, warning him.

Mark looked down at his hand and sucked off some of the blood, making him resemble a vampire. He thrust his leg out again, kicking the dog much harder. Charlotte yelped and a long line of pee and runny shit oozed out of her rear end, coating the carpet.

Mark's face twisted with rage as he ran at the dog and kicked her again, his foot making contact with her hind end. "I will *kill* this fucking animal!" he breathed, his voice a promise, and went after the dog again as Sam screamed.

Suddenly, Nick appeared, yelling, "No!" Sam hadn't even realized he was still there. He watched as his friend grabbed Charlotte by the collar and held her close, putting himself between man and beast.

"What's going on in here?" Patricia Maver had finally been roused from the couch, and was now standing in the entry of the hallway, trying to take in what she was seeing. She had no idea what had caused the sudden eruption of violence, and was particularly surprised to see her son's friend standing in the middle of it all, holding back Charlotte who was so worked up that drool was dripping from her mouth.

"Get out of here, I'm handling this," Mark fumed, and she took a step backwards.

"But sweetheart," she began, noticing that Sam was crumpled in pain on the floor, clutching his knees to his chest.

Mark ignored her, but sensed that he was now out-numbered. He glanced down at his hand which was bleeding from a long gash, then looked at the mess that the dog had left on the carpet.

He knelt down over his son and said quietly, "If I ever see that animal in my house again, I will kill it. Do you understand me? Do you?"

Sam nodded, crying.

"*What*? I couldn't quite hear you over all your blubbering."

"Yes, sir. I understand."

"And if I ever see your friend here again, I will make you both sorry. Do you understand?"

"Yes, sir."

"Good." Mark smiled at Sam and gently ruffled his hair. Then he bent down even closer, looking almost as though he was getting ready to kiss him.

Sam squeezed his eyes shut as his father spat on his face.

"Fucking little prick," he seethed, standing up. He glared at Nick and pushed his wife out of the way, stomping down the hallway, through the living room, and out of the house. All three of them jumped as the door slammed shut behind him. His car pulled out quickly, making the tires squeal.

"Oh, sweetheart, are you all right?" Patricia asked, running to Sam and kneeling down next to him.

Sam could barely move, his entire chest was a white hot pain, and it felt as if his body was being cut in two. He didn't even have the energy to wipe the saliva from his face, and it was beginning to ooze down his cheek and dry there, crusty.

"My poor baby," his mother cooed, trying awkwardly to hold him in her arms.

Even through his pain Sam found himself enjoying the attention and physical contact that his mother was offering. But at what price? She only showed him love after his father had been in one of his rages. Sam wondered if maybe, sometimes, it was worth going through the pain to experience this affection.

"Maybe we should get you to a hospital, baby," she continued, wiping sweat from his brow where it was matting up his hair, making it stick to his forehead like glue.

Sam nodded and winced, not even having the energy to argue with her. His entire body hurt.

Nick came over wordlessly, and the two of them carefully helped Sam to his feet, then walked him out to the car. Patricia buckled the seat belt around him, concerned as always with his safety. He grimaced as the shoulder belt went across him.

"Listen," Nick said, peering into the car. "I'm going to take Charlotte home with me, okay? I'm sure my parents will let her stay at my house. We can make her up a real comfy place in the garage."

"Is she hurt?" Sam asked, his voice coming out in gasps.

The dog had followed them outside and was now standing in the driveway, her tail wagging uncertainly, looking with concern at her owner.

Nick looked down at her and patted her head. "No, I don't think so, but if it looks like she's in pain we'll take her to the vet, okay?"

Sam nodded.

Patricia started up the car and Nick forced a smile for his friend, then gently closed the car door.

Nick and Charlotte stood in the driveway, watching as the car drove down the street.

He bent down and ran his hand over the dog, carefully touching her sides. The dog winced a little but didn't appear seriously hurt.

"You're such a good girl, Charlotte," he said quietly to her. "You and me, we'll take care of him, won't we?"

The dog looked up and licked him on the cheek.

***

"Three broken ribs. Man, that sucks ass."

"Tell me about it. How's Charlotte?"

"She's fine, don't worry. I talked to my parents, and they say that Charlotte can live in our garage." Nick smiled happily, glad to take some of the burden from his friend's shoulders.

"That's great, thank you. I wouldn't trust her being in my house anymore."

"I know."

The boys looked at each other, not used to being around one another in such a serious situation before. It was odd for Nick to see his friend in a hospital bed, looking so weak.

"So, how long are they keeping you prisoner in this joint, anyway?"

"I can go home tomorrow; they just wanted to keep me for the night for observation or something."

"Where's your mom?"

"She's in the waiting room, said her favorite TV show is on right now."

"Oh. Does it hurt?"

"Some, but they gave me a bunch of medicine for the pain, so it's not bad right now. They said I'll be sore for a long time though." Sam grinned and added, "I heard that my father was in here earlier to get his hand looked at. Charlotte really got him good; he needed eleven stitches!"

"That's cool. She's a good dog."

"She is."

Nick nodded, fixing his eyes on the hospital identification bracelet that was circling Sam's wrist. "So, what did you tell the doctors?"

"Mom told them I fell down some stairs."

"Do you think they believed you?"

"I don't know. I doubt it, but no one questioned it."

Nick nodded again, not meeting his friend's gaze.

"Hey, you didn't have to come up here, you know. I mean, it's cool that you did, but you didn't have to." Sam smiled and Nick raised his eyes.

"No, I wanted to. I mean, I -" Suddenly, Nick's voice broke, and he started crying. "It's my fault you're in here. I'm so sorry Sam."

Sam was taken aback, Nick rarely cried, and especially not on his behalf.

"I was so scared. I didn't know what he was going to do to you or to Charlotte, and if I had never suggested getting those dumbass magazines, this would never have happened."

"No man, it's not your fault. Really."

Nick leaned close over his friend, until Sam could smell the potato chips that Nick had recently eaten on his breath. "Listen, man, I'm going to make you a promise. One day, I will kill him."

Sam laughed and looked in his friend's eyes, surprised at the seriousness that he saw there.

"I mean it, Sam. I really will." Several more tears ran down Nick's cheeks, dropped off his chin and landed on Sam's face.

Sam wondered if any remnants of his fathers' spit was still there, and if the tears were getting mixed together with it. One of Nick's tears landed with a splat on his upper lip, and without thinking about it, Sam stuck out his tongue and licked it off, tasting the saltiness on his tongue. He swallowed. Now both Nick's blood and tears were in his own body.

Nick sniffled, embarrassed at his show of emotion, and tried to get himself together. "So listen, my parents are waiting outside, and they want to talk to you. Can I bring them in?"

"Um, okay, I guess."

Nick went to the door and gestured for his parents to follow him inside. Sam was instantly very aware of the fact that he was wearing a hospital gown.

"Hello there, Sam," Pete said, smiling.

"Hi there, sweetheart," May said, her eyes searching. For some reason, the word 'sweetheart' sounded so different on her lips than it did on his mother's.

"Hi," Sam answered, a little uncomfortable, and not just because of the broken ribs.

Pete grabbed one of the armchairs on the side of the room and pulled it over next to the bed, sitting down. May sat on the corner of the foot of his bed, and Nick stood between them both.

"Listen, Sam, May and Nick and I have been talking, and we're all very worried about you. You know that we consider you a member of the family already. And Sam, we'd like to ask you to move in with us. Would you like that?"

Sam's eyes grew wide. He could hardly believe what he was hearing, and tried to make sense of the words.

"We'd talk to your parents about it, of course, but we wanted to talk to you first. What do you think?" May asked. "We'd love to have you, Sam, really we would."

Sam looked at the two people who had been closer to parents than his own mother and father ever had been. He looked at Nick, his brother, who was grinning and nodding enthusiastically.

Sam's first reaction was to say that he could never fathom such a thing, that the mere suggestion of it made him feel like a bother. But suddenly Sam felt a sense of calm wash over him, and he smiled, realizing that the universe was finally trying to piece together the things it had allowed to go wrong. His eyes welled up with tears as he replied, "I can't think of anything I'd love more."

***

A week later, Sam crept through his kitchen and opened a cabinet, wincing as it squeaked on its hinges. Even more than usual, he had been trying to be The Mouse.

Ever since the day when both he and his father had sustained injuries, and especially that night when the Lynch's had their serious conversation with the Maver's, things had been very delicate. Sam felt as though he were walking on eggshells, and every step he took he tried to take with extreme care.

As Sam gingerly reached up for the box of cereal, he thought about his parents. He had actually believed that they might go for Pete and May's idea. After all, Patricia showed little interest in him, and Mark downright hated him. Wouldn't they be happier if Sam was off their hands once and for all? Then he and Nick would really be brothers, and all would be right with the world.

But his parents had scoffed at the idea. His mother had started crying, and his father had kicked over the magazine table in the hospital waiting room, then disappeared. He didn't come home for three days.

The entire time he was gone, Patricia spent half her time in front of the television, the other half pacing back and forth in front of the window, crying and praying aloud that her husband would return. Occasionally, she would ask Sam if he needed anything.

When Mark finally came home, his wife ran to him and threw herself in his arms, weeping with joy. Sam glanced up from where he was trying to get comfortable in the old La-Z-Boy recliner, his chest throbbing.

Mark walked in and said calmly, "Don't you ever be telling our business to anyone else."

Sam thought it best not to mention that Nick had witnessed what had occurred, and had taken it upon himself to tell his parents.

Sam simply nodded and his father continued, "Like it or not, you are a part of this family, and this is where you will remain, do you understand me?"

"Yes, sir."

"Good."

And with that, Mark disappeared, shutting the door of his study firmly behind him. Even from the living room, Sam could hear the click of the lock as Mark turned it.

He dumped some Frankenberry cereal into his bowl, added milk, and mixed it up with his spoon. He watched as the milk took on a pale pink hue. He took a bite and heard the crunching between his teeth. Even that noise seemed to be too loud, and Sam hoped that it was louder in his own head than it was to the outside world. He would hate to disturb his father.

Ever The Mouse, indeed.

CHAPTER SEVEN

The boys were ecstatic. Both of them woke early that Saturday morning, much as dreams of Christmas keep a young boy from actually dreaming. Today was the day, the day Pete had promised to show the boys how to shoot a gun. So technically, as this was an official footstep on the way to manhood, this was actually better than Christmas.

Sam's father owned a few guns. Patricia didn't like them being in the house but he simply declared that as an ex-military man, guns like those had saved his life, and he would not be getting rid of them, and that was his final word. Then, as a more final word, he added that he would use them to protect his family at any expense. Perhaps it was that finalist of final words that caused Patricia to smile and stop her arguments over having guns in the house of a young boy. For if her husband was willing to protect her and their son, that must mean he truly loved them after all, something deep, a primal sense of so much import that it kept him from being nice to them on a day to day basis. Maybe, just maybe, it meant that he loved them so dearly that the idea of losing them would make him lose his very mind, and that's why he kept his family at an arm's distance. Patricia smiled again, this time just to herself. She had finally discovered the truth, that Mark Maver loved his family *too* much, and was so afraid of losing them that he had to keep them both at arms' length. Whether there was any truth to this or not, it allowed Patricia to sleep better at night, and allowed the worry which churned deep in her belly to start to mellow.

Besides, all the rifles were kept in a tall metal lockbox in the side of Mark's study. He did keep a loaded handgun in one of the drawers of his desk (if there is an attacker, he's not going to wait for me to unlock the chest, load the gun, aim and shoot, Patricia. We would all be dead by then. There's no point in even trying to protect this family if I can't be ready for it, he would say).

Sam (and therefore Nick, because who could keep a secret like that) both knew that the gun was in his top right desk drawer. But if Patricia was worried about the boy's safety, she needn't have been; the closest the boys had come to the vicinity of the guy had been when, on a dare, Nick gingerly pulled open the drawer, allowing both boys to ooh and ahh over the instrument capable of ending a man's life. Being so near to it had scared them, though neither boy would admit that to the other one, and without checking with Sam, Nick had simply, slowly, slid the drawer back shut and neither boy had opened it since. Whether it was the harm that the gun itself could inflict, or the harm that Mark Maver would certainly inflict if he ever caught them that was scariest, the boys were unsure. But it was enough to keep them from looking any further. It felt much safer exploring the unloaded gun, safe in its locked case, that let the boys save face.

These feelings were lost on Sam as he pedaled at top speed to get to the Lynch home. It was an early day in September, the balminess of summer still kept the briskness of the morning at bay. His legs pumped faster and faster, warming his body against the morning dew that seemed to envelop his entire being, deep into his lungs; Sam couldn't wait to reach his friend.

When the boys were about three there was a robbery in Stony Meadows, three houses down from the Lynch family. It had been quite the talk of the town, and for many weeks people boarded up their homes like a tornado was near, and no one trusted anyone that was not already a trusted neighbor. Both Sam and Nick claimed to remember this event, though in truth neither of them did. Maybe just hearing all the stories from that period of time made the memories their own, until it was so real that both boys actually believed that the stories of the time were their real, personal memories.

After the robbery, several of the men in town bought guns for protection, and Pete Lynch was one of them. (During this period of time, Mark Maver, never humble, stated how he would never be robbed because it was so well known that he had guns in his home, and that robbers were scared of him, and that it took an event such as this, in which the Dorsey's had lost all of their electronics and fine jewelry to make the neighborhood sit up and take notice and do what they had to do to rid the evilness of the world, something Mark had known all along.)

Sam had always thought that an interesting statement. How could one home possess all the evilness of the world, as well as the means to get rid of it? It didn't add up to him.

At the Lynch home, there was a single hand gun (Pete had said the type of gun, but just like at home the calibers and what not went directly over Sam's head... was this a .45?) locked up in a fancy green case. Neither boy knew how to unlock the case, as they had certainly tried in the past when they were younger.

Now, at fifteen years of age, Pete decided it was long past the time for the boys to learn how to properly shoot a gun.

Giddy with excitement, the boys watched as Pete turned his back and undid a combination lock, the very same one the boys had tried countless times to open themselves when they were about eight or nine years old.

It was odd to see, after all the hours devoted to trying to release the gun, that within a few seconds the case snapped open with a click, and there it was. It looked just like the kind of gun you see in the movies. Checking to make sure it wasn't loaded, Pete allowed each of the boys to first hold the gun to get a feel for it.

Sam was surprised at the weight of it and as he wasn't prepared for that, he nearly dropped it, which would have been oh so embarrassing.

Reading his mind, Pete noted, "Heavier than you expect, isn't it," as Sam nodded.

"That should remind you of the power behind this," Pete continued, taking the gun back from Sam and returning it to its velvet-crushed case lining. "That's the most important thing I want you boys to learn from today. That the gun has power, and therefore the person yielding it also has a certain power. But it's the person that makes it. It can be the power of someone good, wanting to save himself or a loved one in a time of crisis. But if you're not careful, it can also become the power of a bully, someone who believes that just because he knows how to wield a gun, makes him akin to God."

Pete zipped up the lining inside the case, protecting the shiny metal inside, then closed and locked the case around it.

He looked directly in the eyes of first his son, then the boy who was practically his second son. "I mean it, boys," he continued. "This is not a toy, this is serious, and if I ever hear of either of you becoming the latter kind of person I mentioned, you will be very sorry. Got it?"

Both boys nodded their assent.

"Good. Because today is about teaching you how to shoot-"

"Thank goodness, I thought we were never going to get to that part!" Nick interrupted.

Pete glared at him, and he retreated into silence. "More importantly, son, today is about learning how to respect a gun. God help you if you ever forget it."

The boys nodded again, realizing how serious Pete was and not wanting to say the wrong this which could potentially upset him and more importantly, make him change his mind on the gun lesson for the day.

"Good," Pete answered, satisfied. Well then, let's go get some breakfast. Then it's off to the cabin."

Being two fifteen-year-old boys, and especially because one of those boys had a simply insatiable appetite, the three *men* went to an all-you-can-eat breakfast buffet, Pete joking that that was the only way he could afford to feed his son.

The friendly waitress (Sam checked her nametag, it read Mellissa R.) kept their sodas filled and Pete's coffee topped off warm while the three of them went back for seconds, then

Nick went back for thirds. Shoney's must have lost money indeed that day, the owners shaking their heads sadly at their good marketing idea gone bust. The boys loaded their plates with crispy bacon and runny eggs, biscuits with steaming gravy and pancakes loaded in gooey syrup.

His own stomach full, Pete watched as the two boys continued to shove forkfuls of food into their mouths. "I don't know where you two put all that," he commented, watching as Nick paused his waffle exertion just long enough to wash it down with a sip of coke.

His mouth still full of waffle, Nick replied, "Dad, we need to carb-load before learning an important task."

"Ah," Pete answered, trying not to smile. "I didn't realize this was such a serious physical endeavor. Maybe I, too, should get some more of that bacon."

"It's not an endeavor for you, Dad," Nick said as he spooned another forkful of scrambled eggs into his mouth. Pete wondered if he was even tasting anything. "You're not the one learning an important new, manly task today."

"True," Pete admitted, his smile betraying him. "But since I am the man in charge of teaching the manly task, maybe I'll go grab something for dessert. I suddenly feel like I have a lot on my plate." He paused, looked at the boys and saying triumphantly, "Get it?"

Sam looked up and grinned at Pete, but the comment went clear over Nick's head.

As the boys continued to chow down on their breakfast, Pete got up (slowly, which was all his already full belly would allow) and made his way over to the pastries section.

"You've got a couple of great kids there," Melissa the waitress said to him. "Good looking boys, and polite too. Always telling me please and thank you. Not everyone does that, you know."

Without bothering to correct her, and feeling a sense of pride, Pete only stated the truth when he answered, "My wife and I have raised those two right, I think."

"Oh yes, I should think so. Of course, if they keep eating like that I won't have a job to come back to anymore tomorrow," Melissa said, giggling.

"I'll try to keep them in check, before I have to roll the two of them out of here," Pete answered, joining in her laugh. She moved away to refill a pitcher of iced tea, and Pete reached for a Danish covered in more icing than he knew was good for him.

He really was immensely proud of the boys. *His* boys.

***

Pete's father, Nick's grandfather, owned a small cabin out in the wilderness, about two hours' drive from Stony Meadows. The whole drive the boys were chit-chatting excitedly, and the drive there went quickly.

Pete knew he could take the boys to a shooting range which would have been much closer, but he knew the solitude of the cabin would be a better experience, and he was looking forward to sharing this milestone with them as much as they were. In truth, he didn't want a bunch of other people around, stealing attention, he wanted Nick and Sam all to himself, so they could experiencing this bonding moment without interruption.

After an hour and a half or so, they turned off the main road onto one filled with white rocks, which left a trail of dusty smoke in the wake of their car, coating the leaves of the nearby trees in a heavy white film. One might think the trees here wouldn't survive, but they seemed to accept their dusty existence and thrived instead.

After seeing no signs of civilization for about ten minutes, Pete made a sudden left and the cabin came into view. The cabin itself wasn't much, just a small kitchen, smaller bathroom and one lone bedroom, but the porch was to die for. It was twice as big as the house itself, wide and wrapping around three of the four stone walls. He could remember coming out here as a boy; his father had loved this place. Many a night his father had let Pete come here and they would spend the evenings sitting on the cool porch, Pete with his hot chocolate, Bob with his beer, and watch as the stars lit up the clear night sky. Then they would go into the bedroom, there was something so important about being able to share the same bed, and get up early in the morning to fish in the clear stream that ran just a quarter mile or so away from the cabin. If you were extra quiet, you could even hear the water gurgling from the porch.

It was the land itself, and more importantly the fishing, that caused Bob Lynch to buy this small piece of land in the middle of nowhere all those years ago.

After his father passed away and left the cabin to him, Pete dreamed of taking his family out here as he had when he was a child. But May hated the tiny kitchen, and Nick hated pretty much everything else; the long drive, the lack of a television, the fact that he had to sleep on a cot when he was there. And so, the cabin was rarely used, but Pete simply couldn't bring himself to sell what he looked at as the only remaining connection to his late father.

And of course, now the boys were thrilled to use the cabin, as a backdrop to learn to shoot. Now, apparently, the cabin held all the wonder that it did for Pete when he was a boy... apparently all the solitude and peace needed was the addition of firearms to make it an acceptable destination.

Pete parked and the boys climbed out of the car, their long limbs aching from being confined for so long.

"Wow, this is so beautiful!" Sam cried, circling around to see as much of the land as he could.

"Eh, its ok. Believe me it's pretty boring." Nick pointed at the cabin. "There's barely even electric in there, man. No TV, and Dad would never let me have one. Plus its so tiny and cold and just boring."

"Still though, I bet you had fun playing in the creek and stuff when you were little," Sam mused, wondering why the Lynch's had never invited him here before today. "It looks like a fun place to visit when you're growing up."

"Ah, you see that, Nick? Your friend gets it." Nick shrugged and Pete turned to Sam. "Neither Nick or May ever seemed to appreciate the beauty this place held. This one (he ruffled Nick's hair) always just wanted to bring his game boy. And don't get me started on the day that thing ran out of batteries."

"Oh, I remember that," Nick said with a shudder. "You tried to get me to go fishing with you, you wanted me to touch worms and sit in a chair holding a pole all day. That was one of the worst days ever."

"Glad it meant so much to you," Pete quipped, winking sadly at Sam. Sometimes he wished his precocious son had a little more of the sensitivity that Sam seemed to show.

"So, is the trip down memory lane about over? I want to shoot something," Nick whined.

"*So would I,*" Pete thought wryly to himself.

They went a little way away from the cabin, toward where a giant hill full of pine trees formed. About a hundred yards from the base of the hill there were a couple of stone seats in a triangle shape around what looked to be the remnants of many happy bonfires. Sam sat on one of the cold stone benches, the cold shooting through his pants, making his bottom chilly. He kicked at the pile of ash with the toe of his sneaker, watching as it turned a dusky white, the ashes of many happy fires ending up as nothing more than dirt on his shoe.

"Okay, boys, why don't you run and set up those targets we brought against the hill there. You can rest some of them on that log."

"Cool." Nick and Sam filled their arms with empty cans and targets on sticks (one, unbeknownst to Pete, that had a picture of their math teacher taped to the front). Sam set the stakes into the ground, and Nick balanced the empty cans across the fallen log (and one, unbeknownst to Pete, that was not empty, because who didn't want to see what *that* looked like?).

Their hands empty, the boys jogged back over to where Pete was waiting for them.

"All right, good job guys. Now, let's see what you've got."

Carefully, going through all the steps, Pete let the boys watch to see how he released the gun from the case and checked to make sure it wasn't loaded. He showed them the safety switch, how to load the gun, how to hold it and aim and be ready for the back kick.

Nick got to go first. There were just some things that the real blood son got to do first, while the single drop of blood son had to wait his turn.

Nick checked everything he had just learned, then held the gun up, cocked it, and aimed carefully. To his supreme disappointment the bulled just whizzed off the grassy hill behind the log, not hitting a single target, but leaving just the faintest wisp of dirt in the air.

Nick didn't even care that much, though. It was the first time he had shot a hand gun and the power, the kickback of the gun, the supreme noise, was enough to mollify him.

It was Sam's turn next, and after going through the proper steps, he held the gun up toward the target. He took a practice shot, and his bullet, too, hit the dirt in the hill.

"Not bad, boys, not bad at all. Now, Sam, since you saw where that shot hit, why don't you try aiming again, maybe a little to the left and a bit lower than where you think you should, and see what happens."

Sam did as he was told, aiming carefully, and pulled the trigger, elated when one of the soda cans was hit and flew off the log.

Excited, Sam looked up from the gun and grinned.

"Way to go, Sam!" Pete said, watching as Sam clicked the safety back in place. "All right, Nick, it's your turn again. I want to see you do a practice shot, then use the landing of that shot to adjust your sights."

Over and over again the boys took turns, watching as their aim improved. Nick shot through the full soda, causing the can to pop and soda to fizz out the side wall into the air. The boys whooped and smacked their hands in the air. Pete shook his head. He had already decided not to comment on what he was assuming was the picture of someone's teacher, a bad, grainy copy that looked like it had been blown up from a year book picture, smiling out at then. The poor teacher already had three bullet wounds in his still smiling face.

For the better part of the hour the boys shot the gun, learning to load the bullets and working on their aim.

"Alright guys, I think that's enough for today. Let's clean the gun, then I'm going to grab the hot dogs your mom packed and we'll make a fire before we have to drive back into town."

Nick, who still had on his bright orange ear protection pieces, pretended not to hear and kept going, "What? Did you say shoot the gun six more times? Okay, Dad."

Both amused and annoyed, Pete went over and snatched the ear protection away, saying, "I told you Nick, guns are to be respected, and in this case so is the person that let you borrow the gun in the first place."

"Sorry Dad," Nick said, hanging his head.

"Alright, who's ready to cook some hot dogs?"

"Oh yes, I'm starving," Nick said, his anger at having to put the gun away forgotten.

"You couldn't be that hungry, after that big breakfast we had a few hours ago," Pete commented.

"Just like you said, Dad, that was hours ago," Nick moaned dramatically, holding his stomach.

Sam and Pete laughed. "All right, to avoid watching my son starve in hunger, Sam would you go get everything to make the hot dogs while I get a fire started?"

"Will do," Sam answered and jumped up, brushing the dust from his backside. As he walked up towards the tiny cabin to get the bag that May had packed, he could hear Pete and

Nick as they spoke to one another. He couldn't make out what they were saying, could just hear the sounds that were probably parts of words as father and son bonded. A brief hint of sadness washed over him. No one would ever overhear Sam and his father speaking like that, no one would ever wonder what secrets were being shared, and what one person said to cause the other to peal out in a quiet laughter, in a private joke all their own.

CHAPTER EIGHT

Cindy Peterson was beautiful. She had auburn hair that fell gently to her shoulders in soft waves, reminding Sam of the color of the sun setting over autumn leaves. She had the creamiest, smoothest skin he had ever seen, and her eyes were deep pools of blue that a man could easily get lost in. Her body was thin and lithe, with small breasts and a tiny waist. Her laugh sounded like a million little bells.

She was laughing now, a sound that Sam would give anything to hear. He smiled at her and she returned his smile. Her teeth were strikingly white and perfectly straight, thanks to the braces she had had removed just one week previously.

Cindy was fourteen, nearly a year younger than Sam. He was a sophomore and she was a freshman at Roosevelt High School. They had been dating now for six weeks, practically a lifetime, and Sam was smitten.

Gone were the thoughts of May, and in fact he felt a bit silly when he remembered the crush he had had on his best friend's mother. Infatuation and lust were funny things, their course impossible to predict. May was very dear to him, but in no way was he romantically attracted to her. No, those feelings all belonged now to the lovely Cindy with her jingle-bell laugh.

"Would you like to come to my house and watch a movie after school?" Cindy was asking him now, twirling a strand of hair around her fingers. "My dad could give you a ride home after."

"Yeah, I'd love to."

"Great. And I'm sure my parents won't care if you stay for dinner. They're crazy about you."

"Really? I was nervous when I met them the other day."

"Relax, you have no reason to be nervous. You're only, like, the most polite guy in school. They think you're a good influence on me." She dropped the strand of hair.

Sam smiled and brushed the loose hair back from her face and behind her ear, happy to have an excuse to touch it. It was so soft, and smelled of oranges. He decided he much preferred that scent to the smell of honeysuckle.

The warning bell rang signaling that they had only moments to get themselves into their proper classrooms. Cindy slammed her locker shut and gave Sam a quick peck on the cheek.

"See you after school, then," she said with a smile before turning and flouncing off to her class.

Sam had been leaning up against the row of lockers, and now he pushed himself off and sauntered towards his own classroom. Fifth period was history, a subject that he excelled in. Of course, he excelled in most of his subjects. School came as easily to Sam as it proved difficult for Nick. Nick was smart, but he quickly lost focus, his attention easily diverted to anything else that might be going on in the room around him.

Sam didn't mind helping Nick with his homework, as he had been doing for their entire lives, and this helped Nick to scoot by with just-above passing grades.

Sam hurried into the classroom, squeezing through the door just as the final bell rang, and slid into his desk. Nick was in this class with him, and they always sat next to each other in the back row of desks, because Nick insisted that this was the best area to be. Here, they could watch what everyone else in the class was doing, as well as whisper to one another when Mrs. Milwiski's back was turned.

"Hey, dumbass, what's up?" Nick greeted his friend warmly.

"Hey, dumbass. I was just talking to Cindy."

"Ahh," Nick said, a knowing look on his face. "Ms. Cindy Peterson, soon to be Mrs. Maver."

"Shut up, Nick."

"Aw, I'm just giving you shit. Cindy's nice, and she's pretty cute. Nice ass. So, do you think you guys will do it soon?"

"No way," Sam said, shaking his head. They had had this conversation before.

"Mr. Maver, Mr. Lynch, is there something you'd like to share with the rest of the class?" Mrs. Milwiski's voice was only slightly annoyed.

"No, Mrs. Milwiski. Is there something you'd like to share with me?" Nick asked innocently, and the class broke into laughter.

"Always the class clown, aren't you, Nick," the teacher said, wagging her finger. "Keep it down, please, unless you'd like to explain the French Revolution to your classmates."

"I wouldn't like that at all," Nick answered honestly. "And I bet they wouldn't like it, either."

The class tittered, and the teacher said, "That will do, Nick. Now, everyone open your textbooks to page 92."

Grudgingly, Nick opened his textbook along with the rest of the class, choosing a page at random, and turned his attention back to Sam. "Are you and Cindy hanging out tonight?"

"Yeah, we're gonna watch a movie at her place and have dinner with her family."

"Awesome! You know what 'watching a movie' is code for, right man?"

"I think it means that we're going to watch a movie," Sam whispered, not wanting to get into the subject.

"Yeah, *sure* it does," Nick whispered back, and made thrusting movements with his hips. The motion caused his desk to squeak.

"Mr. Lynch, could you read aloud for us? Start at the top of the page, please."

Nick looked up and said politely, "What page was that we were on?"

The teacher sighed. She liked Nick, he was basically a good kid, but some days he could get on her nerves. Today was one of those days. "Page 92, Nick."

Nick made a big show of loudly flipping the pages of his book back and forth, finally settling on the proper one, and began reading.

Sam felt his mind wandering, and the sound of his friend's voice drifted into the distance. Of course, it was easy to daydream when you were dating a girl as sweet and beautiful and pure as Cindy.

Slowly but surely, Sam had increased his knowledge about girls and sex. Most of what he heard from Nick he took with a grain of salt, but much of the information his friend offered was true, since it was coming straight from Pete, who would always answer any question that his son had, truthfully. Occasionally, Nick had even asked Pete questions just because Sam asked him to, then reported back the answers. There were just some things that you couldn't find out about on your own.

The first time Sam had had a wet dream, he woke up believing that he had wet the bed. He spent all day thinking himself utterly childish and grotesque, before finally getting up the nerve to ask Nick about it. Sam was both surprised and relieved when Nick mentioned that something similar had happened to him a few times, and promised to ask his dad for more details on the subject.

In a physical sense, Sam had finally caught up to his friend. Nick was still a bit taller, but only by an inch after Sam had gained a great deal of height practically overnight. His shoulders had filled out, his voice had deepened, and he had several chest hairs which he proudly displayed in the boys' locker room. He had some hairs in other areas as well, but those he chose not to show off.

It still felt that Nick was eons more developed than Sam in other areas though. For one thing, Nick was obsessed with having sex. He talked about it all the time, normally in lewd terms. He allowed the other boys in the class to believe that he had had sex before, but had secretly admitted to Sam that he was still a virgin. Still, though, Nick had gone a lot farther with a girl than Sam ever had. Girls seemed to be drawn to Nick. He was funny and handsome and he always had girls giggling around him in the hallways, or calling him nervously on the phone during the evenings.

Nick seemed to take all this in stride, as though he expected nothing less. He wasn't arrogant, or even cocky, just confident and sure of himself in a way that Sam envied. Nick knew his place in the world, and it was a high place indeed.

Sam was popular as well, partly through his close association with Nick, and partly because he was so pleasant to everyone. Sam was the kind of person who would go out of his way to talk to the geeky girl with the head gear, or take the new kid in school under his wing. Sometimes this habit of his infuriated Nick, but mostly Nick understood and even appreciated that his friend was such a nurturing and protective person.

The two of them had discussed it once. They had been about thirteen years old or so, and it was a warm summer evening, but not too hot. The boys had convinced Nick's parents to let them set up camp in the garage for the night so they could hang out with Charlotte.

They dragged out an old air mattress, pumping it up by hand, and laid sleeping bags on top of it. By this time Charlotte had a nice dog bed, although that evening she happily ignored it in favor of curling up next to Sam.

"Why do you think you're so nice?" Nick had asked, out of the blue, and Sam had burst out laughing.

"What does that mean?"

"You're just nice, you know, to everyone. I've never seen a person be so polite to adults, or so friendly to even the most annoying person at school. I mean, you're nice to that know-it-all, stuck-up bitch, Sarah Connelly, for Christ's sake."

"I don't know, I just don't see the point of being rude or mean or excluding anybody. And Sarah's not that bad."

"You're right, she's not that bad, she's *worse* than that." Nick tossed and turned on his sleeping bag, sitting up and thumping at his pillow until he had made a nice divot to rest his head.

"Besides," he continued, shifting his weight. "What I really meant was, why do you think you're so nice when your dad, you know, treats you the way he does. If my dad treated me like that, I'd probably yell at everyone and try to beat up all people that bothered me."

Sam turned to look at his friend. Charlotte nuzzled closer to him. "I'm not sure, maybe it's *because* he's such a jerk. I know how much it sucks to get treated like that, so I don't want to make anyone else have to go through it."

"Huh." Nick tilted his head back, staring at the ceiling as he considered what Sam had said. "I guess that makes sense. But don't serial killers and stuff usually kill people 'cause they had such a bad childhood? I mean, aren't you ever worried that you'll lose it one day and kill someone?"

"Nick, that's crazy. Of course not."

"Sorry, you're right, I'm being a dick, I guess."

"No, you're not. It's interesting, in a way."

"Yeah."

The boys were quiet, listening to Charlotte's heavy breathing. Only friends as close as they were could ever have such an honest conversation without worrying about what the other person would think of them when it was over.

There was a sudden screeching sound, and Sam jolted.

"Sorry about that, everyone, my hand slipped. There's nothing worse that the sound of fingernails on a chalkboard, is there?" Mrs. Milwiski was saying. Sam looked up with a start and saw that his teacher was copying their homework assignment onto the board. Dutifully, he copied it down in his notebook. Sam looked over at Nick and noted with relief that Nick was doing the same thing, until he took a closer look and realized that his friend was just doodling a picture of a very large set of breasts in the margin of his paper.

"I expect you all to have finished reading this chapter on your own, and we'll discuss it tomorrow," Mrs. Milwiski said sternly, tapping on the board with her piece of chalk, leaving dust marks in its wake.

The bell rang signaling the end of the period, and the students, who moments ago had been lolling lazily in their chairs, immediately jumped up, suddenly full of energy.

Nick rolled his eyes at Sam as he closed his textbook and tucked it into his bag. Sam smiled as he opened his own book bag.

Sam had mowed yards all summer to pay for his new book bag and clothes for the school year. He couldn't bring himself to spend another year using Nick's hand-me-down bag from the year before. It had always been like that; Nick would have whatever was nice and current, while Sam was stuck with something tattered and out-of-date. Even when they were kids, Nick always had an E.T. or Transformers of G.I. Joe bag when it was cool. Sam was tired of always coveting what his friend had. It just wasn't normal to be lugging around an Alf bag during the year that everyone else had already discovered the

Ghostbusters. Being a little kid was tough enough on its own, and Sam had vowed long ago that he would be buying more of his own things once he got older. He had made good on his promise.

Patricia purchased most of his things from the local resale shop, which was fine unless you wanted something remotely current. Sam had realized how long it took to save up money from doing chores around the neighborhood when half of what he made had to be handed over to his parents. The summer he turned twelve, Nick had mentioned that Sam shouldn't tell his parents about every little odd job that he did. Sam had felt guilty at first; he didn't like being dishonest, but Nick's idea had paid off, literally. Sam had been hiding money from his parents for a few years now, and it made his life much easier. He didn't feel so bad about it; it was *his* money after all. Even though he wasn't exactly going by it honestly, it was a relief to Sam as he got more self-sufficient. Every step he could take to gain independence was hard-fought and gave him a feeling of pride.

Sam's bag was a simple black color, because it was very un-cool to have any type of design on your bag this year. He placed his notebook inside as well, then zipped it shut and heaved it over his shoulder. His next class was on the far side of the building; he'd have to hurry if he was going to make it on time.

That evening, he sat on the Peterson's overstuffed couch, his arm slung around Cindy's shoulders. She was cuddled up next to him, her head tucked into the crook of his shoulders. Her knees were bent and she looked so small curled up like that, like a little ball, and he felt protective of her.

He bent his head and kissed the top of her head, and she turned and smiled up at him. She uncurled herself, stretching out her legs, and repositioned herself so that she could kiss him on the lips. Gently, their mouths parted and their tongues darted around each other.

Cindy Peterson was the only girl that Sam had ever kissed, and he very much hoped that she would be the last. Sam knew that he was her first boyfriend, and the two of them were both comfortable taking things slow physically. They enjoyed experimenting with one another, but neither felt any urgency to rush things. Cindy said that she appreciated that about Sam, that he was such a gentleman and wouldn't push her into doing things she wasn't comfortable with.

To date, the farthest they had gone, past the point of making out of course, was when Sam had hesitantly placed his hand on her breast. He did that again now, snaking his fingers under her shirt and bra, until he felt the soft supple skin that waited there. Gently, he flicked her nipple and she cooed and kissed him deeper. She then leaned back and took her shirt off, tossing it behind her, and ran her fingers under his shirt, stroking his chest.

He felt himself get hard, and from the way she was leaning on him, he knew Cindy could feel it too. He wondered how she would react.

She smiled shyly at him, then undid the button and the zipper on his jeans, tugging them down until they were around his hips. She maneuvered his underwear around until she was able to slide his penis out from the top. She loosely wrapped her hand around the shaft and moved it back and forth.

Sam would have preferred a heavier touch, but he was so excited that a girl was doing this to him, rather than it happening by his own hand, that he didn't much care.

Tentatively, she stroked him, starring down at him, not meeting his eyes.

After a few minutes, Sam squeezed his eyes shut and stretched his legs out, clenching his muscles. He felt his body spasm heavily and he let out a groan, thrusting his hips into the air.

After he finished, Sam realized the immediate problem with getting a hand job from a girl… what were you supposed to do with… *the stuff?*

His chest was covered with the sticky mess, and he felt his face grow red.

"Here, use this," Cindy said, reaching over and handing him a tissue from her pocket. Sam didn't even ask her if it was clean or not, he just gratefully used it to wipe away the residue, then quickly buttoned up his pants. Cindy put her shirt back on and sat stiffly on the couch next to him.

For a moment, they both started at the television screen, neither having any idea of what movie it was that they were watching.

Sam wasn't sure what was expected of him. Was he supposed to 'return the favor', as Nick phrased it? Should he simply remain sitting there? Offer up a sincere 'thank you'? Was it possible that he was supposed to leave?

In the end, he said gently, "Come here," and held his outstretched arm toward her.

Cindy looked at him gratefully and scooted over until she was in her original position next to him on the couch, her head tucked into his chest. He wrapped his arm around her and gave her a squeeze.

Without looking at him, Cindy asked, "I've never done that before. Was it okay?"

"Absolutely, it was perfect," he answered, nudging her closer into his chest.

He knew that Nick had already received a blow job. Nick said it was the most amazing feeling in the world, and that until he had felt the wet heat of a girl's mouth for himself, Sam would never be able to understand it. Nick had solemnly advised that Sam try to get himself a blow job ASAP.

Despite his friend's recommendation, Sam was fine with not experiencing things as rapidly as Nick. He was content to take things slow, savor the moment, and see what happened.

CHAPTER NINE

The big homecoming football game was one week later, falling a bit early this year. Nick was ecstatic, as he was the only sophomore on the varsity team. Through all those years of practicing sports with his father in the backyard, Nick had become quite an athlete and excelled at as many sports as Sam did in school subjects.

Sam was in the bleachers, his arm around Cindy, and they were cheering wildly. It was the fourth quarter, and after a difficult first half, the Roosevelt Bulldogs were finally in the lead.

Sam didn't know much about sports, but he could appreciate the hard work that his friend was showing out on the field, and he loved feeling a part of the excited crowd. As people cheered and waved purple and white flags in the air, Sam pumped his fist in excitement, crying, "Yeah, go Bulldogs! Go, Nick!"

The game ended with a win, and everyone in the stands stood up and started jumping around. Roosevelt was a small school, so the crowd was mostly made up of students and parents, with a few unhappy younger siblings in tow.

Down on the field the cheerleaders did cartwheels and toe-touches, and the players themselves formed a massive huddle in the center of the field, cheering and thumping one another on the back.

Sam felt himself getting literally swept away with the crowd as people started making their way through the stands, down toward the field.

"That was so much fun!" Cindy called to him, struggling to be heard over the noise.

"Yeah, that was awesome! Let's go find Nick and congratulate him."

"Okay."

Sam took her hand so as not to lose her in the crowd, then picked his way through the fans until he saw Nick making his way toward them.

As soon as he saw them, Nick's face broke out in a grin. He was holding his helmet in one hand, but with the other he embraced Sam in a hug. Sam tried to hug him back, but it was difficult through all the protective padding that Nick was wearing.

"Way to go, man, that was great!" Sam said, grinning.

Nick wiped some of the sweat off his brow and grinned back. "Thanks, man."

By this time some of the cheerleaders had made their way over and were trying to squeeze their way through to talk to him. Nick grinned and beckoned at them, saying, "My public awaits! I'll catch up with you guys later."

He waved goodbye to Sam and Cindy before being swallowed up by the crowd.

"Whew, that was a rush!" Cindy exclaimed. "And to think that the dance is tomorrow night! I just love homecoming weekend, don't you?"

"Yeah, it's a lot of fun."

Cindy intertwined her fingers through Sam's as they walked away from the field, in the opposite direction of most of the people. "So, listen, I've been thinking that maybe I should meet your parents."

"What?" Sam stopped walking suddenly, nearly knocking both of them off balance in the process.

"I mean, we've been together for about two months now, and you know my folks. I just thought it would be nice, you know? I mean, I've never even seen your house before."

Sam continued walking, picking up his pace a little. "Oh, my house is nothing special. You're not exactly missing out on anything, really."

"I didn't meant it like that, silly, I'd just like to see where you live. Plus I'm sure your parents would like to meet me, right?"

"Uh, yeah, of course they would. I talk about you all the time," Sam stammered. In truth, his parents had no idea of Cindy's existence.

"Great! I can't wait to meet them."

Sam looked at Cindy's face and saw how honest and happy she looked. He hated to crush her spirits, but there was simply no way he could ever bring her home to meet his parents. Not yet, anyway. But the air was charged with an electric current of excitement, and everyone seemed to be in a good mood, and he hated to break the magic. This conversation could wait for another time, but he could see that she was waiting for a response.

"I can't wait for them to meet you, either," he murmured, burying his face into her hair, inhaling oranges.

***

If Sam thought that Cindy was beautiful before, he simply had no words to describe how she looked that evening. He watched her walk through the living room, her dress so long that he could barely make out her feet, which had the effect of making it look as though she were floating effortlessly across the room, flying even.

"Wow," he breathed. "You are breathtaking." It seemed an old-fashioned word to use, but it was utterly true.

The dress was a deep purple color, so dark that it almost seemed black. The bodice was full of satiny, shiny material that twinkled as she moved. Her hair was done up in a fancy twist of some sort, with soft tendrils curling down her cheeks and neckline.

Cindy smiled somewhat shyly at him and did a quick twirl. The dress spun out around her, revealing that she was wearing tiny little high heels, and he caught a glimpse of the draped neckline in the back.

"Wow," Sam said, then remembered the purple corsage that he was holding in a box. He stepped up to her and gently placed it on her wrist, just like the lady at the flower shop had told him to do.

Cindy fingered the delicate flowers and baby's breath that encircled her wrist, and smiled up at him. "You look very handsome."

"Thanks," he replied sheepishly. Nick's parents had been kind enough to pick Sam up from his home and drive him to Cindy's, so he didn't have to make the long walk in his dress clothes. They remarked the entire time about how nice he looked. Sam appreciated all of the kind words, but he was always self-conscious when compliments were given to him.

"Pictures, pictures!" her mother called. "I need pictures! Go stand in front of the fireplace."

The young couple walked to where they were directed, Sam noticing that thanks to the heels, Cindy's head finally reached up to his chin. She was a petite little thing, but he liked that about her.

They turned and smiled as Mrs. Peterson clicked away and gushed happily, "Oh, you two make such a darling couple!"

They posed and smiled, trying not to blink, the smiles starting out as natural as possible but becoming more pasted on as the camera clicked away.

"Sam, I'll be sure to give some of the pictures to your mother and father. I know they will want to see how lovely you two look together," Mrs. Peterson continued, her face partly hidden behind the camera. "I'll have to send some with you when they're developed."

"Actually, Mom, that reminds me. I was thinking of asking if Sam and his parents might like to come over for lunch here tomorrow," Cindy said, smiling hopefully.

Sam could feel the blood suddenly drain from his face, although his smile somehow remained frozen, plastered across his cheeks.

"Of course, that's a wonderful idea! We'd love to meet your family, Sam."

"Great, than it's settled," Cindy said, standing up a little taller.

Whereas Cindy was drawing herself upright, Sam felt himself shrinking beside her. Was he the only one that noticed that the air in the atmosphere had changed? Where it had only moments ago been light and relaxed, it now seemed hot and stifled. Sam tugged at the collar of his shirt, and a tiny bead of sweat formed between his shoulder blades, beginning the long journey of rolling slowly down his back.

As if the decision was now final, Cindy and her mother smiled at one another as the camera continued to click at an alarming pace.

Mr. Peterson got up to stand beside his wife, saying, "Honey, you're going to blind the kids with those constant flashes. Leave them alone."

"Oh, just a few more, I want to remember this moment. Cindy, you're growing up so fast, I just can't get over it."

Seeming to understand that his wife was about to become emotional, Mr. Peterson quickly commandeered the camera and said, "You two should get out of here while you can. Have a good time tonight!"

There was a quick exchange of hugs and a tearful goodbye from Mrs. Peterson as the two finally left the house and let Mr. Peterson take them to the dance.

Sam nervously drummed his fingers across his knees without being aware of the movement. Thinking he was nervous about the evening ahead, Cindy reached over and took both his hands between her own, stilling them.

"We're going to have so much fun tonight, Sam. You look so handsome, and I don't even care if we do much dancing or not, so if you're not a good dancer, seriously, that's ok."

Sam looked down and wondered at how his large hands could seem to be almost fully enveloped in the fragile, delicate fingers of his girlfriend. He knew he was acting strangely, and this sweet, raven-haired beauty deserved better of him during her first homecoming dance.

Sam took a deep breath and gulped down a bit more air than he had planned. He coughed slightly, turning his head away from Cindy's so as not to cough in her direction.

Running his thumbs along her fingers, he said, "I know, it's silly to be nervous about the dancing. No matter how bad of a dancer I am, it's not like anyone will be watching me anyway. They will just be wondering how a guy like me ended up with such a beautiful girl."

"Oh, Sam." Cindy gave him a lazy smile and squeezed his hands as Mr. Peterson pretended not to listen and hummed along with the radio.

Oh, if only things were that simple.

The drive didn't take long, and soon Sam found himself helping Cindy out of the car. He noticed that Mr. Peterson had only waved as he drove off, there were no instructions called out about what time to have her home (they were getting a ride with Nick's family again) or a reminder to keep his hands to himself. Like most adults did, Cindy's father simply assumed that his daughter would be safe with Sam.

The cool October air was an assault on the senses after being in the warm car, and Cindy shivered.

"Would you like my jacket?" Sam asked her as they walked up the steps of the school.

"No, I'm okay for now. It will be warm when we get inside. Thank you, though."

When they opened the doors of the school, faint music could be heard. It got progressively louder as they walked closer to the gym and pushed open the double doors.

The decorations committee had really outdone themselves; the gym had been completely transformed. It was almost hard to think that the sweaty, stuffy-smelling gym and this beautiful room filled with purple and white streamers could be the same place. A tarp had been laid across the linoleum of the gym floor, and several groups of students were already dancing to a fast beat. A disco ball spun, casting flickers of mirrored light onto the dancers beneath. Purple and white balloons were secured to the deejay's booth and the refreshment table, moving around as though they, too, wanted to dance.

It was warm in the gym, and Sam struggled out of his suit jacket and hung it over the back of an empty chair. He had found the suit in the back of his father's closet, and was surprised when he had been given permission to wear it. It was a dark navy blue, a little out of date, perhaps, but Sam had purchased a new tie and new shoes to go along with it. He had spent more time than he cared to admit making sure his tie was straight, and polishing his shoes until they gleamed.

Sam fiddled with his hands, clasping them and unclasping them, noticing that his palms were a little sweaty. He felt a bit shy, not sure what to do with himself. He looked around for Nick, but his friend was nowhere to be seen in the crowd.

Suddenly the fast song came to a halt, and a popular slow song started up.

"Would you like to dance?" Cindy asked, grabbing his arm and tugging him toward the makeshift dance floor.

Sam wasn't good at dancing, not like Nick was. In truth, Nick wasn't that great either, but he made up for his lack of skill by being funny. During fast songs he would do all kinds of silly dances, like The Robot or The Shopping Cart, or moves that he simply made up on the spot. During the slow songs, though, he always cozied up to his date, holding her closer than the chaperones deemed appropriate, and trying to put his hands on her behind.

"All right," Sam conceded, following Cindy. Sam supposed that if Nick could handle slow songs, than he could as well.

He wrapped his arms around her waist, and she put hers around his neck. He could feel the corsage tickling the back of his neck.

They swayed back and forth in tune to the music. Because her head was resting on his shoulder, Sam couldn't see the expression on Cindy's face, but he hoped she was smiling.

They circled slightly, so that Sam was now facing further into the dancers. It looked so odd to see his classmates dressed up; anything other than jeans was out of the ordinary. The perimeter of the dance floor was crowded, full of people who had come stag to the dance, each waiting for someone else to ask them to dance, or couples who were too embarrassed to go out onto the floor.

Sam pulled Cindy tighter to him, feeling happy that he had someone special. It seemed nothing short of a miracle that he was not on the sidelines along with some of his unluckier classmates, watching rather than participating.

He could see the light playing off Cindy's hair and the glittery material of her dress, and he imagined that other boys were envious of him, a feeling he was unaccustomed to.

The song ended quickly, and another fast song began. The couple let go of each other. Cindy started to dance, but sensed Sam's discomfort, and instead suggested that they get some punch.

Together they walked off the dance floor, and Sam said, "I don't know, you might want to steer clear of the punch. Nick told me that some of the senior guys on the football team were planning to spike it with alcohol. Would you like some water instead?"

"It's still early, I'll take my chances," Cindy replied, and Sam carefully ladled some of the frothy red liquid into a clear plastic glass.

"Yum, I don't think they could have poured anything in here. It tastes too good!" she said, licking her upper lip.

Sam got some punch for himself and gave it a sniff. Did it smell a little funny, or was that just his imagination?

"So, I'm really looking forward to your family coming over tomorrow," Cindy said.

Oh, crap, Sam had forgotten all about that. He needed to come up with some sort of good excuse fast, something believable. Unfortunately, Sam wasn't very good at thinking on his feet.

Cindy was looking at him, and he mumbled, "Uh, I don't think tomorrow's a good day for us."

"Why not?"

Oh, shoot. She wanted a reason. "Um, my mom might have an appointment. Or wait, actually, I forgot, I think my dad is getting sick." He knew he was speaking too quickly, and making little sense.

Cindy was looking at him strangely, and she said, "Sam, do you not want me to meet your parents?"

"What? Of course, I do. That's not it at all."

"Really? Because it sounds like you're lying to me, and I don't understand why. You were being so sweet to me just now in the car, and now it's like you've totally changed your mind about something. You aren't the type to lie, Sam, and I want to know what's going on."

Sam looked around the room, hoping an answer would appear out of thin air, or at least looking for something that might serve as a distraction.

Cindy put her hands on her hips and scowled, saying firmly, "Sam, I'm serious. Tell me what's going on."

"I told you, nothing. It's just that tomorrow is a bad time."

"Okay, then when would be a good time? On what day, exactly, will your mother be free and your father be healthy?"

Sam looked at her with a scowl of his own. He wasn't used to Cindy questioning him, although, to be fair, he probably had never given her anything to question. Nick was always talking about how crazy girls were, how they could get all emotional for no reason at all, and how their feelings could change on a dime. Sam hadn't understood before, but could this have been what he meant?

"Look, can we just talk about this later?" he pleaded, still trying to save the evening. "Let's just have fun. I'll even dance to one of these fast songs, okay?"

Sam thought this would appease her, but apparently Cindy was no different than any other teenage girl. She actually stomped her foot as she exclaimed, "Sam, I want to know why you won't let me meet your family. Are you ashamed of me? Am I not pretty enough for you?"

Just what the heck was this? Where was this coming from? Had that car ride only taken place just minutes ago? Sam took a sip of his punch, certain now that there must be alcohol in it.

He took a deep breath. How could he explain that Cindy wasn't the one whom he was embarrassed of? He said calmly, "Cindy, you are the most beautiful girl in the world, believe me. There are just some issues between me and my parents right now, that's all."

"But they would still want to know who their son is dating, right?"

"Um, well -"

"Wait a minute," Cindy said accusingly. "You *have* told your parents about me, right?"

Sam started wringing his hands again, trying to buy time and think of just the right thing to say so that he wouldn't upset her further. Unfortunately though, the pause seemed to have the opposite effect.

"Oh my God, I can't believe this!" she cried haughtily, her emotions wavering somewhere between anger and hurt.

Sam wondered which would win out, and would there be tears? He hated tears.

"I'm going to talk to Linda," Cindy announced finally, turning around in a huff and stomping away.

Sam stood there alone, his mouth agape. Now the sweat was rolling down his back in earnest. He needed to find Nick; he would know what to do.

Sam looked around him. The decorations which had seemed pretty just moments ago now seemed cheesy. Even the disco ball was now sending off sparks of light in a nauseating pattern.

Sam hadn't caught a glimpse of his friend, and decided to check the bathroom. He hurried out of the gym and walked into the closest bathroom, which just had a few boys in it who Sam didn't know. They were standing at the urinals, and only one of the stall doors was shut.

"Nick?" Sam called out hesitantly, but there was no reply. The other boys looked at him strangely.

Sam backed out of the bathroom, wondering what to do. Then a sudden impulse hit him, and he quickly walked to the bathroom on the other end of the long hallway, past all the ill-colored green lockers.

This time when he pushed open the bathroom door, a huge puff of smoke greeted him, and he could hear raucous laughter echoing off the stalls. This must be the right place.

He entered and tried to peer though the haze. There were several older boys, seniors, standing around cracking jokes. His eyes finally came to rest on Nick, who was standing amongst them.

Sam cleared his throat and Nick looked up, giving him a huge grin.

"Sam! Hey there, man, I was going to come find you! Come here and take a swig of this."

Sam walked over to his friend, trying to inch past the senior boys, and reached out for the flask that Nick handed him.

"What's this?"

"It's whiskey. It's awesome, try it."

"How did you get this?"

"Oh, we've got lots of it," Nick said casually. He was speaking too loudly. "Brian's parents are out of town, and Brian smuggled a bunch of stuff from his dad's liquor cabinet. Come on, try some."

Hesitantly, Sam tipped the metal flask up to his lips and took a sip. He had tried beer before, but never hard alcohol, and certainly never straight. The liquid shot down his throat like it was on fire, seeming to burn him from the inside out.

Sam sputtered and coughed, and Nick and the other boys laughed. "You've just got to get used to it, man. The first few sips are rough."

"You could have told me that before I took the first few sips," Sam said ruefully, and the boys all laughed again.

Sam knew that he would never have been welcomed in this bathroom, full of seniors drinking and smoking, had he not been a friend of Nick's. He didn't want to make his friend look bad in front of the older boys. He didn't want Nick to be ashamed of him.

Steeling himself, he took another sip, bigger this time, trying not to wince as he swallowed.

"Atta boy," Nick said, with some pride in his voice.

Sam passed the flask back to him, amazed at the several big gulps that Nick took at once, before passing the flask to another boy. Sam noticed that there were several flasks and even an actual bottle, half empty, being shared.

"So, what's going on in the gym?" Nick asked, wiping his mouth on the back of his sleeve, not seeming to care that he was wearing a suit.

Sam was hoping to speak to Nick privately, and he made a gesture with his head that he hoped his friend would understand.

Fifteen years of friendship paid off, and Nick said to the other boys, "I'll be back," then followed Sam out the bathroom door. The voices of the other boys grew muffled as the door shut behind them.

The sudden quiet of the near-empty hallway was eerie.

"What's up?" Nick asked, his words slurring. He looked a little unsteady on his feet, and seemed to be having a hard time standing still. He shuffled around, then went to lean against the wall for balance. He misjudged the space a bit, and ended up crashing his shoulder hard into one of the lockers, sending a loud bang reverberating down the empty hallway.

Sam watched all this warily, waiting until his friend had steadied himself. "Cindy and I got into a fight; she's mad at me."

"What did you fight about?" Nick's breath smelled of whiskey and smoke.

"She wants to meet my parents, and I don't want her to."

"Hmm," Nick pondered this for a moment. "Maybe you should just let her meet them. It would get her off your back about it."

Sam stared at his friend for a moment before saying incredulously, "Are you kidding? You of all people know how they are, Nick. Plus, I haven't even told them that I'm dating anyone."

"So tell them, then just bring her over for a few minutes."

Sam shook his head, trying to clear it. How drunk was Nick, anyway? "I'm just saying, it could go bad, that's all. And she definitely wouldn't like my parents."

"*I* don't like your parents, but I still like you," Nick said with a grin. "And since I have no intention of having sex with you, I think you had better figure out a way to introduce them, quick. Or better yet, *tell* Cindy you'll introduce them, and she'll let you fuck her 'cause she'll be so happy, then you can break up with her and it won't be an issue."

Sam wanted to grab his friend by the shoulders and shake some sense into him. Obviously, there would be no talking to Nick this evening.

"Where's your date at, anyway?"

"She's dancing with her friends. It's fine, I'll hang out with her later. I told her I had some stuff to do." Nick grinned and pointed at the bathroom. "So anyway, where's Cindy? She's got a nice ass, man. You should go find her."

Sam thought of something, and had a small glimmer of hope. He knew that Nick liked to act tough in front of his friends, but surely he would play nice if he needed to. "Would you go find Cindy and talk to her for me? Just try to make her understand?"

Nick put one hand on Sam's shoulder and inched closer to his face. "Sure I will, man. I'd do anything for you. I love you, Sam."

"Um, okay. I love you too."

Nick started laughing like something one of them said was hilarious, but Sam couldn't think what it might have been.

"I'll go find your girl for you and talk some sense into her. Crazy fucking chicks, am I right?"

"Okay, thanks," Sam said, breathing a small sigh of relief. Girls always responded to what Nick said to them. If Nick, even an inebriated Nick, told Cindy that she should forgive him, then she would. Simple as that.

Nick grinned and disappeared toward the gym, calling behind him, "Just give me ten minutes to work the Lynch magic, then come back to the dance."

Sam nodded and looked at his watch, watching the minute hand slowly creep by ten times, then nervously wandered back into the gym.

He looked around but didn't see either Nick or Cindy. He walked around the perimeter of the dance floor, checked by the refreshment table, and even walked toward the deejay booth. Still no sign of them.

Getting a little anxious, Sam discovered Cindy's friend, Linda, and asked if she had seen Cindy.

"No," came the answer, "but she's pissed at you, I can tell you that much. I think she went outside with your friend, Nick. Why don't you want her to meet your family, anyway?"

It looked like that other thing that Nick had said was also true, that girls always talked to one another. Apparently tonight he had managed to make an enemy of not only his date, but of the entire female population of Roosevelt High.

Sam shrugged off her words and walked out of the gym, towards the front door.

He went outside, the wind blustery against his skin as he realized he left his suit jacket inside. Sam thought it odd that Nick would take Cindy outside since it was so cool, but perhaps he thought some fresh air would do the situation good. Nick always knew best, after all.

Sam wrapped his arms around himself for warmth and looked around. They were nowhere to be seen. He went toward the picnic tables but saw that they were empty. Frowning, Sam continued walking around the outside of the school, stopping when he thought he heard a noise.

Yes, there it was again, a strange noise that sounded something like a mixture of a human and animal. Curious, Sam followed the sound to a small grove of pine trees that sat near the side of the building. He traipsed through the undergrowth of the trees, kicking dead pine needles as he walked, and there he found his best friend and his girlfriend.

Stunned, Sam could only watch at first, unable to tear his eyes away, or even to speak. Nick and Cindy were so occupied with one another that they hadn't heard him as he walked up.

Nick's suit jacket was laying on the ground, and Cindy lay on top of it, her dress hiked up to her hips, her underwear lying next to her. Nick was lying face down on top of her, holding himself up with his elbows, his body moving up and down in quick rhythm. Sam heard again the sound that he had thought was an animal. it was actually coming from Nick; a deep, guttural sound, as he repeatedly rammed his body into Sam's sweet, pure Cindy.

Sam rarely cursed, but suddenly the bewilderment left him and he found himself shouting hastily, "What the FUCK?"

At the sudden sound of his voice, the motion stopped and Nick jerked upward, beyond startled.

"Sam?" he questioned, peering at his friend as though he couldn't quite place him.

"Yes, who the hell else do you think it would be?" Sam cried, his hands clenching themselves into tight fists.

Cindy cried, "Oh God, Sam!" She started crying as she urgently grabbed at her underwear and slipped them on. She stood up, tugging the hem of her dress back down, and trying to brush stray pine needles from it. Her pretty hair-do was messy now, the clip having come unfastened, and a leaf was stuck in her bangs.

Nick stood up as well, but slower, as though he felt he could take his time. Sam noticed with a nauseating feeling that Nick's penis was hanging out of his fly. Nick seemed to notice it at the same time, and lazily tucked it back inside, zipping his pants.

"What the hell are you doing?" Sam sputtered.

Cindy started crying in earnest and tried to apologize through her tears, but emotions seemed to overcome her and she ran off. Not bothering to chase after her, Sam turned his attention back to Nick and glared.

Nick bent down to retrieve his jacket from the ground, giving it several shakes. Both boys watched as a scattering of pine needles and dirt fell from the jacket, coming to rest back on the ground from whence they came.

146

"Sam, hey there, man."

"Really? All you can say is *hello*?" Sam's eyes were wide, his thoughts spinning so quickly that he couldn't choose just one to focus on.

"What else can I say, man? I'm sorry, okay?"

"I sent you to *talk* to Cindy, not have *sex* with her!"

"I know, I know. Look, Cindy was really upset when I found her, she looked like she was gonna cry or something, so I said we should go outside for some privacy, you know?" Nick carefully put his jacket back on as he spoke, adding, "I told her that you were crazy about her, and she said 'really?' and I said of course, after all, look how pretty you look, and she said, 'do you really think I'm pretty' or something like that, and I said sure I did, and she smiled and hugged me, and I could feel myself getting turned on, and one thing led to another. You know how it is."

"No, I *don't* know how it is," Sam spat, angry and humiliated. "She's never even had sex before, you asshole. And for that matter, neither have you."

"Well, everyone's gotta have a first time sometime, right? Hey man, at least this way there won't be as much pressure on you."

"What? How can you even say that to me?"

"I'm sorry, I'm a little drunk," Nick confided in a whisper. As if that was news.

"You're an asshole," Sam said again, because he couldn't think of anything else to say. He wasn't good with words, English wasn't his strongest subject, and he couldn't figure out how to convey his feelings properly. Instead, he turned and stomped off in the opposite direction that Cindy had gone earlier.

Perhaps trying to lighten the mood, or perhaps because he meant it, Nick called after him, "A real friend would have at least let me finish!"

Sam kept walking. He knew that if he turned around he would punch Nick, and he didn't want to become his father.

CHAPTER TEN

Sam and Nick had never gone so long without speaking before. Certainly, they had had arguments; fifteen years of growing up with a person will do that. But the skirmishes were always minor, quickly apologized for or simply forgotten.

This was something new, it was more than just an argument, it was a shift in their relationship, and neither boy was prepared for it. After virtually having grown up together, suddenly the absence of the other friend was very acute, their missing presence palpable.

It was especially strange because no one else was aware of the new dynamic, at least not right away. They still had assigned seats next to each other in some of their classes, and one of their teachers thought she was being nice by assigning them to be partners on a project together. Their friends automatically saved two seats for them on the bus, as 'Nick-and-Sam' were considered a package deal. The idea of seeing one of them without the other was simply unthinkable; the idea would have been more of a believable possibility with a pair of conjoined twins. For the boys were essentially that - conjoined in everything but the physical sense.

Cindy had given several tearful apologies and begged forgiveness from Sam. She offered many different excuses for her behavior, ranging from low self-esteem to spiked punch, but Sam would have none of it. It was odd, but much like they had in the past for May, Sam's feelings for Cindy had simply evaporated. Had someone told him the morning of the dance that his feelings for Cindy would disappear, he never would have believed it. But the truth was, he could no longer look at Cindy without seeing Nick, and that was an image that would have taken the loving feeling out of any circumstance.

The irony of the situation did not escape Sam. He had asked Nick to get Cindy back together with him, to melt away her anger and lead her into Sam's arms. He had also wanted Cindy to stop caring about meeting his parents. In an ugly, round-about way, Nick had managed to accomplish exactly that.

For his part, Nick was keeping a respectful distance. He, too, had offered apologies and excuses, ranging from being highly intoxicated to being a slave to his own dick. Again, Sam did not want to hear these things. He was upset with Cindy, but that was nothing compared to the utter betrayal that he felt from his best friend.

Their sixteenth birthdays came and went, and the boys still didn't talk. This was especially troubling because Nick had inherited his mothers' old suburban, and could now officially drive in his own right. Not only was this thrilling on its own, but it meant that Sam (who had not yet been able to save enough for a car) didn't have to ride his bike or wait for the bus all the time. He had been immensely looking forward to the chauffeured ride to school, but now that the boys were in the biggest fight of their lives, he still walked to the bus stop, feeling ever much like the little kid while his friend went on to become an adult, leaving Sam behind in every way possible.

Over the next three weeks Cindy gave up hope, but Nick tried everything he could think of to get back into Sam's good graces. Nick hadn't realized before how much he relied on his friend. (Also, his grades were seriously starting to fall.) Nick attempted reverse psychology (without knowing there was a name for the behavior), ambivalence, even downright sincerity. Nothing worked. It was as though Sam had wrapped a shroud of secrecy over himself, allowing no one in, in the ultimate act of privacy and self-survival.

One day at the end of November, Sam noticed (without much interest) that Cindy was absent from school. Then she was absent again the next day. That was odd, because she was a good student who normally took school seriously. On the third day when she wasn't there, Sam started to wonder if she was ill. He didn't care about it from an 'ex-boyfriend' standpoint so much as he did from a 'decent human being' standpoint, and he hoped she didn't have anything serious.

Sam caught up to Cindy's best friend in the lunch room. "Hey, Linda, I noticed that Cindy hasn't been in school for a few days. Is she sick?"

Linda turned to look at Sam with such venom in her eyes that he was taken aback. "I don't know why you would give a shit about that, Sam. You don't give a shit about anything else."

With that, Linda tossed her hair over her shoulder, turned and flounced off, slamming her lunch tray down on her table with such malice that her little box of milk rattled.

Sam should have known better. It had been unofficially decided by the three parties involved that the 'situation' outside the school with Nick and Cindy never actually happened, at least not to the general population of the high school. Right after it happened Cindy had gone to Nick and asked that he not say anything, for fear of her reputation and of further hurting Sam. Nick had readily agreed, as he wanted Sam to have no reminders of the events of that evening. Plus, even though he had finally had sex, it just wasn't cool to do your best friend's girl. This was one conquest he would be keeping to himself. Nick and Cindy had both gone privately to Sam and told him they wouldn't be saying anything. Sam had simply shrugged.

Unfortunately, since Sam and Cindy were no longer together, and since Cindy had been acting, well, *strange* lately, the student body at large assumed that the ever-pleasant Sam had dumped Cindy. Now he had somehow become the bad guy in all this.

The weirdest thing about the whole situation was that Cindy never did return to school. Sam heard that she had transferred to a different area high school, but he couldn't figure out why. Surely things between them weren't that bad, were they? Was she just so ashamed of her behavior that she couldn't stand to see Nick or Sam again? According to the rumor mill, she had left school due to a broken heart, but Sam didn't think that could be the case. Or could it? Was he really worthy of having a broken heart over?

He tried once or twice to get in contact with Cindy, even going so far as to call her house. Mr. Peterson had told him not to bother calling again, than practically hung up on him.

Sam spent many nights awake, pondering how someone who was supposed to love you from the start, like a parent, and someone that you fell in love with on your own, people who were once (or should have been) so completely important in your life, could just fall away. Sam wasn't even sure if he was truly ambivalent toward Cindy, or if it was some kind of survival trick of the human mind. *If someone treats you badly, you don't care about them. It simply stops, and you are a better person for it.* Although it sounded good psychologically speaking (Sam was getting an A in that class) he figured that no, it was probably just a bunch of horse shit. But Sam had spent literally his entire life pretending, making himself believe until it actually became truth, that if a loved one hurts you, you simply stop loving them in return.

Maybe it was because Cindy was no longer present, but gradually Nick was able to work his way back into Sam's good graces. In the middle of November Nick simply set his lunch tray down opposite from Sam's and sat down, as if they had never stopped being friends.

"Hey there, man. How'd you do on that algebra quiz? I bombed it," he said, nonchalantly picking up his hamburger and taking a massive bite. Ketchup squirted out onto his chin, and he swiped Sam's napkin to wipe it off with.

"I think I did all right on it, actually."

"Well, there's a surprise!" Nick answered, laughing. "You always do pick this stuff up so much more than I do."

"If you want, I can help you with the problems we got for homework," Sam said graciously.

Nick looked up and grinned, relieved, in more ways than one. "That would be a huge help, man. My math grade is pretty bad right now."

Sam smiled and said, "I can come home with you after school, if you want."

Nick nodded. "Hey, the lunch lady gave me an extra brownie. Do you want it?"

"Sure, thanks."

Sam took a bite of the nearly stale brownie (he had gotten spoiled by May's desserts) and chewed thoughtfully. If Nick was offering to give his dessert away, than he must truly be sorry indeed, and ready to make up.

And after that, the fight was over with. Both boys had missed the company of the other, though neither felt very comfortable admitting to it. Perhaps if Sam had actually hauled off and punched Nick, the problem may have gotten out of their systems a lot sooner. But as it was, enough time had passed and they both agreed, without the benefit of the spoken word, that everything was back to normal. The truth was, each boy needed the other. Brothers, no matter how many drops of blood they may share, belong to one another.

After school that day, Sam rode the bus home with Nick, and the two of them entered the Lynch house together, chatting and laughing.

May looked up from the mixing bowl she was working with and gave a sigh of relief. She had been concerned when Sam had stopped coming by the house, worried that that nasty father of his had done something. Upon asking her son about it, May had been assured that Sam was quite healthy, just busy with a new after-school activity. As the days turned into weeks, Nick admitted (after much prodding) that they had had an argument, but no amount of persuading would get him to admit what it had been about. Now, May was delighted to see Sam back in her house. She had missed him; he was as much a part of the family as any of them. Plus, she knew that he was a good influence on her son. May rolled her eyes up to heaven. There was no telling what Nick might have gotten into by this point in his life if it wasn't for their friendship; he had always been one to push boundaries.

"Hello there, Sam, I'm making fish for dinner. Should I set you a place?" she asked. May had already realized that it was best not to bring up the fact that he had been mysteriously absent from their home for so long. Whatever their little dispute was about, she was certain it couldn't be over anything serious, and she didn't want to draw their attention back to whatever had come between them.

"Sure May, I'd love that, thank you," Sam answered, smiling.

May quickly searched his face and arms for any signs of bruising or scarring, but saw nothing there, for the scars he had now were the kind that couldn't be seen, and smiled more easily as she answered, "Great, dinner will be ready in about an hour. Why don't you go take Charlotte for a walk before we eat?"

"Absolutely!" Sam grinned and led Nick to the garage. As soon as the dog recognized him, she barked joyously and ran to Sam, licking his face.

He laughed and tried to wipe off the saliva with one hand while petting her with the other.

Nick watched the happy reunion with a smile. Although it had never been mentioned, it had just been assumed that he would look after Charlotte while Sam was away. No matter what two best friends are fighting over, no matter how serious an argument, some things are simply understood.

"Do you want to go for a walk, girl? Do you?" Sam was asking now, laughing as the dog pranced around happily. Nick attached her collar and the boys set out.

Despite the cold, Nick was feeling warm as he said, "I've been walking her every day, you know."

Sam glanced at his friend and said, "Thank you for taking care of her."

"Anytime, man. I love Char, you have a really good dog there."

"*We* have a really good dog," Sam corrected, and Nick smiled.

They continued walking, at a faster pace than normal due to the chill in the air. Charlotte was oblivious to the temperature, happily running ahead of them as far as the leash would allow, then doubling back to see what they were doing, then running ahead again.

"So how have things been going with your folks?" Nick asked, not sure if this was acceptable subject material.

"Not too bad, I guess. I mean, things are the same with, well, you know. But I've been staying late at school a lot, spending time in the library mostly, then taking the late bus home. Then I grab a quick dinner and go to my room. I always tell them I'm in there doing homework. It's not so bad, really."

"I don't know, it sounds pretty boring to me. The library followed by homework? That sucks, man."

Sam laughed. "I don't mind the library."

Nick shuddered as if the very mention of the word did him physical harm, and Sam punched him lightly on the shoulder.

It was true, things had been slightly better at home, but only because Sam made an effort to spend as little time there as possible. When he was home he would call out that he was either leaving for or returning from school. His mother rarely glanced up from the show she was watching, and his father would only grunt in reply. Sam often wondered if they would even notice if he didn't bother to come home for days at a time. Sometimes he missed the violence, at least it was attention, at least it was proof that his parents knew he existed.

Sam sometimes felt as though he were simply surviving at his house. Not living in it, not making happy memories, but simply surviving, floating through time until something better came along. Seeing May today only served to remind him how other families, normal families, behaved. There were smiles and hugs and laughter, there was conversation. There were arguments and apologies and forgiveness. There was *interaction*, there was love. Sam didn't have any of those things, and he constantly wondered what his life would have been like if that had been different.

Some of the kids at school envied him. He could stay out late if he wanted without asking permission (which he never did). It didn't matter if he got a bad grade (which he also never did) because his parents simply didn't care. Of course, that meant that they didn't care when he did well either, and therefore he never received praise. He had learned when he was young not to bother showing off his good grades, for there would be no test papers or art projects hanging on the refrigerator in the Maver household.

Sam could remember being in the third grade and receiving his test back; he had been the only student in the class to have a large red 'A' scrawled across the top. Sam had tossed the paper in the trash on his way out, and his teacher had rescued the paper from the wastebasket and chased after him, saying that she knew his parents would want to see how hard he had worked. Sam learned after that to throw his papers away when the teacher wasn't looking, or to wait until he got home, then shove them into the trash can out back by the garage.

"Man, it's freezing out here, let's turn back," Nick said, doing a quick about-face.

"Okay." Sam followed, sorry that their walk would be ending soon. It was nice spending time alone with Nick and Charlotte again after all this time, despite the chill in the air. He had been wondering if the conversation might change to the elephant in the room, so to speak, but bringing up Cindy's name now didn't feel right.

The two boys shuffled along, their pace quickening as they drew nearer to the house. They were quiet as they walked, each consumed with their own thoughts, and breathing heavily. Their warm breath left great puffs of white in the air before they faded away, only to be found again with the next breath of air they expelled from their lungs.

Charlotte kept pace easily, walking next to Sam, her tail wagging the whole time. A random squirrel darted past, chattering away, and for once the dog chose not to chase it.

She was far more excited to be spending time with Sam than she was interested in the animal's whereabouts.

"Welcome back, I've got hot chocolate for you." May smiled when the boys traipsed back into the kitchen, offering them two steaming mugs.

"Are there marshmallows in there?" Nick asked with concern.

"Of course. I wouldn't dare serve it any other way." May laughed and winked at Sam, who smiled back and gratefully took his mug, cupping it in his hands for warmth. He still adored May, but the same wink that would have sent his emotions into a tailspin just a few years ago now caused him to feel nothing in particular. Strange, how feelings worked. Idly, Sam wondered if he would ever fall in love again the way he had loved May, and later Cindy. Or was that real love at all? It had certainly felt like it at the time.

Sam blew lightly on his hot chocolate, then gingerly took a sip. The liquid rushed down his throat, warming him. For a brief moment he was reminded of the feeling he got the night of the dance when he had sipped from the flask, but this experience was much better. Instead of fiery and unpleasant, this warm liquid felt comforting.

"We're going to go watch TV," Nick announced, and his mother nodded.

Carrying his mug carefully so as not to slosh anything over the sides, Sam followed Nick into the living room. Nick sprawled onto the couch, his lanky body taking up almost the entire thing, so Sam sat on the rocking chair. With the toe of his shoe he gently tapped the ground, causing his chair to rock back and forth ever so slightly. He sipped his cocoa and watched as Nick flipped through the channels, not stopping on one thing long enough to even see what show was on. From the garage, Charlotte let out a brief howl, unsure if Sam was going to disappear again, then she settled down and fell asleep.

"God, there isn't shit to watch," Nick complained, scrolling through all the channels for a second time. Louder, he added, "I wish my parents would finally get cable television in this house!"

"I wish my son would finally do his chores, but we can't all have what we want in life," May's voice called from the kitchen.

Sam laughed as Nick scowled. Imagine, being able to skip one's chores. Sam wouldn't have dreamed of doing such a thing, for there would be hell to pay. It simply wasn't worth it.

The front door made a slight creaking sound. "Yum, is that fresh fish I smell?" Pete's voice boomed.

"Sure is," May replied. Without having to look, Sam knew that she had gone over to her husband and stood on her tiptoes to kiss his cheek. He had seen it happen many times before, and he used to think it odd that a wife would go and greet her husband when he arrived home from work.

"And guess who will be joining us for dinner?" May's voice continued.

Pete walked into the living room, squeezing out of his jacket as he went. "Sam, I was hoping it was you! How have you been?"

Sam stood up and held his mug with his left hand, shaking the hand that Pete offered with his right. When he was younger the greeting would have been a hug, but as Nick had told his father, they were men now, and men didn't hug other men.

"I'm doing very well, thank you. I hope Charlotte hasn't been a bother to you."

"No, no, she's very well behaved, and quiet. I only wish we could keep her in the house, but you know me." Pete shrugged his shoulders helplessly.

"It's no problem, really. I'm just happy you're willing to let her stay here."

Pete leaned closer to Sam and whispered in his ear, "Sometimes I even sneak out there and pet her. It makes me sneeze like crazy, but she really is a good dog. Now don't go telling May that I said that."

Sam grinned and nodded his agreement. He had nearly forgotten how nice it was to spend time in the Lynch household. It was just so *easy* here.

"Nick, pick a channel, for goodness sake. This is giving me a headache," Pete said good-naturedly, spinning around to see the channels on his television whipping past.

"Or go start on your homework!" May suggested from the kitchen.

At that, Nick instantly found a channel that he could live with.

Pete playfully knocked his son's legs from the couch so he had room to sit, and together the three of them settled back to watch television. They were enjoying the scents of dinner that were floating in from the kitchen, their stomachs grumbling in response.

Soon May announced that dinner was ready, and the three stood up and stretched, ambling into the kitchen. Sam picked up his empty cocoa mug, then walked over to the coffee table to collect Nick's as well so he could place them in the kitchen sink.

The dinner table at the Lynch home was set for four, as the universe had always intended.

Sitting down and placing his napkin on his lap, Sam said eagerly, "This looks delicious, May." He had been eating school lunches and microwave dinners for the past month, and his mouth was watering.

"No it doesn't, you know I don't really like fish," Nick chimed in.

May sighed and replied, "Just eat some of it, all right? Goodness, it's like dealing with you when you were three years old all over again."

"You always say I'm growing up too fast, so you're welcome," Nick said, grinning mischievously. Sometimes Pete and May wished their son could be a little more like Sam, and all four of them knew it.

Pete scooped a heaping pile of fresh green beans onto his plate, saying, "So, Sam, how is that pretty girlfriend of yours doing? It's Cindy, right? She seemed very nice when we dropped you off at her house before the dance."

The boys froze, Sam's mouth hanging agape, Nick's forkful of fish halted in mid-air halfway to his mouth.

May noticed the sudden change but Pete was oblivious as he continued serving himself, adding, "Nick goes through girlfriends so quickly, I can hardly keep up. It's nice that you were able to find someone special."

"Um," Sam stammered, his face flushing. "We're not exactly together anymore." He dared to glance at Nick, who was now watching him intently.

"Oh, I'm sorry to hear that. What happened?"

Sam shifted uncomfortably in his chair, and May interjected, "Sweetheart, it isn't our business to pry into Sam's personal life."

Sam said a silent prayer of thanks to May, but Pete said, "I don't mean to over-step my boundaries, Sam. I guess I just think of you as a member of the family."

Pete was looking at him expectantly, and after he worded it that way, how could Sam not respond?

"We just had a falling out, I suppose."

"That's a shame. I had assumed that after the dance when Nick told me that neither of you would need a ride home, that things were going rather well." Pete raised his eyebrows up and down, grinning at Sam, who nearly knocked over his water glass. Nick started coughing uncontrollably.

That night he had ended up walking home, a journey that took over thirty minutes by foot, scuffing up his new shoes and getting mud on his pants. When his father had noticed it the next morning, he had shoved Sam into a wall and yelled that he would be paying for the dry cleaning bill.

Sam had been forced to retrieve his suit jacket from the lost and found during the next school day. Sam had no idea how Cindy had gotten home, had she possibly called her father? Perhaps that was why Mr. Peterson had been so abrupt with him over the phone.

After receiving a curt look from his wife, Pete decided to let the situation drop, and the conversation switched topics.

When Sam arrived home that evening he wondered if his parents would comment on how late he was. Normally he had to adhere to the bus schedule, and arrived home before dinner.

It had been so long since he had eaten at Nick's house that he felt certain his parents would notice his absence.

Sam walked into the door and kicked off his shoes so he wouldn't track mud into the house, being sure to line them up carefully in the shoe caddy.

"Mom, Dad, I'm home!" he called, shrugging off his coat, smoothing it free of wrinkles, and hanging it on the hook behind the door.

He could hear the television on. He walked over and saw both his parents watching the same movie that he and Nick and Pete had been watching earlier.

Feeling elated at having his friend back, being welcomed back into the Lynch household, and even surviving the first mention of Cindy, Sam decided to try again. He hadn't realized until spending the evening with the Lynches, how much he missed human interaction.

"I just had dinner with Nick and his family. We had catfish and it was delicious."

"Huh," his father said.

"That's nice, dear," his mother answered, never turning her head from the screen.

Sam was tempted to utter, "Just kidding, we actually ate blowfish, raw. I hear that stuff can kill you if it's not cooked properly. So we decided not to cook it at all, just to be safe." But he knew he would probably get the same 'huh' and 'that's nice, dear' no matter what he said. It wasn't like he was being listened to.

Finally giving up, Sam let out a deep sigh and headed to his room, closing the door quietly behind him.

CHAPTER ELEVEN

Mark Maver was an army brat, then followed in his father's footsteps and joined the service himself straight out of high school. He had a love-hate relationship with the army; he enjoyed the stability it offered but despised the more menial tasks that were often assigned to him. Mark felt that he was able to give much more of himself to his country. His father had seen action, and he often spoke of defending one's country as the single greatest honor that a man could achieve. Mark didn't feel that keeping a latrine clean amounted to much of an honor for anyone, except perhaps to the next man who visited the bathroom.

After much patience Mark finally started to move up the ranks and he no longer found himself having to do the tedious tasks; instead he was the one assigning others to do them. This gave him a huge surge of pride.

During a leave Mark followed along with some of the other commanding officers and they arrived at a bar. It was one of those dingy, hole-in-the-wall places, most of the patrons being the regular customers. It was dimly lit and the air swirled with smoke. The smell of stale beer permeated the air, and the floor was sticky from countless spilled drinks that no one had ever gotten around to mopping up.

The men sat down at a corner table and a pretty young waitress walked over to take their order, then scurried off to fill pitchers of cheap beer for them.

As soon as she was out of earshot a man named Dave spoke. "Dang, she's the purdiest little thang I've seen in a long time." Dave had a thick southern drawl, and the drunker he got the more difficult it became to understand him.

The other men nodded their agreement, then the conversation quickly turned to the utter hopelessness of the new set of recruits.

Mark wasn't really paying attention to his buddies; his eyes were following the waitress, watching as she picked up two frothy pitchers and carried them to their table. She set them down silently, glancing warily at the men as she did so. Mark tried to meet her eyes to offer her a smile of thanks, but she looked away before he had a chance, seeming anxious to leave.

Mark took a long slug of beer and felt himself immediately relax. He was always sober at work, but anytime he was off-duty Mark enjoyed this particular vice. He had learned the behavior from his own father, yet another thing that was passed from father to son. Mark's father often drank beer but preferred scotch. Perhaps one day Mark would prefer it as well, but for now he stuck with the cheaper option.

Mark's father had been a tough man, one who you didn't dare to defy. He believed in obedience, and he believed that the only way to keep order was with his belt. When he was a boy, Mark feared the man but was a bit awe-struck by him as well. Everyone did what he said; he possessed so much power. Now that he was older, Mark respected his late father, and hoped that one day he too would rise to the rank of a colonel. His father had done the army proud, and Mark knew that he would accomplish great things as well.

The men drank their beer quickly and Dave beckoned the waitress over. "Heya, sugar, we'll take two more, won't we fellas?"

She nodded and reached for their empty pitchers, and this time Mark took the opportunity to lightly touch her arm.

Startled, she glanced at him and he smiled and said, "Thank you. What's your name?"

Hesitantly, the waitress pushed her curly dark hair behind her ears. It was so short that it simply tumbled back out again, brushing her cheeks. "I'm Patricia."

"It's nice to meet you, Patricia. I'm Mark. I have to say, you seem a little nervous."

The girl started practically shaking at having been called out on her behavior, and she answered shyly, "It's just that last weekend we had some army boys in here, and quite a fight broke out. Some glasses and a chair were broken, the other customers complained, and my boss yelled at me. I had to pay for the broken dishes out of my own wages."

"I see," Mark said, leaning back in his chair and steepling his fingers together. "I'll tell you what, I will personally vouch for the proper behavior of these boys here." He gestured at the other men.

Dave nodded and added, "We ain't here to cause no trouble, ma'am." He grinned, a smile that might have been nice had it not been for the gap left by the front tooth he was missing.

Visibly relieved, Patricia smiled and said, "I appreciate that. I'll be right back with some more beer."

When she returned Mark was able to strike up a conversation with her, and when her shift ended he insisted on walking her home, with a single purpose in mind. It could get lonely being surrounded by men all the time, and everyone knew that men had needs.

Without too much trouble, he convinced Patricia to sleep with him. It was amazing what a little hand-holding and sweet talk could do. Then he slipped out of her tiny apartment in the middle of the night and headed back to the base, assuming he would never see the woman again. He was wrong.

Some weeks later Patricia tracked him down at the barracks and informed him that she was pregnant. Mark had gone through all the emotions: denial, anger, resentment, and eventually acceptance. Mark knew what his father would say if he were alive; he would say that a man needed to accept the consequences of his actions, no matter what those consequences happened to be. Mark felt as though his father was looking down on him, watching to see what decision he would make. Scared that his father might have some input with the Lord Almighty, and fearing for his very soul, Mark married Patricia a few months later.

For a while after Samuel was born, things were going all right. Patricia wasn't a bad woman, although certainly not the wife he would have picked for himself. She was far too timid. Then when he was about two years old, Sam fell ill with a case of pneumonia and spent quite some time in the hospital. The insurance offered by the army didn't cover all the medical bills, and other areas of their lives suffered as the young couple tried to move money around to pay off the hospital. Even after the boy was sent home with a clean bill of health, the other bills that had fallen by the wayside still mounted up, causing their debt to grow ever deeper.

When the electric company literally turned off the lights on the Mavers, Mark had to admit that what Patricia had been hinting at was right - he simply didn't make enough money through the army. His brother, Ned, worked at a steel factory somewhere in Missouri, and he offered Mark a job, one with good benefits and a decent starting salary.

Mark hated to leave the army. He knew that given just a little more time he would surely rise up, prove himself, and do great things, just as his father had. But this woman, and this baby, had robbed him of ever knowing how great of a man he could have become.

It was with a heavy heart that the family moved. Mark knew he was responsible for keeping a roof over the heads of these two people that had somehow snuck their way into his life, and he hated them for it. Patricia knew this, she saw it in the way her husband looked at her, with revulsion in his eyes. She could feel it every time he was near her, his skin nearly crawling with the resentment of dreams unfulfilled.

Patricia had always been shy and timid, but now she folded further and further in on herself until she became so fragile that she barely recognized herself as a human being anymore. She tried to be as quiet as possible, for since the move, the smallest little thing could set her husband off. She had always known that Mark had a bit of a temper, and that perhaps he liked the drink a bit too much, but she had always been able to deal with it. Lately, though, things seemed to be snowballing, and it was impossible to stop it.

If the baby cried, or if Patricia acted as though she didn't appreciate his sacrifice, Mark's face would turn red with anger and he would often lash out. Once she had to stop him from shaking the baby, but when she intervened he turned his hatred on to her, shouting, "This fucking baby is the reason we're here! *You're* the reason we're here! I should be a Goddamned major by now!" Then he would stomp off in a huff, no doubt on his way to get drunk with Ned.

It was true that Mark was earning much better money at this new job, but he just assumed to drink it away as to put it toward paying off any of their debts, so really they were no better off now than they were before the move.

Patricia would try to keep both herself and the baby out of his way as much as possible, and quiet. Maybe if he forgot they were there, he wouldn't hate them so. Eventually it seemed like her plan had worked almost too well, for she felt that neither of them really existed at all, and she started to wonder if they ever had to begin with.

***

"Hey, man, I've got a surprise for you," Nick whispered, a gleam in his eye.

Oh boy, Sam thought to himself. A surprise from Nick could mean just about anything.

It was Saturday night. Sam had spent the day doing odd jobs for some of the neighbors in their homes. Business was typically bad for him at this time of the year, as the normal jobs he could depend on weren't an option. There were no yards to mow, for what was left of the grass was yellowed and sparse. All the leaves had already been raked into steep piles and hauled away. All Sam could do was hope that it snowed soon so there would be sidewalks and driveways to shovel.

He had just arrived at the Lynch home, having walked there from the Dixon family who needed a crib to be re-painted. Sam still had specks of white paint scattered on his clothes, and there was a smear of it on his arm that he had been trying to pick off with his fingernail during the walk over.

Nick had opened the front door and called to him to enter through the garage, and that was where Sam now stood. He pulled off his heavy jacket, the blue one stuffed with goose down that his grandmother had sent him for Christmas last year. It was his warmest coat, yet he still felt the cold air that had seeped through the stuffing and found its way directly into Sam's bones.

Shivering, he rubbed his hands together and tried to blow hot air on them, waiting for the numbness to dissipate. Charlotte sat at Sam's feet, her tail wagging expectantly, and with what was surely a smile on her face.

"What's the surprise?" Sam asked, too cold to play guessing games.

Nick grinned. "It's in the tree house. Let's go up!"

"What? Are you serious? We're way too big for that thing, and it's freezing out. I've been outside walking. You just watched me take my coat off."

"Well, put it back on."

"Nick, I want to stay where it's warm. Just tell me what the surprise is."

"Nope, c'mon!" Nick threw Sam's coat back towards him, and he reluctantly caught it. There was a heavy winter coat hanging on a hook in the garage. Nick and Pete used it for doing outdoor work in the wintertime, and Nick quickly put it on.

Sam sighed loudly, irritated. He knew that there was no use arguing. One way or another Nick was going to get him to do what he wanted to do, even if what he wanted was as ridiculous as shoving two teenagers into an outdoor house built for children in the middle of December.

Grumbling, Sam and Charlotte followed Nick to the backyard. Charlotte had thought they were going for a walk, but was dismayed when she watched the boys carefully picking their way up the steps of the ladder. The dog knew what this meant. She relieved herself next to the tree, then lay down beneath it to wait for them to come back down.

Nick's lanky body was swallowed up by the door of the tree house, and Sam carefully followed him inside and looked around.

It was strange, but somehow the tree house had shrunk. Sam remembered there being far more room in here, enough for three or four boys to stretch out comfortably. Now, the walls felt as though they were closing in, and the floor joints squeaked each time one of them moved.

"Are we even sure this is safe?" Sam asked warily. "No one has been up here in years."

"Of course it's safe, dumbass." Nick crawled to the side of the tiny room and sat down, cross-legged. Sam begrudgingly did the same, crawling to the opposite side. It was hard to believe that they used to be able to stand up in here.

Nick had obviously been up here earlier; there were fresh blankets piled up in the corner, and he tossed one to Sam. He grabbed it and gratefully bundled it up around him, trying to ward off the frigid air.

"Do you want to tell me what this is all about now?" Sam asked, starting to lose his patience.

"Yep," Nick said, reaching under the remaining blanket and pulling something out, shouting triumphantly, "Ta-da!"

"Where in the world did you get that?" Sam asked in astonishment, his eyes widening.

"My buddy Brian from the football team. His older brother bought it for him. I put in a good word with the chick Brian's been crushing on, and now they're dating, and Brian said he owed me one. Well, I just cashed in the favor. Here, take this."

Sam accepted the icy cold beer that Nick offered him from the six-pack of bottles.

"Brian drove over here earlier and dropped it off, and I hid it up here right away. Pretty awesome, huh?" Nick looked profoundly proud of himself as he opened a beer.

"Yeah, it's cool." Sam twisted the cap off his bottle and took a sip.

"Ahh, now this is refreshing," Nick sighed contently, looking for all the world like an old man who had just gotten off a hard day at work and needed to settle back with a stiff drink. "Just what I needed."

Sam laughed and took a few quick drinks. He didn't much like the taste of beer, but he had tried it before and Nick had promised him that he would grow accustomed to the taste. Ruefully, he wondered when that would happen. At least it was better than whatever had been in that flask.

"Look what I found when I was up here earlier," Nick said with a grin. He reached over and lifted an old milk crate, snatching up a magazine that was hidden underneath, and tossed it to Sam.

"Wow, I can't believe this thing is still here!" Sam said, laughing. Gingerly, he flipped through the pages, fragile from their years of being stored in extreme temperatures. The pages were so weathered that it felt as though they would crumble in his fingers.

"Yeah, crazy, right? I actually went through and found the picture that had been my favorite, and I jerked one off up here earlier when I hid the beer."

"Nick!" Sam cried. He knew he should never be shocked by the things that came out of his friend's mouth, but sometimes Nick still managed to surprise him.

"What?" Nick asked, grinning. "Getting off for old times' sake, ya know?"

Sam laughed, shaking his head, and drank more. The beer seemed to be going down easier now, and he could feel his body warming up, despite the cold.

"Hey, I'm between girlfriends right now so you can hardly blame me for taking matters into my own hands." Nick grinned, checking to see if Sam had picked up on his pun.

Sam rolled his eyes and laughed. "Yeah, it sucks that Mandy broke up with you."

"She's in our class, and a senior asked her out. I can't compete with that. Figures." Nick threw his arms up in a what-can-you-do gesture. "Whatever, I'll find another chick to date soon enough."

For the millionth time, Sam found himself marveling at Nick's confidence, at his general attitude towards life, certain in the knowledge that everything would somehow or another work itself out. Of course, for Nick, things always had.

Sam took a long drink. He could feel the alcohol coursing through his body, warming his blood and emboldening him to approach a subject that he never had before. "So... what was it like?"

Nick glanced at him. "What was *what* like?"

"You know." Sam hesitated and for some reason found himself lowering his voice, even though it would have been impossible for anyone to overhear them. "The *sex.*"

"Oh." Suddenly more alert, Nick leaned forward. "Well, it was great, man. Kind of hard to describe. But honestly, it was about the greatest orgasm I ever had."

Sam's forehead wrinkled as he said, "Orgasm? I thought you said that you didn't... er, *finish.*"

Nick's face flushed and he shifted his weight around, raking a hand through his hair. It took a lot to make Nick feel uncomfortable, and Sam wondered worriedly what his friend was about to say.

"Well, I didn't cum the, uh... second time."

"What? You mean you guys did it *twice?*" Sam was appalled.

"Well, the first time was over pretty fast, if you get my drift, and we were both still in the moment, and it just happened." Nick shrugged.

"Christ, Nick." Sam leaned back and tried to process this information. "It was bad enough when I thought you were caught up in the heat of the moment, but now I find out that you did it a second time!"

"Well, not exactly. I mean we were interrupted, remember?" Nick joked, trying to get Sam to crack a smile.

Sam shook his head, feeling the anger drain out of him. "Whatever, Nick. It's over and done with now. Just swear to me on our friendship that you won't ever do anything like that again to me, okay? And I mean not *ever*."

Nick hung his head, remorseful, and was silent for a moment. He fiddled with the label on his beer, slowly peeling away strips of the paper, before he spoke. "It was a really shitty thing what I did, man, and I'm sorry. I fucked up but I won't ever do it again. After all, we're blood brothers, right?"

Sam was surprised that he had mentioned that. They hadn't discussed their childhood ceremony in so long that Sam had doubted Nick even remembered it. He met Nick's eyes and saw real regret there.

Tentatively, Nick stuck out his hand to shake and Sam smiled and reached for it.

***

"I'm going to bed. Goodnight!" Sam called to his parents. He had just arrived back from Nick's house, his body chilled from being in the tree house for so long followed by the walk home.

It was late, and he just wanted to crawl into his bed and bury himself with covers.

Normally this plan would have worked fine, except that on this particular night as Sam was walking down the hallway on the way to his bedroom, he happened to pass his father who was emerging from the bathroom.

Sam tried to pick up his pace but Mark said, "Wait a minute, there."

Sam stopped dead in his tracks and turned around, pursing his lips together and trying to breathe through only his nose without being obvious about it.

Mark walked closer and sniffed the air, then leaned closer still and inhaled near Sam's mouth. Sam stood perfectly still.

"That's beer on your breath."

Since this wasn't a question, Sam wasn't sure if he was expected to respond. He nodded, knowing that lying wouldn't help him.

"Where did you get alcohol from?"

Sam didn't want to get Nick into trouble so he eliminated the middle-man, so to speak. "I got it from one of the older students; his brother bought it for him. I didn't drink that much, sir."

"I really don't give a flying fuck how much of it you drank," his father sneered. "What is the legal drinking age in the state of Missouri?"

That one was definitely a question, though an obvious one.

"Twenty-one," Sam said meekly.

"And how old are you, Sam?"

Sam sighed. "Sixteen."

"I'm sorry, what was that?" Mark asked, cupping his hand behind his ear.

"I said I'm sixteen, sir."

"That's right. That means that what you did is illegal. For fuck's sake, what in the hell were you thinking?"

Sam shuffled his feet, hoping to come up with the answers that would get him in the least amount of trouble. Unfortunately, he doubted that anything he said would save him now. Why, oh why, hadn't he spent the night at Nick's? Of all the stupid things he could have done. Apparently having three beers had messed with his better judgment.

"Un-fucking-believable. You never do a thing right. You're a Goddamn waste of my time. "

Sam squeezed his lips together again, tighter this time, to stop himself from replying.

"Goddamnit!" Mark suddenly yelled, seeming to get himself angrier. He grabbed Sam by the shoulders and pushed him into the wall.

Knocked off balance, Sam stumbled and his shoulder knocked hard into the wall behind him.

"Fucking pussy!" Mark yelled, raising his open hand back and smacking it hard against Sam's cheek. "I can't leave you alone for a second! You don't even take hits like a man!" Mark pushed him again.

Normally Sam took these outbursts passively, but tonight he screamed, "Leave me alone!"

Surprised that his son had offered up a response of any sort, Mark halted long enough for Sam to wiggle out of his grasp and run to his room, slamming the door shut behind him.

He hurled himself onto his bed and sat there shaking, both with anger and fear that his father would follow him into the unlocked room.

Astoundingly, no one else entered the room that evening. Eventually Sam grew tired of holding vigil for himself and fell into a tormented sleep.

CHAPTER TWELVE

Sam was remembering a time when he and Nick were younger, probably around seven or eight years old. They had been sitting on the Lynch's back porch, eating watermelon and spitting the seeds out into the yard.

That had been an especially good watermelon, one of the really sweet ones that was so dark pink it was almost red. The boys had been taking enormous bites, not noticing or not caring that they each had sticky juice dribbling down their chins and onto their laps, turning their clothing a none-too fashionable shade of pink.

Nick had just spit several seeds out in a row, having stored them up in his mouth like a chipmunk. Now he heaved them out one at a time with a dramatic 'fftt, fftt' sound, watching as they landed scattered in the grass.

He wiped his mouth with the back of his hand and turned to his friend, saying proudly, "My yard is going to be full of watermelon trees now."

"Watermelons don't grow on trees, dummy, and even if they did, they wouldn't grow just from those seeds."

"Why not?" Nick asked, noisily slurping some juice before taking his next bite of watermelon. "What if I take care of them?"

"I'm not sure, but I don't really think it would work," Sam answered doubtfully.

"But what if I watered the seeds real good?" Nick asked, standing up and grinning wickedly.

Sam watched, open-mouthed, as Nick unzipped his fly right there in the yard and started peeing in the general direction where all the seeds had landed. He haphazardly swayed his body back and forth so that the stream covered as much ground as possible.

When he was through he simply zipped his pants, sat back down next to Sam, and said, "There. Nice and fertilized."

Then the boys looked at each other and burst into uncontrollable fits of giggles. For the next several weeks, if one of them mentioned the newly-coined word 'piss-melons' they would both howl with laughter, their faces turning as pink as that melon had been, tears forming in the corners of their eyes.

Now Sam smiled to himself at the memory as he stood over the dirty dishes in the sink. He picked up a well-worn sponge and began to scrub the food remnants off the dinner dishes, watching absent-mindedly as the little bits of tomato sauce softened in the hot water and turned his sponge red and greasy.

Sam often wondered about memories, how they could be so important one day and seemingly gone the next. Then years later, right out of the blue, they would sneak up on you and reappear, making you realize they had never been truly lost after all.

That evening after a quick spaghetti dinner with his parents, eaten in front of the television where no one spoke or even looked at one another, a commercial for watermelon-flavored Kool-Aid had come on. That was all it took to make the memory come flooding back to him, which Sam thought was especially odd since he had obviously heard the word 'watermelon' mentioned on many occasions since he was a boy. What was it about today, about this one particular moment, that caused Sam to recall that specific time in his childhood? Strange, memories were, always lying dormant until for some reason, your brain decided that you needed to recollect something from your past.

"You about done with those dishes?" Sam's father called gruffly from his place on the couch.

"Almost," he called back. The store-bought spaghetti sauce always seemed to stick and smear more than the homemade kind that May always served.

"Bring me a beer, will ya?"

"Yes, sir." Sam dried his hands on a dish towel and went over to the fridge, plucked out a beer and wordlessly handed it to his father, who accepted it automatically without looking up.

Sam glanced at the TV. Currently there was a commercial on for laundry detergent, and it seemed to involve an entire family that was incredibly excited about the possibility of doing their laundry together. Sam waited to see if another happy memory from his childhood would surface, but none came to mind. It appeared his brain had no obvious connections with either a happy family, or clean clothes, that it felt Sam needed to think about this evening.

Mark Mavers took several huge gulps of his beer at once, then let out a deep burp. He shifted his weight on the couch, readjusted his crotch, and took another long swig. His wife turned up the volume on the remote.

Sighing, Sam returned to the kitchen and to the rest of the dishes. As he put his hands into the sink, the heat from the water scalded him and he pulled his hands out again quickly. As he added some cold tap water into the mix, Sam realized that the exact same water hadn't bothered him at all just a moment ago as the sink was filling. Perhaps it was all in what you were used to. Only when you left and then returned to a dangerous situation did you realize there was ever any danger at all.

***

"This is bullshit," Nick declared, throwing his hands up in the air in frustration. "I'm never gonna learn all this. I'm not smart like you are." He glared at Sam accusingly.

"Sure you are, you just have to pay more attention in class. Or any attention, for that matter."

"Hey, it's not my fault that Mr. Edwards is the oldest teacher in the world and can't explain anything through all of his coughing fits. I'm honestly concerned that one day he's just going to die, right there in the middle of class."

"Yes, I'm sure Mr. Edwards' safety is your utmost priority," Sam muttered. "But if you don't figure out how to do these equations, your grade will also be in danger of a sudden death."

"Yeah, yeah, whatever. Fucking algebra."

The boys were sitting on the floor of Nick's bedroom, leaning against the bed, various textbooks and notebooks creating a moat of education around them.

Nick stretched out his legs, kicking several of the books to the far side of the room in the process. "I need a break."

"Nick, we literally just started. You have yet to even pick up your pencil."

"It doesn't matter how much work I've *physically* done, Sam. I'm in need of an *emotional* break from math, you know?"

Sam did not know. If his friend could work out such 'logic' from absolute nothingness, Sam couldn't understand why Nick wasn't a whiz at the logic of numbers. He opened one of the textbooks and started to point out an equation, but Nick wasn't even looking at him.

"Sam, would you say you're a boob-man or an ass-man? 'Cause I feel like I'm more of a boob-guy myself, but that doesn't mean I don't appreciate a good butt. Or a nice set of legs. Or a nice stomach. But tits, man, I tell you…"

Sending up a silent prayer to the God of Frustration, Sam closed his book and turned to his friend.

"Fine, it's your grade, not mine. What is it you're wanting to do, exactly? I don't really feel like talking about boobs and butts all day."

"I dunno," Nick whined, the cry of the truly bored. "You should come up with something."

"I already came up with something, remember? It was called, 'Nick doesn't fail algebra'."

"Nah, come up with something else."

Sam rolled his eyes and began piling his books into his bag, realizing that the idea of doing homework had flown completely out the window by this point.

"Fine. Maybe your mom will drop us off at the mall?"

Nick sat up straighter, brightening instantly. "Now, that's a more promising idea. I'm sure she won't care."

As the boys stood up and made their way into the kitchen, Nick kept mumbling, "I can't wait until the fall, when I'll be able to drive myself around. I'm sick of getting rides like a little kid."

"Yeah, that will be pretty sweet," Sam agreed.

"Did I hear someone say 'sweet'?" May asked, grinning. "Because I just tried out a new recipe this morning, and I need some guinea pigs. Here, take these."

The boys each held out their hands to accept some kind of chocolate cookie bar.

"Thanks, May," Sam said, taking a bite and swallowing. "Delicious!"

"Will you take us to the mall?" Nick asked, by way of thanks. "We're bored."

"I was under the impression that you two were in there working on homework," May answered, putting the lid on the cookie jar and pushing it back to its rightful place on the counter.

"We're done."

"Nick," May said in her sternest voice, which really wasn't very stern at all. "You boys just got home about five minutes ago. I seriously doubt that."

"Sam's just that good of a teacher, I guess," Nick answered, grinning. There was a smear of chocolate covering one of his front teeth.

"Now that I don't doubt," May replied, winking at Sam. "But whether or not you are such a good student remains to be seen."

"Very funny, Mom," Nick said. "If you will just drop us off at the mall for a couple of hours, Sam can spend the night here and help me with my homework later."

"Oh, can he now?" May asked, amused.

Sam grinned and shrugged. They all knew that he would choose to spend the night at the Lynch home any time he could. And of course, he was always a sucker for helping Nick with his homework, no matter how unwilling of a pupil he could be.

May sighed good-naturedly and said, "Oh, all right. Let's go before I change my mind."

She grabbed her purse and her keys from the table and added, "I can't wait until your car gets out of the shop and you boys can start driving yourselves around again."

"Neither can we, Mom, neither can we," Nick answered mournfully.

Twenty minutes later the boys were waving their goodbyes and shouting out promises to not be late, to not purchase roller skates then ride through the mall wreaking havoc ("That was a one-time thing!" Nick had cried indignantly) and to not allow themselves to be kidnapped.

Satisfied, May drove away and the boys rushed into the giant building, enjoying the sudden freedom.

Because it was a Thursday evening in the middle of January, the mall wasn't very crowded. Most people avoided the mall during this time of the year, being thoroughly sick of shopping after the Christmas season, then returning all the gifts they had received right after the new year.

Without having to ask one another where their first stop should be, the boys immediately turned to their right and hurried into the Boon Dockers' store, where upon entering their pace noticeably slowed.

Boon Dockers sold many questionable items, and had a rather forbidden feel, almost as though they were sneaking in even though they had simply walked in through the front door.

Aisles of hip T-shirts and novelties quickly gave way to products covered with marijuana leaves and alcohol slogans. As one progressed even further into the store, the light dimmed and all the black light and neon signs were for sale, pink and blue lights beaming out a swirl of color and strobe lights blinking rapidly in the corner.

As fascinating as all of these things were, it was the last aisle that truly drew the boys' attention. Here were vibrators and various sex toys, most of which Sam wasn't sure what their purpose was, but Nick had a grand time coming up with what those uses may be. You could purchase posters with topless girls on them, flip through erotic books, and laugh hysterically at the Jell-O molds shaped like penises.

Nick grabbed a long-stemmed feather with ridiculous bright pink plumage and used it to tickle Sam's cheek.

"Cut it out, asshole," Sam grunted, wiping at his face.

"What's wrong, turning you on too much?" Nick asked innocently, jumping away as Sam playfully swatted at him.

"You wish."

Nick replaced the feather and picked up a package of edible underwear, throwing them at his friend.

The package hit Sam square in the forehead and he quickly picked them up and tossed them back, saying, "Here, the cherry is your favorite flavor, right?"

"Nah, I'm more of a fan of the strawberry body cream."

"Geez, do people really use all this stuff? Or is it just like, for jokes and stuff?" Sam asked, gingerly running his hand along a shelf that seemed to be entirely devoted to fuzzy handcuffs.

"Of course people use this stuff, dumb ass. They're sex aids, you know. For when shit gets boring, like after you get married. Or if a guy can't keep it up. Although, I never have that problem." Nick thrusted out his pelvis and grinned.

"Yes, some lucky girl is going to snag you up," Sam quipped, laughing.

"I'm only gonna be with a girl if she's willing to wear these," Nick said, grabbing a pair of crotchless panties from a rack and carefully placing them on his head, so that he could see out of the opening where the crotch should be.

Sam doubled over in laughter, crying, "I really hope whoever buys those things washes them like a hundred times. Put them back, dumbass."

"Never!" With the lacy women's underwear still sitting haphazardly over his face, Nick continued to look through the clothing rack, loudly admiring the selection.

Sam gestured to the items behind him, saying, "What I want to know is, how can there be so many different kinds of vibrators? I mean, don't they all do the same thing?"

"That's because woman are incredibly indecisive," Nick answered knowledgeably. "And they like a lot of choices to suit their many, many moods."

He walked over to where Sam was standing and picked up a package, then said in a sing-song, high-pitched voice, "Oh, Sam, my lover, tonight I'm in the mood for an extra-long one with variable speed pulses!"

Sam cracked up as Nick replaced the package, then picked up another one.

"Oh, Sammy, tonight I'm feeling blue. I need this Blue Rabbit to get me off! Only having a teaser for my clit will do the job!"

Sam kept laughing while saying, "Keep your voice down, Nick!"

Nick ignored him, selecting another package and attempting to chase Sam around with it, calling, "Sam, don't go! This one is waterproof, and I'm feeling dirty! Momma needs a shower!"

"Hey! Just what in the hell do you think you're doing back here?"

The sudden bark of a man's voice startled both the boys, and Nick dropped the vibrator he had been holding.

"Nothing," they both answered in unison.

"Oh, really?" the man's voice sneered as he walked over and plucked the underwear from off of Nick's head. Both boys were trying hard to contain their laughter, erupting little hiccup sounds with the effort.

"You're bothering the other patrons," the man continued.

Nick made a big show of glancing in both directions, then answered in a conspiratorial whisper, "There *are* no other patrons. Why, do *you* see someone? Do you often see people that aren't really there?"

"All right, smartass, I'm tired of you kids parading around in my store and playing around without ever buying anything."

"And how do you know we weren't planning on buying anything?" Nick argued, his tone daring.

"C'mon Nick, let's just get out of here," Sam urged, tugging at his friend's arm.

"Uh-uh. I'm a paying customer, and I expect to be treated with the respect that I deserve," Nick said decisively, staring at the man.

"Oh really?" he said sarcastically. "And what exactly was it that you were planning on purchasing?"

"These underwear," Nick said matter-of-factly, grabbing them back out of the owner's hands. "I need a birthday gift for my mother."

Sam lost it at that point, doubling over with laughter as the man's jaw dropped open, then quickly became a scowl.

Nick flounced over to the register and slid his wallet out of the back pocket of his jeans, calling nonchalantly, "How much?"

Somewhat flabbergasted but still pissed off, the owner stomped over to the other side of the counter and rang up the purchase, answering snidely, "Twelve bucks, kid."

If Nick was shocked at the price he chose not to show it. Instead, he carefully counted out twelve one-dollar bills, being sure to lick his fingers between reaching for each bill, and said,

"Great, that's far less money than the pair I bought her for Mother's Day."

Glaring, the man typed some numbers into the register, causing it to ding and making the cash drawer open up. He shoved in Nick's money, slammed the drawer shut with his hip, and put the underwear and the receipt into a bag.

"Thank you," Nick said sweetly, taking the bag and patting it protectively. "It's been a pleasure doing business with you."

Then he turned and walked out of the store, Sam hurrying along behind him, leaving the owner shaking his head.

"Oh my God, I can't believe you just did that," Sam cried once they were safely out of earshot from the store.

Nick grinned and said, "Hey, twelve bucks is a small price to pay for shutting that prick up."

"But… it's his store, and he got the money, so didn't he sort of win?"

Nick sighed, then said in a voice like he would use when explaining something to a small child, "No, Sam, *we* win. That guy was forced to admit that he underestimated me, and he had to wait on me."

Sam laughed. Again, with the Nick logic. "I'm not sure if that's how it works, but whatever, man. So, what are you going to do with those anyway?"

Nick glanced thoughtfully into the bag, admiring the frilly black and red panties. "I don't know right now, Sammy. But I'm sure there are many uses. They just haven't made themselves known yet."

"Sure," Sam answered, smiling. "While we are waiting for the underwear to make themselves useful to you, what do you want to do in the meantime?"

"Food court?" Nick suggested. "I'm hungry."

"Shocking."

The boys did an about-face and speed walked through the long expanse of the mall. As they neared the food court their noses were suddenly consumed with the mixture of smells that comes from multiple fast food restaurants cooking in such a small area of space. Greasy burgers, fries and pizza smells mingled with the more exotic ones coming from the China Express, then combining with the sweetness wafting over from that new trendy frozen yogurt and smoothie stand.

The entire thing was a nauseating assault on the senses, but to two teenage boys, it smelled like heaven.

"McDonald's?" asked Nick, although he needn't have bothered. Despite the many choices, the boys always ended up at their tried-and-true.

Sam nodded, and they walked over to the golden arches, both ordering a burger, fries, and a soda. While Nick wadded up the change from his twenty-dollar bill and shoved it back into the folds of his wallet, Sam carefully lined up the two dollars that he had received in change and placed it back into the proper section of his own wallet, sliding it back into his pocket carefully. When it came to money, Sam was always more cautious then his friend, because unlike Nick, Sam couldn't simply ask his parents for some 'kicking around' money. Each of Sam's dollars represented a yard mowed, a walk shoveled, or a wall painted.

Filling up their sodas at the fountain (Root Beer for Sam, Coke for Nick), the boys cautiously carried their trays to one of the many empty tables in the middle of the food court and sat down.

Nick unwrapped his cheeseburger and took an enormous bite, saying, "This sucks, man. There are no hot girls around here to look at."

Sam popped a ketchup-smeared fry into his mouth and looked around. "There's not much in the way of people-watching," he agreed.

"I wanted to feast my eyes on some sexy chicks while I'm feasting my stomach on this sexy burger," Nick added, his mouth full.

Sam rolled his eyes and took a drink of his soda.

Nick continued to look around him, then gestured to Sam and nodded toward a rather obese woman waiting in line at the China Express. "I bet you're fantasizing about her wearing those undies, aren't you?" Nick joked, patting the Boon Dockers bag where it rested on the table next to his tray.

"Shut up, man."

"Ooh, I knew it," Nick continued, leaning in toward Sam. "You're probably thinking about all those rolls of fat being squeezed out of the top of all that lace right now." He sat back in his chair, pleased with himself.

"Put a lid on it, dumbass. That poor lady is probably really nice, and here you are making fun of her just because she's a little overweight."

Nick shrugged and tossed a French Fry at Sam, answering haughtily, "My best friend, always the bleeding heart."

"Yeah, yeah," Sam retorted, throwing the fry back to its owner. As it flew through the air Nick ducked his head, opened his mouth, and expertly caught it, chewing it with satisfaction.

Sam smiled. "My best friend, always the attention-seeker."

Nick swallowed and smiled back. "I guess we all have our little roles to play, don't we."

The boys ate the rest of their dinner in a comfortable silence, leaving Sam to ponder Nick's last remark.

CHAPTER THIRTEEN

The day dawned dark and dreary, and there was such a small amount of light coming through the blinds in Sam's bedroom that he believed it was still the middle of the night when his alarm clock went off.

He sat up and stretched, then curiously bent back the blinds and took a peek outside, his eyes opening wide as he looked out.

The three to six inches of snow that the forecasters called to fall overnight looked like a foot instead. Deep mounds of snow covered the entire yard, and a large drift had completely covered the small bush that grew outside Sam's window. Now, it just appeared as a curious white mound, standing taller than everything else in the yard, and if a person hadn't known beforehand, they would have wondered what the snow hid beneath.

Fully alert now, Sam threw off his covers, crammed his feet into his too-small slippers, and wandered down the hall and into the kitchen.

Both of his parents were up, sitting on the couch and sipping steaming cups of coffee. Sam took note with a sinking feeling that his father was also in his pajamas, and assumed that he had been unable to go into work that day.

"Good morning," he said, walking into the living room to stand beside them.

Sam's mother glanced up from the television. "Thirteen inches of snow fell overnight; they're calling it the 'Surprise Blizzard'. Your school is cancelled."

"Thirteen inches? Wow!" Sam said, truly impressed. He sat down next to his mother on the couch, watching as the meteorologist on the television explained to the viewers that besides the massive amount of snowfall, the temperatures had dropped and it was dangerously cold. Sam wondered why they were making the poor newscaster stand outside, so bundled up that you could barely see his face, in order to tell people that the wind chill was minus-eleven and that people should stay indoors.

"Wow," he repeated, inhaling deeply to catch a whiff of his mother's coffee. "Looks pretty bad out there. I guess I will go back to my room and read one of the books I got from the library the other day."

Sam stood up and was about to leave the room when he caught sight of the disgusted look on his father's face.

"The hell you are," Mark replied. "You're gonna get your ass out there and start shoveling the driveway."

Patricia glanced at her husband and said quietly, "It is pretty cold out there; maybe it could wait till later?"

Mark turned the same disgusted look to his wife, as if he couldn't believe he had to deal with not just one, but two idiotic people in the same household. Mark spoke slowly, in a patronizing voice, "If he doesn't shovel the driveway, I won't be able to get the car out to go to work tomorrow either, and I need to support this damn family, don't I *dear*?"

He put so much emphasis on that final word, normally a term of endearment, that Patricia shuddered involuntarily and answered meekly, "Of course, you're right."

Sam's mouth fell open, but only for a moment before he remembered to clamp it shut again. Sometimes it was still surprising how much his mother refused to fight for him, and how she always gave in to his father, no matter what. It had been going on for so many years now that Sam figured she probably didn't even register what was happening anymore. His mother was simply going through the motions of what it took to survive in this household. Well, Sam could understand that, at least. He was an expert at it as well. He supposed he learned from the best.

Sam spun on his heel and headed back to his bedroom, where he proceeded to get all of his warmest clothes out of his closet. He put them on one at a time, layer upon layer, until he was fat and poofy. He walked back to where his coat and scarf were hanging and added that to the mix, checking to see if his parents were appreciating the amount of clothing he was wearing. They weren't.

He zipped his coat, wrapped the scarf securely around his neck, added a hat and gloves, and waddled his way out of the door.

As soon as Sam got outside, a wall of frigid air hit him in the face so forcefully that it nearly knocked the wind out of him. He stepped off the porch and sunk almost to his knees in the snow.

He trudged over to the shed, having to walk by lifting one foot high off the ground and letting it sink into the snow in front of him, then doing the same with the next foot. The shovels and rakes were kept in one of those tiny, heavy-duty plastic bins that Sam had often felt resembled having a porta-potty on their lawn. The brief walk to the shed was exhausting and seemed to take forever.

Once there, Sam realized that in order to *retrieve* the shovel, he would basically *need* a shovel. He stared in dismay at the massive show drift that had blown in front of the shed, rendering it nearly impossible to open.

Sam took a deep breath than exhaled slowly, watching as the air became puffs of steam around him. Then, using his hands and feet, he attempted to burrow through enough of the snow so that there was room for the door of the shed to swing open.

The snow was higher than his boots, and Sam could feel his sweatpants, and his jeans under that, turning wet and cold as the snow soaked in.

Finally, he was able to swing the door open just wide enough to reach in and grab what he needed, the shovel with the bright red plastic end.

Triumphant, he began the walk back to the driveway, doing his best to place his feet in the same footsteps that he had made on his way there.

Sam reached the garage, dug the shovel into the snow, and heaved it upward. He was surprised at the weight. This snow was wet and heavy, and Sam had to use all his muscles to hurl it out of the way.

He dug the shovel in again, enjoying the scraping sound it made as it moved along the driveway. He heaved upward again, tossing the snow to the side. He did this a few more times, than dared to look behind him. Dismayed, Sam realized he had barely made a dent in the driveway, which now seemed longer and more daunting than it ever had before.

Sam squeezed his eyes shut for a moment, then kept going.

As he worked, Sam's arm muscles began aching and getting stiff. The wetness of his jeans was beginning to freeze over, encasing his legs in a cold so desperate that he could feel his limbs growing tingly and throbbing with pain.

The snow was cunning, able to find even the smallest cracks to seep through, and soon it had squeezed through the cuffs of Sam's gloves. Within moments his hands and fingers began to hurt as well, making him feel almost nauseous.

The driveway was about halfway shoveled when Sam decided that he could take it no more. He stood the shovel up against the garage door and went into his house.

His parents hadn't moved off the couch, but they did both look up as their son entered the house.

"Is the driveway all done?" Mark asked.

"Um, not yet, sir. It's very cold out, and there's so much snow, that I thought maybe I could change into dry clothes and get warmed up before I finish the rest." Sam had been saying all this while facing the ground, but now he looked up and saw a mixture of disappointment and contempt on his father's face.

"Are you serious?" Mark sneered. "You are the laziest, whiniest kid I know. A little bit of snow and cold, and you take that as an excuse to slack off."

"No, sir," Sam stammered, "I promise I will finish the driveway just as soon as I -"

"Do you not care if I get to work tomorrow? Well, *do* you?"

Sam fought the urge to remind his father that it was only ten in the morning and that he had an entire day in which to work on the driveway. Instead, he answered, "I care."

"Well, perhaps you better start acting like it. Unless you don't like eating the food that my job provides you. And all this bitching that you're doing about the cold? How would you like it if you didn't have a roof over your head at all? I suggest you get back out there."

Patricia was looking closely at Sam, and quietly suggested, "Maybe it would be a good idea for him to warm up a bit. Look how red his face is."

Mark turned to his wife with a glare and answered, "He's just being a sissy, and you coddle him too much. When I was his age I was doing twice the work in far worse conditions."

Sam didn't have time to wonder what that meant before his father turned back to him, adding, "Get out there and finish the job. Do NOT come back into this house until it's done or you will be sorry, you hear me?"

Sam nodded and tightened the scarf around his neck, then turned to go back outside.

"And when you're done with the driveway, you can get in here and mop up this mess that you've made standing here belly-aching and letting dirty snow melt all over the floor," Mark called after him.

Sam trudged back outside, not sure if he was more pissed off or sad.

He continued shoveling, and wondered what Nick was doing. Probably relaxing with his family. Sam thought back to that day when the Lynch's had offered to let Sam move in with them, and he idly thought of how much happier he would be right now, in this very moment, relaxing in the cozy house of his best friend. No, it could have been *his* house too, not just the house of his best friend, just as the universe had intended. Sam never had understood why his parents had insisted he continue to live here. He supposed that if he were currently residing in the Lynch residence, there would be no one else to shovel the driveway. Perhaps that was reason enough for them.

Sam hadn't realized it, but angry tears were streaming down his face, freezing on his cheeks in the icy air.

His hands were getting sweaty, but at least they were no longer hurting. In fact, he could barely feel them at all. He simply watched as someone else's hands held the shovel, working it in and out of the snow.

He kept working automatically, no longer caring about the pain. Sam simply watched the shovel. In and out, in and out.

***

Frostbite was a tricky thing. That's what the doctor said as he examined Sam's fingers. He kept shaking his head and tut-tutting, gently turning Sam's hands this way and that.

"Son, I just don't understand what you were doing in those temperatures for so long. Especially with wet hands!"

"I was just trying to shovel the driveway." Sam glanced at his mother, who was in the corner of the room, sitting on a chair, her eyes glassy with unshed tears. "I guess I didn't realize it was so cold outside, or that I had been out there for so long."

The doctor shook his head again and sighed.

When Sam had persevered through the entire driveway, he had gone to his bedroom, changed clothes, and fell asleep, his entire body aching. When he woke up, his limbs were stiff and his body was hot with a fever.

After Sam had shown his mother that his legs and face were red and raw and blistering, and the tips of a couple of his fingers were turning a strange dark color, they made a trip to the emergency room. Luckily by that afternoon most of the roads had been plowed. As his mother backed the car out of the garage, Sam thought ironically that at least the driveway was clear of snow.

Sam was laying stiffly in the hospital bed while the doctor checked over the blisters that had formed on his legs. An IV was poking out of his arm, sending warmed antibiotics through his veins.

Sam lay his head back on his pillow and concentrated on staring at the ceiling as the doctor and several nurses went in and out of his room, always seeming to be in a hurry.

Allowing his body to be examined over and over again, his hands poked and prodded, Sam thought about how nice the nurse was who had gotten him the quilt, and how it was nicer than the one in his own bedroom at home.

He was suddenly in such a dreamy state, Sam barely registered the things that were being said around him. Words like 'too late' and 'can't recover' and 'remove' floated around him, the words themselves becoming a palpable thing, rising up. Sam watched as they traveled up, higher and higher, until they became hazy and were swallowed up by the swirls in the paint pattern above him.

Sam wondered at the simplistic beauty of his ceiling, how all the different circles of white paint made up a truly beautiful scene, and he hoped that he was not the only patient who had ever noticed or appreciated it.

This is what he was thinking about as he nodded at the doctor and watched his mother sign a paper, her sobs real this time, and this was the last thing he remembered.

***

"All right man, I've been dying to see this. It feels like those bandages have been on your hands forever."

"I know, it sucks. I've gotten so used to them being on, I think it's going to feel weird once they're finally off."

"If you think you're going to miss them that much, Sam, I will be happy to send some extra gauze home with you," the doctor said, smiling at Sam. "Now, let's take these off for the final time, shall we?"

"Absolutely."

Sam leaned forward in his chair, anxiously watching as the doctor carefully removed the final bits of bandage. Nick peered closer still, extremely excited to be invited to witness the unveiling.

Sam had an idea of what to expect, his bandages had been changed twice already, but he had never had the time to truly examine his wounds. Watching as the doctor slowly unwound the final piece of gauze, Sam felt an excited, nervous apprehension in the pit of his stomach.

"There now, your left hand has healed up nicely. It was lucky that we just had to remove the tip of your index finger on that hand. Now let me take a look at your right hand."

As the doctor began the painstaking task of removing the larger bandages from his right hand, Sam held his free hand in front of his face, turning it back and forth so he could see it from both sides.

"Dude, your finger looks so wicked!" Nick said, truly impressed as he gently took hold of Sam's wrist to move it closer.

"Um, thank you?" Sam replied.

Grinning, Nick dropped his friend's wrist and leaned in closer to the doctor, waiting eagerly to be exquisitely grossed out.

The final bandage was peeled away and without meaning to, Nick cried out, "Holy shit!"

The first two fingers of Sam's right hand had been completely removed from the second joint up, leaving each finger about half an inch shorter than it had been previously. The healing process had been long, and now Sam's hand felt naked and vulnerable.

"Man, that is fucked up!" Nick said in appreciation, gaining a "hmph" sound from the doctor. "Does it hurt?"

"Not anymore, it just feels weird, you know?" Sam said as he wiggled the stumps of his fingers back and forth at his doctor's instruction.

"Well, it looks wicked cool," Nick continued, trying to be helpful. "So how will you, like, hold a pen and stuff?"

"Sam will be able to do everything he could always do," the doctor interjected as he made a few notes on a clipboard resting on his lap. "The human body is remarkably adaptable. Sam's hand will relearn how to do all those things. He was lucky, being able to keep a majority of the portion of both of the fingers. That will really make things easier."

"Oh yeah, look at him, super lucky," Nick replied, grinning. "But c'mon doc, admit it, there are some things he won't be able to do with that hand anymore. Like, point at someone for instance. Or give someone the finger."

In response, Sam held up his middle stump and said to his friend, "This is half a 'fuck you'. If I'm truly pissed, I will give you the finger with my good hand. This way you'll know the difference."

Nick laughed and even the doctor cracked a smile. "I must say, Sam, you really have healed quite well. I did a good job, if I do say so myself. Now get out of here, I don't want to see you again for three months."

"Awesome, thanks!"

The boys hopped up and raced out of the hospital room, to the waiting room where May was waiting, a magazine in her lap.

She looked up as she heard the quickened steps of two teenage boys rounding the corner, closed her magazine and smiled.

"Well, let's see it!" she said encouragingly, standing up.

Somewhat proudly, Sam threw his hands out in front of him and waved them around in the air.

"Wow, they look good Sam, really good."

"May, you don't have to lie to me," Sam answered, laughing lightly. "I know what it looks like."

May leaned in to give him a hug. "It looks like you're a survivor, that's what it looks like."

"Ah geez, Mom, don't get all sappy on us," Nick said, rolling his eyes. "Let's get out of here and have that lunch you promised us."

"Sounds good to me," May agreed, smiling. "Sam, the restaurant is your choice."

Ten minutes later the trio was seated around a cozy table in Pete's Tavern, and the waitress was setting a steaming plate in front of Sam.

"I can't believe I'm having such a fancy steak for lunch," Sam said, his mouth salivating as his eyes took in his food.

"Well, you deserve it. And if you boys are going to play hooky, you may as well do it right," May replied, winking at him.

Sam's doctor appointment had been for 1:00 in the afternoon that Thursday, and May had offered to take him. In honor of the occasion she had allowed Nick to leave school early as well, and she had picked both of the boys up from the school on the way to the hospital.

"You should let us leave school more often," Nick suggested, shoving a mouthful of baked potato into his mouth in between words.

"Nice try, this is a one-time thing," his mother answered. "And don't talk with your mouth full."

"My mouth is always full," Nick countered as May nodded her concurrence. "So, since Sam is missing some fingertips, that means he has no fingerprints, so as long as he commits all his crimes with those two fingers he could never get caught for anything, right?"

"I don't think that's exactly the way it works, Nick. And please don't hold your friend to a crime spree in the name of science."

Nick and May had been so busy speaking to one another that they hadn't noticed as Sam attempted to pick up his knife and fork, struggling to balance the silverware against what remained of his fingers. Finding some semblance of balance, he tried to cut into the steak but was dismayed as the knife dropped from his hand and landed on the table with a clatter.

Mother and son looked up at the sudden noise, and tried not to wince as they saw what was happening. May wasn't sure what to do. Offer to cut the steak for him? Pretend not to notice his difficulty?

In the end, she simply leaned over and patted Sam's arm, saying softly, "Sappy or not, you're a survivor, Sam."

Nick nodded and raised his water glass. "To Sam!"

The three raised their glasses and clinked them together, smiling and laughing as all they all shouted, "To Sam!", Sam included.

Then Sam put his fork between his thumb and good fingers on his right hand, stabbing it into the meat and securing it into place. Then he picked up the knife with his left hand, the knife feeling unfamiliar, and slowly cut off a piece of the meat. Adaptable, indeed.

CHAPTER FOURTEEN

Sam couldn't remember how old he had been, he could have been five or seven or anywhere in between. For that matter, it could have been a dream; maybe it had never actually happened at all. Sometimes Sam found that his dreams and his reality tended to intertwine together, and that the more time passed, the more he realized he wasn't sure what was real and what was not. Perhaps they weren't dreams or memories at all, maybe just musings or fantasies that his brain had somehow come up with. But either way, they felt real enough, and even if Sam's brain had concocted the whole thing, well, wouldn't it have done that for a reason? For some purpose, real or imagined, Sam's brain wanted him to accept certain occurrences as having happened, so he decided to believe that the day when he was five or seven or somewhere in between had actually taken place.

It had been a hot summer day, the kind where when you left the comfort of the air conditioning and went outdoors, a wall of heat hit you so forcefully it nearly knocked you backwards. The less resilient would shake their heads and go back inside before the door had even shut behind them. But Sam had always been a fighter, even against the radiant summer sun, and he had pushed through until he no longer even felt the heat.

He busied himself playing in the yard, using his fingers and a metal spoon he had swiped out of the back of the silverware drawer to dig a hole that he imagined was just shy of allowing him to drop through where he would fall directly into China. Of course he would deeply be surprising the Chinese family who he imagined was picnicking beneath him, either inches or thousands of miles away, it really didn't matter. He dug and dug, his fingernails caked with mud, sweat beading off his forehead and falling into the giant hole he was working on. Or was it tiny? It could have been, but to Sam's mind he had worked on it for so long that at any moment, a young Chinese boy would peer up and him and say, "Why hello there, American boy, I was just having a Chinese picnic with my Chinese family. Jump on down and feast yourself on all the fortune cookies you can eat!"

Suddenly, out of nowhere, the sky grew dark and ominous, rumbles of thunder promising that a summer storm would be breaking soon. The wind picked up, swirling Sam's hair into an unruly dance atop his head, and instantly cooling his wet forehead that was bathed in sweat.

Hurriedly, as large droplets of cold water began to cool his body, and right before he would have dropped down into that Other Place, Sam used his arms to scoop all the dirt he had so painstakingly removed and pushed it back into the hole. Even though he had purposely dug as far back from the house as possible, he knew his father would be upset if he tripped into it. The Chinese family would probably not be as welcoming to Mark Maver as they would have been to Sam.

Jumping on the dirt, partially to stomp it back into place and partially because it was fun, Sam realized that he was getting so wet, from sweat or from rain he wasn't sure, that his clothes were sticking to him and he made a mad dash for the safety of the house.

"Oh, Sam," his mother said as he entered, being sure to kick off his muddy shoes and leaving them outside on the porch so he could hose them off later. "You are a wet muddy mess. Get in the bathroom now and get cleaned up. Your father -"

"Your father what?" Mark interrupted, walking into the room.

"I was just telling Sam that he needed to go take a bath right away. Look at him, he's a mess." Patricia answered, nodding toward their son.

"Oh, I thought I heard thunder," Mark answered, looking Sam up and down. "Thank goodness, it's been hot as hell out there. Maybe this will finally cool things down."

Sam nodded, not sure where this was going. Dirty water dripped from his hair onto the floor. Nonchalantly, Sam changed his stance so his father wouldn't notice the growing puddle.

Then, just as quickly as it had started, the rain stopped. It was as if someone had simply pushed the 'off' button. Curious, Sam peeked behind him and sure enough, the downpour had come so fast and so heavy that it seemed to have tired itself out, the water all used up.

"It looks like it stopped already, sir."

"You don't say? That was fast, it's probably still hot as shit outside."

Sam fought back a smile and decided against asking exactly how hot shit might be, certain he would discuss it with Nick later.

Mark moved past his son and opened the door to the porch slowly, as if worried that all the summer heat would screech past him and settle over the living room.

"Well hey," Mark said to the porch, "It's cooled off quite a bit out here! Wow, when did it get to be dusk already?" He stepped outside and stretched, taking a deep breath and letting the unnaturally cool air fill his lungs.

"Sam, Patricia, come on out here. The temperature must have dropped twenty degrees! May as well enjoy it while it lasts, what with this damn heat wave." Mark strode out onto the porch, walked down the steps, and stood in the dewy grass.

Mother and son shared a Look, wondering how this would end, but Sam quickly followed his father outside and Patricia turned off the television and copied her family's movements out the door.

"Well, would you look at that," Mark said, pointing.

Sam joined him and looked and looked, squinting, trying so hard to see what his father could see, but there was nothing there.

"What is it, sir?" he asked nervously, wondering if he had just failed some type of test. Patricia stood on the porch, surveying the scene.

"Lightning bugs; can't you see them?"

Sam shook his head forlornly, wondering if his father was drunk. That would certainly explain this odd behavior, and the fact that his father thought he could see bugs with lights blinking out of their butts or something.

"C'mere, look toward the front of the bushes, where it's darker," Mark said, squatting down so he was at Sam's height, pointing.

Sam looked closer, and sure enough! Little lights were flashing on and off near the bushes. He blinked, and rubbed his eyes, but they were still there, flying around, never lighting up one place for more than a few moments.

"Wow!" he cried, truly excited by the fact that there actually were bugs that apparently *did* have lights shoved up their butts. He could not *wait* to inform Nick.

"Haven't you ever seen lightning bugs before, Sam?" Mark asked and Sam shook his head. Who would have mentioned them to him?

"When I was a kid we used to try to catch them so we could put them in a jar and watch them light up. Hey, Patricia, go grab us a jar, will ya?"

With that, Mark took Sam by the shoulder and guided him toward the line of bushes, saying, "Here, watch me."

Dumfounded and fascinated all at once, Sam watched eagerly as his father cupped his hands and grabbed one of the little bugs, completely out of thin air, gentle as could be.

"Look," Mark instructed, kneeling down in front of Sam and slowing unclasping his fingers.

Sam watched, captivated, as they gave way to a black bug, bigger than what he had been expecting, sitting calmly in his father's palm. The bug made his little butt light up, casting the smallest of bug shadows onto Mark's hands, then languidly flew away, blinking a path of light as he went.

"Here you go, this was the best I could find," Patricia said as she walked out to where her family was standing, handing them an empty mason jar. "I poked some holes in the top with a knife." Wordlessly Mark took it from her and unscrewed the cap.

"Well, what are you waiting for?" he asked Sam. "Let's go catch some lightning bugs!"

For the next five minutes (or was it closer to an hour?) Sam and his father ran around the yard chasing after the bugs, scooping them up and adding them carefully to the growing population in the jar. Sam took to squealing every time he caught one, because it was exciting, and because it made his parents laugh. Five minutes or an hour later, after the mosquitos came out thirsty for blood, the family went back indoors.

Sam sat on the couch between his parents, carefully spinning the jar in his hands, watching bugs crawl and fly around. "So what do we do with them now?" he asked, continuing to examine the entire ecosystem (he had put some grass and a small stick in there for their comfort) of which he held.

"We can put the jar by the side of your bed when you go to sleep tonight, and you can watch them."

"Really? Wow!" Sam cried, utterly impressed. He imagined even Nick Lynch didn't get to sleep next to a whole city of bugs.

"Sure, go take your bath and we'll get you and the bugs to bed."

Sam sprinted off to the bathroom, taking probably the world's quickest bath, but being sure to remove all the dirt from his body so that he wouldn't be ordered to take a second one.

Putting on a freshly laundered pair of pajamas, he eagerly jumped into bed, for once happy to be there even though his father was in such a good mood.

Mark came in and set the jar on Sam's nightstand, as promised, and sat crisply on the corner of the bed.

Sam didn't take his eyes off the jar as he asked, "So what happens to the light bugs in the morning? Can I keep them?"

"First thing tomorrow we will open the jar up and let them go. Then they can spend the rest of their lives flying around in our backyard, and you'll get to see them every night."

"Okay," Sam said decidedly, a little sad they these wouldn't be his permanent pets, but mollified with this agreement.

Mark affectionately ruffled Sam's hair, told him goodnight, and left the room.

As the door closed behind his father and the light from the hallway receded into just the tiniest sliver of yellow next to the doorway, Sam was alone in the dark with his bugs. True to their name, they moved around and around, each lighting up at different intervals, so that even if one was resting, another was lighting his way.

Sam fell asleep, and even in the darkness he dreamed of light.

***

The month that the universe had intended May to be born started out with rain, and the rain didn't stop for a week. The only thing that seemed to change in the weather was the type of the rain itself. It would sprinkle, little droplets that clung to your hair made it just a little too annoying to go outside. It would rain constantly, a steady steam beating down on the pavement, clanking onto tin roofs and causing the ground to become a solid puddle that refused to dry. Occasionally it would storm, complete with thunder so loud you could feel it in your chest, and bolts of lightning that gave the tiniest glimpses of light into a world that had become nothing but shadows moving about.

It was storming the night that Sam was sitting on his bed, trying to get comfortable by propping himself up with his flimsy pillows, and losing the battle. A geometry textbook rested open on his bended knees, and his notebook and pencils, their edges as dull as the weather outside, lay beside him.

He flipped a page in the textbook, studied it momentarily, and picked up his paper to copy the equations, wishing he could find his recently lost pencil sharpener. Sam thought about writing a note to remind himself to buy a new one the next time he was out, then thought wryly that he shouldn't waste the lead he had left to write a note when it was needed more for homework. Chuckling to himself, he decided to make it a mental note instead.

Just as Sam was picking up his protractor to trace the angles he was working on, there was a mighty boom of thunder that seemed to shake the very foundation of the house, as if God himself was showing off the power he held over humanity. This was followed by a quick crack of lightning so bright that it was nearly blinding, then everything went black. The loss of electricity was even more obvious after the powerful bolt of lightning, pushing everything into brightness, only to have it immediately bathed in dark. Sam thought God must now be showing off, by thrusting forth such a massive beam of light, only to have it immediately shushed by complete darkness. The Lord giveth, and the Lord taketh away.

Sam gave a deep growl of frustration. He knew he had a flashlight somewhere (Why was it that he only thought about the location of said flashlight when it was too dark to go searching for it?). Feeling in the darkness for his books, Sam closed the textbook and piled everything onto his nightstand. Unless the power came back on soon, which seemed unlikely judging by the screaming sound of the wind outside, Sam would just have to fill his brain with knowledge at another time. He hoped his teachers would be understanding if his homework wasn't completed tomorrow, and felt a quick burst of apprehension (Sam *always* had his homework ready) but he relaxed himself by realizing that probably all of the area was without power as well. He was also comforted by the thought that his teachers would be forgiving to no one if not to Sam.

Out of habit Sam glanced at the digital clock which resided on his nightstand, then felt silly as he realized that there would be no glowing numbers shining back on him this evening.

He stood up carefully so as not to trip over his slippers and stretched, feeling somehow comforted by the darkness and the hammering of the rain. There was a grumble and for a brief moment Sam thought another torrent of thunder was beginning, but then he chuckled in earnest as he realized the sound was coming from his very stomach.

Holding his hands out in front of him and sliding his feet across the floor, Sam made the memorized journey from bed to doorway, hallway to living room, kitchen to refrigerator.

His stomach growling more angrily this time, giving the thunder a run for its money, Sam pulled open the door of the fridge, again being mildly surprised when the contents didn't light up. Stupid electricity. It was funny how used you could get to something, something that you never thought of or appreciated, but once it was gone you realized how dependent you were on it to start with. Sam used to like to think that he would have liked to have been born in an earlier time period, the pioneer days perhaps, but as he was shoving his hand through the darkened refrigerator in an attempt to find something edible that had not yet expired, a bit worried at what his fingers may touch, that he thought perhaps he wouldn't have made a good pioneer after all.

Sam had the door wide open, his head buried inside as his hands searched the back of the shelf where he thought he had noticed a pudding cup earlier. He was so intent on his pursuit that he didn't hear the footsteps behind him, and perhaps he thought that growling sound was his stomach again, or more thunder getting ready to erupt. There was an eruption, but it was of a different kind.

What started as a growl turned into the voice of a man, and when the refrigerator door was slammed and came into contact with Sam's head, he was completely taken by surprise and at first didn't even realize what he had been hit with.

"What in the FUCK do you think you're doing? The power is out, you moron. Are you *trying* to make all the food go bad?"

Still stunned from the sudden contact of the door hitting him in the side of the head, he had not yet changed his position, so Sam was completely unprepared for his father to open the door and slam it shut again, so hard it bounced back open off of Sam's head, this time causing a more forceful contact. A glass bottle of ketchup and a jar of pickles fell from the door and smashed to the ground, both shattering, their contents mixing in a disgustingly syrupy goo which hid shards of glass beneath the sweetness.

Sam toppled over, knocked off balance by the force, and his bare foot slipped in some of the goop on the floor. He fell to the ground, landing sharply on his rear, tiny pieces of glass embedding their way into his foot. The smell of the acidic ketchup, the salty pungency of the pickles, and the sweet smell of Sam's bloody food intermingled ad nauseum.

"Do you think I work my ass off all day, every day, so that I can provide food for you, to just let you stand there literally watching as it all goes bad?" The contempt in Mark's voice was palatable.

"No sir, I'm sorry. I was just hungry and I couldn't see -"

"*No*. None of these whiny little excuses, I'm sick of it." Mark gave the door another solid kick, and this time since Sam was no longer in the way, it closed with a bang, the entire refrigerator shuddering with remorse.

"You had dinner, you don't need to eat anything else. You're just saying you're hungry so I have to work more hours to pay for extra food. Do you know that in the army, you eat what you get and you don't ask for more, you simply say thank you. *Thank you*. Have you ever once thanked me for providing for you? Now get up and clean up this mess. It smells like ass in here."

Mark turned on his heel and walked out of the kitchen. Sam heard a kitchen chair squeak across the floor as his father caught it on the toe of his shoe, yelling, "Damnit!"

Sam nodded, then realized his father couldn't see him, and said as stoically as possible, "Yes, sir." Then Sam gave his father the finger. The full one, not just on the hand where his finger was missing the tip. As he had explained it to Nick, that's how you knew he really meant it.

Sam wondered how he would get a mess cleaned up that he couldn't even see, and how he would go about picking out the slivers of glass he could feel implanted in the sole of his foot. No matter, he wouldn't need his sense of sight to do that. You didn't need to be able to see to feel where the things inside of you hurt the most.

***

"This is seriously, like, the coolest thing that's ever happened," Nick said happily. "I mean, have we ever gotten a day off school before just because there's no power?"

"Not that I can remember," Sam answered, kicking at the carpet with the toe of his good foot so his chair would rock back and forth, back and forth.

"I'm surprised they didn't make us go anyway and just learn in the dark or some shit. Some of those teachers can talk, talk, talk, all day long and probably wouldn't even notice if there were no lights on."

"I think there's more to it than that," Sam answered. "They have to worry about stuff like people flushing toilets."

"Ooh," Nick said, sitting up from where he had been stretched out on the couch. "I didn't even think about that.

What if, like, every student had to take a dump? Ew, that would be wicked gross." Nick shuddered in glee at the disgusting possibilities.

"Yeah. They definitely don't want Nick Lynch in school with no flushing toilets."

"Ha, very funny." Nick swung around so that he was backwards, with his back on the couch, his feet spread across the backrest, and his head on the floor. "How long do you think we will be without power? Like a week maybe? Like, past the test we are supposed to have in history on Friday?"

"I don't know, it will probably be fixed before that. I wouldn't stop studying if I were you; even if they had to cancel, they would still have the test when we got back."

"*Stop* studying? Hah, I would have had to *start* studying to do that," Nick said with a laugh.

Sam rolled his eyes.

"So, what do you want to do? Watch a movie? Oh wait, that's right, no power. Hmm, do you want to listen to my new tape? Oh wait, that's right… well, we could pop in a frozen pizza - oh shit, that's right…"

Sam grinned as he listened to Nick's train of thought, not at all surprised when he ended with, "Well shit, what in the hell can we do? This blows."

"Two minutes ago you said it was the coolest thing ever."

"Yeah, not going to school is awesome, but what good is it to have a day off if we can't do shit during it?"

Sam shrugged. "At least it's daytime, so even though it's raining we can still see each other."

"Oh, yeah," Nick answered, laughing. "Just what I want to do all day, look at your ugly mug."

Getting light-headed from his position, Nick let his legs fall off the back of the couch, then stood up and sat back down as a normal person would position oneself on a couch, and he peered at his friend.

"Say, now that you mention it, what's that mark on the side of your head? It looks like dirt that you didn't see to wipe off 'cause it was too dark."

"It's nothing, just a bruise." Sam didn't mention that he also had a large, painful knot on the side of his head, and gauze wrapped around one of his feet as well.

"Oh, gotcha," Nick answered, understanding when not to press something. If Sam wanted to discuss how he got the bruise, he would. It wasn't as if Nick couldn't figure it out on his own anyway. Ever since they were kids Sam would show up to his house with some form or another of an injury, everything from bruises and scrapes to stitches and broken bones. Although the particulars of every incidence were slightly altered, the perpetrator remained the same.

Despite the calmness of the dark, quiet house, with nothing to hear but the steady rain falling outside and the tiny squeaking sound coming from Sam's chair as he rocked, Nick could feel his blood pressure start to rise. It made him so mad; no, that wasn't right. There was more venom in his thoughts than that. It *pissed him off* that Sam's dad was such a complete dick. Sam was always so loyal, no matter how lousy of a friend Nick could be sometimes, and yet someone could treat him like garbage. And not just someone, but his own *father*, for Christ's sake.

Nick could feel his fingers balling themselves up into fists. If someone at school said or did something to disrespect

Sam (unless that someone was Nick himself, of course), that person would be dealt with. Nick would pull them aside, do whatever he had to do. Not that this was a usual circumstance, by any means. Everyone loved Sam, and besides, if someone did have a problem with him they would know they would have to contend with Nick first, so no one would bother trying. At school, Nick could protect Sam from anything. Unfortunately, however, school was not the place that Sam needed protection from.

"What are you thinking about, dude? You look totally zoned out over there."

"Oh, sorry." Nick forced his hands to relax, wiping the sweat on his jeans. "I don't know, I was in another world for a second there."

"Was it a world with electricity?" Sam joked. "Cause I'm starting to get pretty bored myself."

"Geez, soon it will be dark outside and then we will really have nothing to do," Nick whined.

"We could always go outside and try to catch lightning bugs," Sam quipped.

Nick turned and screwed up his face as he looked at his friend. "Yeah, that only sounds like the most boring, kiddy thing I could ever possibly ever think of."

"Yeah, I know. I mean, I just remember one night when I did that as a kid."

"Yeah, I did that too when I was little. And what do you mean one night? You only did it once?"

"Only once."

"You know, that's right," Nick mused, adjusting his position once again on the couch so that he was laying down on his stomach, his chin propped up in his hands. "I can remember trying to get you to do that with me and dad when we were kids but you didn't want to. So, uh, why did you only do it one time? It's not like sex, like if you were a lightning bug virgin and then you weren't."

Sam raised his gaze to the ceiling, neglecting to comment on the absurdity of that statement, and answered nonchalantly, "Oh, I don't remember. Just didn't have much fun with it, I guess."

"You are such a dweeb," Nick responded, thinking his friend was acting very strange indeed, and started bemoaning again about his lack of anything worthwhile and *adult* to do.

Sam had stopped listening. Nick's words drifted off into the distance until they became not words at all, but just the rhythmic bass symphony sound of Nick's voice.

Sam thought back to when he was five or seven or somewhere in between. He rarely lied to his friend, but in fact, he did remember.

That next morning when he had woken up, Sam had said a quick "good morning" to his bugs, then gone into the kitchen in search of cereal.

The cereal was on a shelf just barely out of Sam's tiny reach, so as he usually did, Sam grabbed one of the kitchen chairs, carefully dragging it over to the cabinet, and stood on the top.

The box was pushed back further in the cabinet then he was used to, and Sam had to scoot his bare feet closer to the end of the chair to reach. As his fingers curled around the cereal box, Sam felt the chair shift under his weight.

With no warning, the chair seemed to fall out directly from underneath him, causing Sam to pinwheel his arms back in a crazy attempt to achieve his balance.

The chair landed on its side with a thud, the cereal box tipped to the floor and fell open, its contents (which were in the tiny shape of little balls, which was most unfortunate on this particular day) pouring all over the kitchen floor.

"What in the hell was that noise?" Mark asked, still in his bathrobe, padding into the kitchen.

He looked down at his son with a freshly scraped knee of his own making, the chair tilted at an angle which looked to have scraped the tile floor, and the little balls of cereal rolling every which way.

"Goddamnit, Sam! What in the fuck? I'm trying to get a little more sleep before I have to get to work, then I *just* want to have my coffee and read my paper in peace, and instead I wake up to this fucking disaster. What in the hell do you think you're doing?"

"I'm sorry," Sam whimpered. "I couldn't reach the cereal and -"

"And, and, and then, let me guess, *this*." His father interrupted, spreading his arms out as he surveyed the mess. He took a step toward Sam, his bare feet crunching on several pieces of loose cereal.

"Ow, God*damnit*!" he roared, reaching over to pull Sam up by the collar of his pajama shirt. "Go get the broom and the dust pan. Sweep up this fucking mess. If I so much as see one grain of cereal on this floor, there will be hell to pay."

Sam nodded, starting to make his way toward the broom closet.

Meanwhile, Mark began purposefully grinding his feet on the kernels of cereal, imbedding them into the tile. "And you had better figure out a way to buff that scratch out of the floor. I swear to God, if I can tell where that chair landed by the time you are done, there will be hell to pay."

Sam nodded again, wondering how much hell a single person could have to pay in a given day, and he went to fetch the broom.

Disgusted, Mark wandered back into his bedroom, wiping cereal remnants on the carpet of the hallway as he went. "And vacuum this up, too!" he yelled before slamming the door of his room.

For the next two hours, Sam swept using the broom that was way too tall for him, and vacuumed using the vacuum that was way too tall as well, and hard to push at that. Then he got on his hands and knees, happy to have a job that was finally his height, and scrubbed and scoured the gouge that the chair had made in the floor, trying to get it as much erased as possible. He crawled around, looking for balls of cereal that may have inadvertently rolled under the table or behind the trash can or anywhere else that a tiny cereal ball could possibly end up.

And then he remembered about his colony of light bugs.

"Oh, no, I need to put them outside!" Sam thought to himself as he hurried down the hall to his bedroom, scurrying for the jar.

He had wondered if the fun, nice father from last night had been real or just a figment of his imagination. Alas, it had been real, however short lived. The proof was in the jar he was holding, the bottom littered with the bodies of dead bugs, their eyes empty of life, their bodies void of light.

The boy picked up the gun, not noticing how much his hands were shaking as he did so. Carefully, on auto pilot, he placed it between his fingers, grasping it tightly, as he had seen in the movies. It was heavy, so much heavier than he had expected, as if it weighed a hundred pounds, as if it was the weight of one's very soul.

CHAPTER FIFTEEN

Nick's hair had been getting longer, and he put a backward baseball hat on his head to keep it from falling into his eyes. At first it had just been pure laziness, but it seemed the ladies reacted well to his longer locks, so now Nick was keeping it that way on purpose. He felt like a rock star each time he dramatically tossed his head back to keep the hair out of his face. He swore he could literally see girls swoon when he did this, so he did it far more often than was actually necessary. But today, Nick didn't feel like dealing with it, so he went with the hat. Although, he was pretty sure girls would still pay attention to him, they tended to like the backwards hat as well. Or the front-words hat. In fact, it seemed as if Nick could do no wrong when it came to the fairer sex.

To date, Nick had had sex with not one, not two, but *three* different girls. As he happily kept track of his rising number, he thought with satisfaction about his sexual prowess. No other boy in his class had had sex with not one, not two, but *three* different girls. In fact, many of them, like Sam, had never had sex at all.

Nick was immensely proud of his conquests, (well, except for that first time… he cringed… maybe not that first time) but his skills seemed to keep improving, and the guys in his class were quite impressed.

Nick had had his dick sucked four times, by *four* different girls. (He had tried to get girl number two to sleep with him as well, but she stated she wasn't a whore and refused him. He wasn't sure how one could state that one wasn't a whore, when one had cum streaming out the corner of her mouth, but he hadn't pushed it.) No, Nick would never push a girl into having sex, and he never offered false promises to them or proclaimed his love for them. He would talk pretty words and try his darndest, but if a girl didn't want him (rare) there would certainly be another girl to come along who would.

Nick wasn't sure how he had gotten so lucky in this department. His looks helped, for sure. Practically every girl in his class had a crush on him, a fact that he was well aware of, which boosted his confidence into bordering on arrogance. This confidence/arrogance was attractive to girls, and they would find reasons to hang around him, getting all giggly and blushing when they did so.

Sometimes girls called him at home, and he would chit chat for a moment then find a reason to get off the phone. After all, he had heard of phone sex but he was just interested in regular sex, and that couldn't happen over the phone, so Nick was not interested. It wasn't that he was disrespectful, he was always polite, but if he had to listen to a girl jabber on about one thing or another, it had to at least be in person so he could steal peeks at her boobs.

Nicked liked girls. Not just one girl, but girls in general. He liked how their bodies curved, how their hair always smelled good, how soft their skin was, the way their lips looked as they wrapped around his dick.

"It's amazing, seriously. You've only had the one chick, but honestly man I could easily find a girl to give you a BJ. There are plenty of girls that would do that for you, man."

Sam scrunched up his face and shook his head, his eyes skyward. "I really appreciate the offer," he said sarcastically to his friend, "but I'm good, thanks."

"I mean it, though. Girls think you're sweet, and the missing fingers thing gets you some serious sympathy points. You could totally get a girl to open her mouth and -"

"Yes, I understand the offer, thank you," Sam interrupted his friend wryly.

"Whatever, man, have it your way. More for me." Nick folded his hands behind his head and stretched out, knocking his hat askew.

The boys were sitting on Nick's porch, Charlotte between them, laying with her head resting on Sam's lap.

Absentmindedly petting the dog, Sam took a deep breath, inhaling the fresh air around him. "Girls are more your department, anyway."

"Oh, come on, do you really want to go to college as a virgin?"

"It wouldn't bother me."

"It would bother *me*."

"What would bother you, if you went to college as a virgin, or if I did?" Sam asked, grinning.

"Both," Nick answered, smiling back. "That's just the kind of friend I am."

"Yeah, I'm very lucky," Sam answered, rolling his eyes, but at the same time knowing the truth of it.

Scratching Charlotte behind the ears, Sam half listened as Nick continued on about the benefits of being sexually active, and instead thought of the basis of their friendship. Obviously, it had started out of sheer convenience, since the boys lived so close together. Idly, Sam wondered if the boys had just met, right now today, if they would still be best friends. They were different in so many ways, and what with Nick being so popular, among boys and girls both. If they met now, today, Sam figured Nick would be obligatory decent to him, but would probably not befriend him seeing as they traveled in such different circles otherwise. Nick was a jock, Sam often had his nose in a book. Nick was a social butterfly, whereas Sam often liked to have time to himself.

Not for the first time, Sam felt how lucky he was to have Nick, and Nick's parents, in his life. Thinking back on all the major events of his life, good and bad, Sam wasn't sure how he would have gotten through everything if not for his best friend. Nick was there for the bad, and most often was the one that created the good.

"So," Nick said loudly, drawing Sam back into the present. "It's Saturday, there's a party tonight at Dylan Murphy's house, life is good, man."

Sam nodded his agreement. The April day was unseasonably warm, with a cool breeze rustling the branches of the tree that held the old playhouse, tousling the tips of Nick's hair that stuck out from the sides of his hat, cooling the back of Sam's neck. No matter how bad life could be, on a day like this, sitting on a porch with your dog and your best friend, it was hard not to simply breathe and take in the day. Sam felt that overall, life was good indeed.

This led Sam's mind to wander, to a day when they were much younger, when the days were just turning sunny and balmy.

The boys must have been in the fourth grade or so, when the girls in class suddenly took to doing gymnastics in the playground. The girls who were able to do cartwheels and flips, backbends and stand on their hands, created a new crack in the class system. Suddenly they became the more popular ones, the ones with more confidence, and surely the prettiest.

The girls who weren't able to twist and bend, to defy gravity itself, were doomed to sit on the grass, watching from the sidelines, to be outside looking in.

It was at this time that Nick decided he simply had to learn to do a cartwheel, to impress them. This wasn't a difficult goal, seeing as Nick was as stubborn as he was athletic, and after a few practice turns in his backyard, Nick was spinning away at recess. This was much to the delight of the girls, who pointed and giggled at his over-exaggerated spins, as of course was the intention.

Realizing the girls were riveted to his actions, Nick took delight in his own gymnastic endeavors, pretending to be silly but secretly loving the way his feet left the earth, the colors of green and blue becoming a swirl around him until he was upright once again. It was a rush, in every sense of the word, as he could practically feel the girls falling for him with every cartwheel he did.

Sometimes, Nick liked to ham it up, purposefully falling over or landing in a dramatic spill at the end, long lanky limbs splayed out around him, moaning loudly. This caused the girls to shriek in hysterics, and whisper amongst themselves in awe as Nick Lynch grew cuter and cuter.

"I could totally teach you how to do a cartwheel, we could do them together," Nick had often suggested to Sam.

"No thanks, I can't even do a straight somersault," Sam would counter.

"That's why I'm going to teach you, Sam. No one knows how to do something until they learn how to do it."

Sam couldn't argue with that logic, but he had known even then, on some level, that this was just the start of Nick surpassing him on one of those life stages that aren't maybe so important, or perhaps are the most important of all.

Despite Nick's protests, Sam never learned to do a cartwheel, he never even tried. While his friend liked to defy gravity, Sam preferred to keep his feet firmly planted on the ground.

Charlotte had temporarily fallen asleep on Sam's lap and she whimpered quietly as dogs do when they are chasing squirrels through Never-Never Land, and Sam was jerked back to the present.

Nick was saying something, and Sam struggled to find his place in the conversation.

"Think about what I said tonight, Sam," Nick instructed, taking off his cap, smoothing his hair back, and putting it on again. "I could probably get a girl to do it for you at the party."

"No thanks," Sam said again, trying to be stern but ending up laughing, realizing the conversation hadn't really changed at all in his mental absence. When Nick set his mind to something, it was often hard to get him to realize it was a bad idea. "I'm all set in that department."

"Sure, if by 'all set' means 'no action whatsoever', then you're good," Nick quipped, looking at his friend searchingly.

"I will just live vicariously through you."

"That's a dumb way to look at it."

"Getting your friend to have a girl suck you off is a dumb thing to do."

"Dumb or not, the results would be the same. You'd get off; maybe that would help your stress level."

Sam shook his head in wonder at his friend, laughing. "My stress level comes from having to do my own homework as well as yours."

Nick grinned, saying, "Well, you have a point there."

Of course, both boys knew the source of Sam's real stress, the problem that no one wanted to speak of. It seemed like to bring it up, to put a name to it, would put an imperfection, a small black mark, on this beautiful day.

Nick decided to change the subject. "So, what time do you think we should get there tonight? I don't want to be too early 'cause that would be dorky, but I don't want to get there so late that all the food is gone."

"Ah, wanting to make an entrance as well as eat as much as possible. What to do, what to do…"

Nick playfully swatted Sam on the leg, waking Charlotte, who nuzzled in closer. "This is serious man. The last time I got to a party I went too late, and there was one piece of pizza left. *One*, Sam. I can't let that happen again."

"No, that would be tragic," Sam said as Nick nodded, the sarcasm lost on him.

"I know. It starts at seven, so I'm thinking maybe eight? Or seven-thirty? I just don't know."

"Why don't you make it 7:45 then, split the difference," Sam suggested.

"Oh, good idea! Split the difference, I like that." Nick raised his eyebrows in approval.

The problem solved, Nick took his hat off and laid down flat on the porch, placing his hat over his eyes. "Cowboys do this all the time in movies when they're trying to take a nap. It keeps the sun out of their eyes," he said informatively.

"Yeah, but they probably aren't as antsy as you," Sam answered, watching as Nick wiggled around to get comfortable, knocking the hat onto the porch. Nick scooped it off, gave it a quick dusting off for good measure, and balanced it back onto his face.

"No, it works. For real, it's like it's nighttime under this hat. I could totally take a nap, it's so dark."

Nick stopped talking then, not to sleep, but simply lost in his own thoughts of girls and cowboys.

Sam gently patted Charlotte's head, appreciating the soft fur against the nubs on his fingers, and gazed at what he could see of his friend, a body without a face. In the sudden calm, with the calls of a few far off birds the only ones to break the silence, Sam thought about the remark his friend had made about the hat. If only there was some way to do that in reverse, to have a dark world surround you, but to put something over your eyes that would bring back the light.

***

When Patricia Maver was young, she often dreamed of the day she would get married. It would be to someone tall, handsome, with hair so deep brown it was almost black. He would be so in love with her it would melt her heart, and her friends would be so jealous, and she would swoon with pride.

The wedding itself would be a thing of beauty; her in a simple but elegant long white gown, a single strand of pearls around her neck. There would be a church, stone on the outside, high wooden beams on the inside, brimming with her loved ones. The priest would announce them as husband and wife, and the flashes of light from a multitude of cameras wanting to capture this supreme happiness would be nearly blinding.

Her new husband would whisper sweet nothings to her, take her hand and walk her down the aisle, two people merged into one single being in front of God, in front of the world.

When Patricia Maver was young, she often dreamed of the day she would have a baby. First she would have a daughter, a beautiful daughter with a thick head of dark curly hair and eyes that were startling blue. She would look up at her mother in wonderment, and Patricia would know that she had created a beautiful creature, one full of love for her. Her husband would stand over her in the hospital bed, completely devoted to wife and daughter, one hand letting the baby suck on his finger, the other stroking Patricia's hair. "I'm so proud of you, I love you so much. Look at this beautiful new person we've created," he would whisper to her, and Patricia's heart would swell with love.

When Patricia Maver was young, she often dreamed of the day she would be sitting out in the sunshine, on a white wicker rocking chair, watching her daughter catch butterflies in the grass, and holding her newborn son to her breast.

He husband would go back and forth, from daughter to mother and son, always devoted, always caring, always so full of love.

"I love my family so much; my beautiful wife, my brilliant children, my wonderful home," he would say, gazing at her adoringly. She would smile back, knowing that it was all true, that she had the life that other people envied. Her husband, her daughter, her son, all glorious in their own way. Her yard, surrounded by a white picket fence and the greenest grass in the neighborhood, a cherry tree in the back that always seemed to be in bloom. Her house, a big white two storey with a sweeping porch wrapping around the whole thing like a hug.

Hers would be an amazing life.

When Patricia Maver was young, she never dreamed of having a husband that ignored her at best, hit her at worst. A son, such a dreamer, such a handsome boy, but his face always marred with pain, sometimes physical, but mostly the kind of pain that was deeper, eternal. He would look at her, was it with pity, or anger? Definitely not infinite love, although there still was love there, whether she had earned it or not, which made her often feel even worse.

The house, small and run down, with walls that needed to be repainted and carpet that was badly in need of repair. The yard, smaller still, the grass always seeming to be on the verge of dying, growing yellowed and dingy no matter how much rain washed over it.

Her world, not a fairy tale, but often a nightmare, the story you tell your children to scare them into a different life, a better life.

Sometimes Patricia hated herself, for getting into the mess to start with, and for allowing her son to live in it besides. But as far as she could see, there was simply no way out, no better options for them. Sometimes, in her wildest thoughts, she fantasized about leaving her husband. But it could only ever be a fantasy, as Patricia knew that her husband wouldn't allow her and Sam to leave him. What life would there be for her anyway? No job, no way to support herself much less a teenage son.

And so she stayed, they both did, under a roof where fist ruled above heart, where fear was present over love. Although… she did love Mark. At least, she thought she did. Sometimes, he would make love to her, or praise her for a tasty breakfast, or tell her that her hair looked nice. And the love grew. But those times were few and far between… and the love wavered.

When Patricia Maver was young, she never dreamed of living a nightmare.

***

The boy thought his hands steady but as the gun shook between them, he realized that wasn't the case. "C'mon, you've done this before," he told himself, trying to calm the knot that had formed in the pit of his belly, trying to see clearly as sweat dripped into his eyes. Carrying the gun at his side, he turned to the commotion behind him, a million thoughts going through his head. Was this for protection? Or was he being a bully? And at this point, was there even a difference between the two?

CHAPTER SIXTEEN

Dylan Murphy's party was in full swing by the time the boys showed up, but as Nick noted, there were plenty of sandwiches and pickles and olives left, so the timing had been perfect.

Filling his hands with food, and ever the horny social butterfly, Nick walked over and took up post near a table where several pretty girls were standing.

Sam knew he would be able to follow in his friend's footsteps, literally, for it was a well-known rule that Sam was welcome in any social circle that Nick found himself in. The school body at large seemed to accept that they were basically a package deal.

Tonight, though, he simply didn't feel like talking to a bunch of girls, so he ate a salami and swiss cheese sandwich, enjoying the way the two flavors combined in his mouth, and stood anchor at the food table.

"Hey, Sam, how are you man? Glad you and Nick could make it."

Swallowing quickly, Sam turned around and looked into the eyes of his smiling childhood friend. "Thanks, Dylan. This is a cool party."

"Yeah. Hey, I haven't asked you about her lately, but do you still have Charlotte? How's that dog doing, man?"

"Yeah, I do, and she's great. She lives over at Nick's house, you know, but I'm there all the time so I see her all the time, so I still feel like she's my dog."

"She probably likes you more than she likes Nick anyway," Dylan chided. "I bet he forgets to walk her and stuff."

"Well, between me, Nick, and his parents, I think Charlotte gets pretty spoiled," Sam laughed, thinking about his dog.

"I bet." Dylan watched Sam take another bite of his sandwich, staring openly at his hand. "So, do your fingers still hurt and stuff? Your hands are so wicked, man."

"It's weird," Sam answered, looking down at his fingers, or what was left of them, splaying them apart. "Mostly, I'm used to it so I kind of forget it's there, you know? Like, I relearned how to hold a pencil and a pen and a fork and stuff, and type on the computer, so it's really not too bad most of the time. But sometimes it's like the tip of my fingers hurt, but there're not really there, so it doesn't make sense that they hurt. The doctors say it's a real thing, phantom pains or something."

"That's so messed up, man. But cool though, you know? Like having a tattoo."

Sam thought that in no way was losing your fingers to frostbite anything like choosing to get a tattoo, but he just nodded at his friend.

"So," Dylan continued, getting warmed up to his subject. "Does it feel different when, you know…"

Sam looked at him blankly. Dylan looked around, lowered his voice, and continued, "You know, jerk off or something."

Sam could feel himself blushing, maybe he should have followed Nick after all, but Dylan was a good friend who was simply curious. Sam always appreciated Pete being upfront with him about uncomfortable topics, so Sam decided to answer honestly.

"It did feel weird, at first, cause it wasn't like, *my* hand, you know. But just like everything else, I got used to it."

"So, do the ladies like it?" Dylan continued. "I mean, it must feel different for them too in that department, right?"

Feeling a little uncomfortable with the way this conversation was going, Sam just shrugged and finished his last bite of sandwich.

"Speaking of, you have yourself a new girlfriend yet? After that Cindy chick moved, you haven't really been with a lot of girls, amiright?"

Sam shrugged again, not wanting to get into exactly how right Dylan was on this particular subject matter.

"What is it, man, is it the hand thing? Cause a lot of girls think you look cool. I know for a fact that Laura in geometry has a crush on you."

"Laura from geometry just likes watching as I try to use my pencil and my protractor at the same time."

"No way, man, she's sweet. She likes the whole no-fingers things. Apparently she told Courtney about it and Courtney's best friends with Julie, so she knows all about Laura liking you." Julie was Dylan's on-again, off-again girlfriend.

Sam's head was starting to spin a bit, and he excused himself from Dylan to go see what Nick was doing.

Nick was standing with a boy and two pretty girls from their class; no surprise there. Sam walked up to the group, thumping Nick on the shoulder as a greeting.

"Hey there, man. Jessica was just telling me that her parents are gonna be out of town the weekend after next. Isn't that cool?"

"Yeah, that's pretty cool," Sam conceded.

"Yeah, it's like, super cool," the wordsmith Jessica added, swinging back her long mane of brown hair. Sam watched as it fanned around her head in tiny tendrils.

"So, Jessica and her best friend, Carrie, are supposed to be house sitting or whatever that night, and they might want some company. I mean, just sitting in a house sounds pretty fucking boring, am I right?" Nick commented.

"Yeah, it's like, so beyond boring I could just scream," Jessica said, moving her head so that her hair whipped around in the other direction, nearly smacking Sam in the face.

"You guys should definitely come over and hang out. We could order a pizza and watch movies and stuff," the other girl, a blond with short curly hair chimed in. Sam guessed her to be Carrie. He thought he recognized her from his geometry class. He wondered what was meant by 'and stuff'.

The other boy who was standing in the group, Tom, was looking reluctant to leave although he was obviously not still an active participant in the conversation. Carrie was looking at Sam, and Jessica hadn't averted her attention from Nick all evening.

"Um, I don't know, I may have to help my parents with something that weekend," Sam offered sheepishly. Tom brightened up; maybe he was back in the game after all.

Nick glared at his friend, saying, "No, you must be mistaken about the weekend."

"I don't think so, Nick. In fact I -"

"No, no, I distinctly remember when we were talking on the porch earlier today, you were mentioning how bored you were going to be the weekend after next. *Remember?*"

Tom looked forlornly at the ground.

"Nick," Sam said slowly, as it was quite obvious to him and he was sure it was obvious to the others as well what Nick was trying to do (well, on second thoughts, maybe it wasn't obvious to Jessica), "I don't think I can make it that weekend."

Nick glared at him, astonished that Sam would let an opportunity like this pass by, but Sam only shrugged. "Sorry, ladies, but Nick obviously forgot what else we talked about today. I won't be able to come and keep you company that evening. But I'm sure Nick and Tom can help you find something to do, so you won't, like, die of boredom."

Jessica nodded at the accuracy of the statement. Carrie huffed but then turned her attention to the elated Tom. Nick shook his head in wonder at his friend, then turned back to Jessica with her long, swinging hair.

***

It was a crisp morning in late April when everyone in Stony Meadows awoke to a sea of fog. It was a cool, dewy blanket of white that covered the area, so thick you could breathe it in, letting it cool your lungs. As a person walked through it, taking a child by the hand to the bus stop, or with a tiny dog on a leash, droplets of moisture clung to their hair, their skin, made their glasses blurry. Visibility was terrible, and all the cars were covered in a wet sheen, the people too.

As Sam walked through the fog he had a notion of what it must be like to go through a cloud. Sam never had, but Nick had been in an airplane several times for family vacations. (Sam had often been invited to go, but for reasons he couldn't fathom (wouldn't his parents like him out of the way for a week on end?), he had never been allowed to tag along.

His curiosity getting the better of him, Sam once asked Nick to explain what it was like to fly through the clouds, and the way Nick had described it, Sam believed it must be very much like walking through a heavy fog.

Therefore, as he picked up his pace and stretched out his arms to his sides, letting as much of the vapor cover him as possible, Sam felt like a bird, flying through a cloud. He imagined this is the closest he would ever come to touching the sky, to seeing up from the top to the bottom, to look down upon the earth and have sky both above and below.

He slowed his pace and walked slowly to the bus stop, wanting to reside in this private cloud for as long as possible. Nick had been given a car when he turned sixteen which was wonderful, but on days like today when he called to say he was sick and wouldn't be going to school, Sam was once again a slave to the bus route. He was excited about this, for Sam knew the chances of him being allowed to purchase a car of his own, despite his savings, were slim, and he missed these early morning walks. Just him, his book bag slung over his shoulder, and an air of solitude.

It gave Sam a much needed chance to think, about thoughts both deep and mundane, when he was alone with himself and the world. Much as he loved his friend, Sam enjoyed having time to himself as well, something he didn't think outgoing Nick would ever truly understand.

Allowing his backpack to swing side to side with the rhythm of his movement, Sam smiled into the day ahead. The fog was so dense it hid any of his neighbors that were out and about, and Sam felt that he was truly alone in this world.

He used the time to ponder his life, much more deeply than a sixteen year old should, and thought about his parents, his old girlfriend, his friend, his time here on earth. He had often wondered if he was put here for a special purpose.

Sam's grandmother was religious and every birthday and Christmas she mailed him a card about how much he was loved by God. Sam wasn't sure about whether there was a God or not, but it felt strange to know that if there indeed was, then He loved Sam more than Sam's own family ever did.

He wondered, if there was a God, did this being love him more than Nick, than Nick's family, than Charlotte? Did God remember the day, so long ago, that amounted to the single drop of blood that the boys shared? Of course, a sixteen-year-old boy knew that the idea of 'blood brothers' was silly, childish, but in Sam's mind it still lingered as being something of grave import.

If there was a God, why did he sit around, watching as Mark Maver raged and bullied like a storm himself, a storm every bit as big and furious as one that God could create? Why did God allow his mother to sit like a stone, seeming to be in a world all her own half the time, perhaps wracked with pity or guilt or shame or maybe with no feelings at all?

All these things made it hard for Sam to accept a God, an all-powerful being who still watched as bad things happened to the good people of the world, all while the bad people of the world seemed to flourish. Still, though, he kept all of his grandmother's card in a shoebox in the top shelf of his closet. Every October and December he would take it down to add a new card to the collection, but periodically he would open the box just to try to feel the hope that he believed the cards themselves should carry. Sometimes it almost seemed to work, the mere act of opening the box bringing with it a sense of peace that would hang over Sam for several moments, the same way the fog was hanging over him now. Other times, Sam knew he could be enveloped in it, in the fog, in the peace, but it was just out of his reach, the cloud always ahead of him, never right in his line of sight. He couldn't feel it, but he knew it was there. The feeling of calm.

Realizing the slowness of his pace could make him late for the bus, Sam quickened his movements once again, not wanting to miss his transportation. He had missed it once before, and had been forced to walk the rest of the way to the Lynch house in shame, head lowered, falling on the mercy of May to take him to school.

The thought of May made Sam's train of thought move in a different direction, and he considered Nick's parents. May, still beautiful in her own right, although long since the object of Sam's affections. Pete, still jolly and good natured, ever the doting father. It was true, the Lynch's had become more parents than Sam's own parents, and he was grateful to them for that.

Was it God who had brought the entire Lynch family into his life? If so, he was eternally thankful, for Sam believed that without the three of them he may not have survived his circumstances, physically or mentally.

But if it was God that had brought this family into his life, then didn't he realize that it was because of Sam's own family life that he needed the Lynch's in the first place?

All this seemed very confusing, too heavy of thoughts for a foggy Wednesday morning, and Sam was determined to think of something else.

He arrived at the bus stop, and heaved his backpack over his shoulder, letting it rest on the damp ground, giving his body a break from the heavy burden.

***

Holding it with both hands, the boy raised the gun. He pointed it at the man who was screaming, who was threatening to kill, and whose eyes showed an evil which made all involved feel he meant it. The boy looked at his friend, at his best friend, and for just the briefest moment their eyes locked.

Though only a few feet apart from one another, the boy wondered about the amount of space between him and his friend. In fact, what was the space between friendships and family? One drop of blood and all the rest, between right and wrong, the space between what was good and needed and what was pure evil.

His body taking over where his mind could not, the boy aimed carefully, right at the chest of a raging Mark Maver. He knew what he had to do, had known it his whole life. Carefully, he squeezed the trigger. The shot was enormously loud, and everything came to a stop.

CHAPTER SEVENTEEN

May that year came through Missouri hot and heavy, as if someone had told the month itself that it was actually August, and had therefore better act like it. It was as though the weather couldn't keep control of itself; one day it was sticky with heat, the next raging with a storm so powerful it would knock thick tree limbs over as if they were merely sticks.

Instead of introducing the residents of Stony Meadows lovingly into the next summer season, that May screamed it in, in a way that no one could ignore with the most wild weather ups and downs.

"Mom, take it easy on the people out there," Nick would joke to his mother, hers being the namesake of this most treacherous of storm seasons mixed with uncannily hot temperatures that anyone had seen in a long time.

"Sorry there, son. If I had any control over this craziness, you better believe I would stop it!" May answered, laughing.

Sam and Nick were at the Lynch household, watching as May was putting the final preparations on the salad they were having with dinner.

"Your father will be home any minute, even with this crazy storm, and I'm sure he'll want to eat as soon as he gets in the door. You two better go wash up."

"What if the power goes out? We wouldn't have to wash our hands then," Nick bantered.

"Yes we would, dumb ass, the water would still work," Sam scoffed.

"Oh yeah? Well, with no lights it would be too dark for her to see if we were dirty or not," Nick interjected, pleased with his logic.

"Wash. Now." May interrupted, ignoring her son as she stirred in the last of the tomatoes. She always liked to add the tomatoes last so they wouldn't bruise as she stirred the rest of the salad, squeezing out their juice to make the lettuce wilt.

The boys ran for the bathroom, elbowing one another and giggling as they went. It appeared as though the weather was making everyone a bit crazy.

It seemed that each day this month had been either dry and raging hot, or had storms so severe that there were often tornado warnings, in which case everyone had to hightail it to the basement until the weatherman deemed it was safe to emerge again. Today it was a storm, one so angry and fierce the sky was a milky black, the storm clouds hanging so low May thought she could almost taste them.

May carefully folded the salad over onto itself, satisfied that it had been mixed properly, and added another sprinkle of shredded cheddar on top for good measure.

A boom of thunder cracked as soon as her husband walked in the door, startling her.

"Honey, I'm home," he called out in a sing-songy voice, making May giggle. The boys heard him as well, and rushed back into the kitchen, their sleeves wet up to their elbows. May sighed. You definitely had to pick your battles with those two. She supposed at least they were clean, even if they were all wet.

Actually, looking at her disheveled husband, who was now shaking off in the hallway like a dog, water droplets flying everywhere, it was May that was the odd one out simply by being dry. Laughing to herself, she went to help Pete with his coat, placing it on the coat rack and grabbing an old towel to put over the floorboards to catch the drips.

"Goodness, it must still really be pouring out there, huh?" she asked, giving him another towel for his head.

"You don't know the half of it. Sorry I was late getting home, but traffic was a mess. No one knows how to drive in a storm, it would seem, although you'd think people would be used to it by now!" Pete answered, rubbing his wet hair into the towel.

He glanced at the two boys standing in his kitchen, their sleeves completely soaked as well, but made no comment as he grinned at his wife, who just shrugged.

"All right, sweetheart, do you need any help with dinner? I'm starving."

"Nope, everything is all set. We're all ready to sit down."

"Perfect."

The family of four, which was as God and the universe always intended it should be, went into the dining room and took their rightful places around the table, always in the same four spots.

"Yum, fried chicken is one of my favorites," Pete said, taking a big bite and chewing it thoughtfully.

"I know all my boys like fried chicken," May answered, "and what with this crazy weather we've been having, I felt like we could use a treat."

"Good idea, Mom," Nick replied, his mouth full. "In fact, I think we could use a treat every day this month."

"Don't push your luck, kiddo."

As the family continued to eat and give one another light ribbings, as only a family can do, the lightning show continued to do a dance in the background, casting patterns on the walls of the dining room, the thunder punctuating every sentence.

And then, suddenly, the light above the table went out, and the house was shrouded in blackness

"Whoa, cool!" Nick exclaimed. "Did I call that, or what?" His mouth was full, as it often was, but luckily no one could see it. Only the muffled sound of his voice gave him away.

"I'll go fetch some candles," Pete said, smiling, scraping his chair across the tiled floor as he got up. "Tonight's dinner is going to be romantic."

This made the boys crack up, and May blushed, although the darkness saved her from being caught.

***

So strange, how one day you can wake up, and it's just like every other day, and you don't feel any different. But stranger still is how that one day can change your life forever, because after the events of that single day, waking up a boy but resting your head on your pillow that night as a man, nothing would be the same again. You never know you're in the 'before' until looking back in time from the 'after'.

It was the perfect storm of things that could go wrong.

It was the beginning of April, and unseasonably it was quite hot. Just the wrong time for the air conditioner at the Lynch home to go out. It was a Saturday, and Sam and Nick were hanging out in the living room watching TV, deeming it too hot to venture outside. So when the AC puttered and whined its final breaths of cool air, it didn't take long for the sun to soak through the windows and transform the Lynch house into a furnace of sorts.

"Oh man, this royally sucks. We can't stay here, I'm gonna melt," Nick moaned dramatically, so loudly that May had to shush him while she was on the phone with the repairman.

"Well, we could go to the community pool, that would cool us down. We haven't been there since we were kids."

"Nah, all the little kids piss in that thing, I don't feel like swimming in a big vat of pee."

Sam rolled his eyes. "Okay then, let's just go cruise around in your car; we can turn the air on or put the windows down."

"Nah, I'm short on gas money this week. I don't want to waste it just driving with no destination in mind. That sounds almost as bad as pee-swimming."

Sam offered up idea after idea, and Nick scoffed at each one, and as the temperature rose so did the boys' patience with one another.

"We could always just go to my house. It's not like we do that very often, and my dad's out day drinking with my uncle," Sam offered up, more as a joke than anything else.

To his surprise, this caused Nick to sit up and he said, "Wow, come to think of it I haven't been in your house in like a year. Let's stop by, I want to see how dorky your room is. Plus we could take Charlotte, show your mom how well she's doing."

"Seriously?" Sam asked, incredulous. "Of all the things we could do today, *that's* what you pick?"

"I just mean to stop by for a while is all, and Charlotte could use the fresh air and a change of scenery."

"I don't think my house is the scenery change she would be looking for," Sam answered wryly, remember why Charlotte lived at the Lynch home to start with.

"Oh, c'mon, your dumb shit father isn't there. Let's just see if you have anything interesting hidden away in that room of yours, then we can take Charlotte to the park or something."

Well, that part of the plan sounded good, although Sam wasn't entirely sure Nick didn't realize that he would be no cooler at a park with the sun beating down on him than he was in his own living room, but Sam wasn't about to interject. His friend could get very moody and hard to be around when he was bored. Or hot. Or hungry. Or horny. Or really, any combination thereof.

"Okay, lets go to my house. I do have a couple of cool new games for my game boy, and I just bought a new CD."

Nick nodded eagerly.

"But we're only staying a few minutes, okay?"

"Deal."

The boys gathered their things, sweat oozing out of their pores already.

"Mom, we're heading to Sam's for a minute, then we're taking Charlotte to the park," Nick cried to the empty kitchen.

If May wondered about their unusual destination she made no mention of it, as she was still on the phone with the man from HVAC who was apparently not free to fix the air anytime in the near future. She was running around trying to open all the windows that the cord on the phone would allow her to reach.

Sam put a leash on Charlotte and ruffled her fur, then the three of them climbed into Nick's car. For Charlotte's sake, they put the windows down so she could stick her head out and soak in her surroundings, inhaling all the new and unfamiliar scents along the way.

Nick turned the radio up so loud that the boys had to fight to hear one another, and Sam almost wished he could stick his head out the window to get some fresh air too, and a break from the blaring music.

The drive was a short one, of course, and Nick expertly pulled into the Maver's driveway. Making sure Charlotte's leash was securely fastened, the three got out and walked into the open front door.

"Mom?" Sam called, his voice carrying above the din of the TV. "Nick and I are here. We brought Charlotte; do you want to come see her? She's doing so well."

"What was that? You brought company? Oh Sam, the place is a mess."

"Relax Mrs. Maver, I'm not real company," Nick stated, helping himself to an apple that was sitting in a fruit bowl in the middle of the kitchen. There was a large bruise on the side, that he either didn't notice or didn't care about. The apple had been sitting there awhile.

Two boys and a dog made their way into the living room, where Patricia sat in a housecoat, her feet embedded into a pair of old and tattered slippers, watching TV.

She turned as the boys entered, and when she saw Charlotte a smile crept up her face, leaving one to get a hint of the pretty woman who those features once belonged to.

"Oh, boys, Charlotte looks wonderful!" she cooed, laughing as Sam undid the leash and the dog bounded over to her, licking her face, while Nick crunched noisily on his apple.

Sam smiled at his mother's sudden happiness. Maybe this had been a good idea after all. Seeing his mother smile, a real smile and not a pretend one, made his heart swell, and for that moment he felt happy too. It had been him who had made her smile. Well, maybe it was mostly Charlotte, but he was the one who owned the dog after all.

Thinking back after the fact, he wondered if that was the last time he would ever feel true happiness, the kind that you don't have to fight for or think about, the kind where there isn't an anxiety deep in the pit of your stomach. Where every smile doesn't have a frown ready in its wake, lying in wait for the owner to just… remember.

Because at that moment, the doorbell rang.

Curious, Sam left Charlotte with his mom and went to answer the door, and that was when his world changed. Everything prior to that door opening was the 'before', and everything since would become the 'after'.

Standing there with tears in her eyes, her angry father seething behind her, was Cindy Peterson.

At first, Sam didn't notice anything peculiar, except of course the fact that his old girlfriend who he hadn't seen since she had left school back in October was now standing at the foot of his stoop. Maybe he should have felt it odd that her father was standing protectively behind her, his arms folded across his chest, anger in his eyes.

Completely dumbfounded, Sam raised his hand in an odd and socially awkward greeting.

"Oh my God, Sam, what happened to your hand?" Cindy asked, the first person to speak, staring outright at the missing fingertips on Sam's hand.

Normally when people posed that question to Sam, if Nick was around (which he usually was), Nick would start shouting out all sorts of silly answers, each more ridiculous than the last. "It was a crocodile!" "It was a shark attack!" "He tried to use a chainsaw while blindfolded!" And the always popular, "You should see how the other guy looks!"

"Oh, uh, frostbite, actually," Sam stammered, having no clue as to why Cindy was suddenly here, now, in front of him, discussing his missing fingers. It almost felt as though no time had passed at all between them, that she was his girlfriend and they were looking forward to the big homecoming dance and everything was right with the world. Almost.

"Well, aren't you going to invite us in?" Mr. Peterson more stated than asked, as he put his hand on the small of his daughter's back and shoved his way past Sam into the house. Sam was jerked back to reality as he opened the door wider and stepped back.

"What is this?" Sam asked, totally bewildered, and Cindy started crying in earnest and whispered, "Oh Sam, I am so, so sorry about all this. I couldn't stop him, and I didn't get the chance to -"

Before she had time to finish her sentence, Nick and Patricia wandered in to see what the commotion was about.

Mr. Peterson gave a curt not to Nick, then said in a grueling voice, "Hello there, Mrs. Maver. Is Mr. Maver around as well? Because much as my daughter has tried to avoid it, the time has come to have a little chat about what your son did to her."

It seemed strange, thinking back on it later, that Sam hadn't noticed Cindy's bulging belly until right at that moment. Synapses started firing, connections were made, and Sam realized that Cindy Peterson was in fact one very pregnant Cindy Peterson.

"Your son needs to make this right. We just moved back into town, despite my daughter's wishes, because you need to make amends. Cindy can't do this alone, financially or otherwise. It's time to be realistic about the situation -" (here he gestured wildly at Cindy's belly, and she seemed to shrink down into herself - quite a feat considering her size) "- and it's high time that your son stand up and be a man about the situation. Where's your father?"

Sam couldn't have imagined it, but the storm got worse at that very moment. As if when Mr. Peterson spoke his name, it conjured Mark himself, who had unfortunately overheard the last words that had transpired.

Mark Maver, becoming the storm himself, swept into the kitchen where his family and Nick stood in bafflement, their mouths hanging agape. Some teenage girl, her belly ripe with pregnancy, stood crying miserably, her shoulders heaving up and down, snot running from her nose. And then there was another man, around Mark's age, who looked ferocious, guarding his young from harm... and the harm apparently consisted of his son.

"Just what the fuck is going on here? Who are these people in my kitchen?" Mark growled, trying to make sense of what was before him. Any time he didn't understand a situation, that meant he couldn't control the situation. And *that* was a situation that was unacceptable.

"I'll tell you what happened. Your son took my daughter to the homecoming dance last fall, and knocked her up. Cindy was so upset that we took her to a new school for a while, but now we've moved back to the area so that your son can step up and take care of our daughter. He needs to do the right thing. After all, it takes two to tango, so to speak..."

"Wait, what in the fuck are you talking about? My son doesn't even have a girlfriend," Mark said, angry and confused, the confusion fueling his anger.

Cindy glared at Sam through her tears.

Nick was staring at Cindy's protruding stomach, not able to avert his eyes, wondering if this were a dream or a nightmare or some kind of cosmic joke.

"Oh, they were definitely together, all right. I've still got the pictures my wife took of the two of them on their way to the homecoming dance to prove it. Cindy was crazy about your dumbass son, who clearly took advantage of her that night." Mr. Peterson pointed at his daughter's stomach for proof. She looked at the floor miserably.

"What in the fuck, Sam, is this true?" Mark glared at his son, his words spitting venom. "Were you and this whore together?"

"Don't call my daughter a whore. It was your son who -"

"I'm not talking to you," Mark said curtly to Cindy's father, his teeth gritted, his tone enough to make Mr. Peterson clamp his mouth shut.

"I thought you were at the bar with Uncle Ned?" Sam said meekly by way of an answer.

Mark laughed, but it wasn't a happy laugh, it was sinister. "Really, you think you can get out of this by asking where *I* was? They cut me off from drinking too much, they sent me home. *That's* why I'm here. Are you happy with that, you little shit? But thank God I came home when I did, to find out that my son is a complete disgrace."

"Maybe we should let your family talk this through. We will be back tomorrow afternoon to discuss logistics," Mr. Peterson was saying, some of the wind taken out of his sails when he saw who the dominant male of the room was.

"I think that's a good idea," Patricia said, finally adding something to the conversation. "Let me walk you out; we can talk a little more outside."

Mr. Peterson nodded, turned on his heel, and left through the open door that he hadn't bothered to close.

Cindy had just but a moment to whisper to Sam, and within ear shot of Nick, "I'm so sorry, they just assumed it was yours since we were together, Sam, and I couldn't bear to let them think I was with another guy that night. I'm so sorry I didn't say anything, I -"

"Cindy, get your butt out here, now!" Before she could say anything more, Cindy hurried outside to where her father and Patricia were standing, closing the door softly behind her.

Nick had yet to say anything at all, his thoughts were still churning, a wild ocean of questions and emotions. Remembering that day back in October, at the dance. The cool ground, the pine needles, the smell of oranges. Was it possible?

"You fucking idiot. You fucking little shit. You God damned whore," Mark was saying, his words coming out slowly, making them all the more frightening.

Charlotte let out a low growl.

There were still breakfast dishes on the kitchen table, and Mark picked them up, throwing them one at a time against the wall, watching with satisfaction as each shattered.

The boys could only watch, as gooey yellow egg remnants slithered down the kitchen wall, finally coming to rest in a sea of glass.

"This is un-fucking-believable," Mark said, his voice getting louder. He picked up a glass, still half full of orange juice, and slammed it against the wall, shards of glass flying in every direction. The orange and yellow may have been pretty, a work of art, if it wasn't so nauseating as it dripped down the wall.

Breaking the dishes seemed to get Mark more worked up, and he was warming to the idea of violence.

"How old are you, Sam?" he asked, slurring his words.

"Sixteen, sir," Sam replied meekly.

"I said, how old are you, you fucking moron? Speak up!"

"Sixteen, sir," Sam said, his voice louder and clearer than he had expected.

"Do you think a sixteen-year-old should be raising a child?"

"No, sir."

"Damn right they shouldn't. This girl's parents are gonna want a fortune from us. You know that, right? God damn money grubbers. This is going to ruin my reputation, ruin it! All because you couldn't keep your dick in your pants!"

Nick opened his mouth to speak, to correct the situation, but he found that his voice had deserted him, and he was too numb and terrified to speak. He could only watch as the situation unfolded, like he was watching a movie on the TV.

Mark opened the refrigerator with a clang and grabbed a beer, opening it and chugging half of it down with a few gulps. As if he was too angry to control his own body, he started pacing; kitchen to living room, living room to study, back to living room.

Unsure what else to do, the boys silently followed him at a safe distance.

"Sixteen years old. *Sixteen* fucking years old. My son, the asshole." Mark was muttering to himself, drinking another gulp of beer, already drunk even though it was about ten in the morning.

Charlotte came in and stood beside Sam, shaking, not understanding the loud voices but knowing her owner was upset.

"Goddamned dog, what is that mangy thing doing in my house?" Mark asked, finally noticing Charlotte.

261

"She was only supposed to be here for a few minutes. We can take her back to Nick's right now-"

"The hell you are; you aren't leaving."

He finished his can of beer, chucking it at the living room wall, and turned toward his son, his first born, his only connection to the world after he passed on from this life, and the hatred Mark felt was immense, incalculable. Mark went and stood beside his flesh and blood, calmly. A stranger looking in would have said that father and son must be sharing a bonding moment, since both of them were standing so near one another, so stock still. A moment that would bond them, perhaps, but not in a way that anyone would desire.

The abrupt calmness was eerie, the calm before the storm, when suddenly the proverbial skies opened. Something seemed to snap in the father, something that could be felt but not heard by the son.

"YOU FUCKING IDIOT!" Mark reached out and slapped Sam across the face, hard. Charlotte let out a whine.

"What in the *fuck* were you thinking? You are such an embarrassment. I wish I'd never had a son at all." Mark shoved Sam into the living room wall, causing him to lose his balance and fall hard on his bottom.

"Mr. Maver," Nick started weakly, but Mark was in such a trance he had forgotten Nick was even there, and seemed unable to hear him.

"Fucking cunt," he sneered, grabbing Sam by his left arm and dragging him upright again. Sam's arm twisted at a painful rate, and he felt a snap, followed by an immense amount of pain.

Not noticing or caring that Sam was now in tears, nauseous and light-headed from the pain in his arm, Mark dragged him by the arm through the living room and into his study. There he threw Sam into the base of his desk. Sam was on the ground, heaving, when his father grabbed him by the hair with one hand, the other hand around his neck, choking him.

Nick was in the doorway, and cried, "Please, stop. You're hurting him!"

Ignoring Nick, Mark spat on Sam's face as he squirmed, gulping for air. "I should just kill you right now, you son of a bitch," he hissed, his face red, droplets of saliva shooting out with each syllable.

Mark stood up, leaving Sam writhing against the desk, trying to catch his breath, terrified. He was no stranger to violence, to be sure, but this time felt different. Even the air in the room stank of hatred and pain.

Mark stood up and stretched, as if he had just finished a workout, and wandered to the other side of the study while Sam tried to stand up, Nick doing his best to help him.

The boy knew what he had to do. He realized he had known it his whole life, so it didn't even come as a surprise. He calmly went to the desk drawer, opened it, and picked up the gun. Without thinking it over, he pointed and shot once, twice, watching as Mark Maver fell to the floor, blood spurting out of his chest in a fascinating and gruesome arc.

CHAPTER EIGHTEEN

The sound of the gunshots reverberated, bouncing off the walls as the dishes had just moments earlier.

The boys stood staring at each other; the gun dropped to the floor. It was eerily quiet.

The quiet was stopped by the sudden sound of people as they hurried frantically into the house, alerted by the harsh noise. Patricia, Cindy, and Mr. Peterson ran through the house, each with the hair on the back of their necks standing up, and each knowing there was something to fear, without knowing exactly what.

Running into the study, the events started happening fast, too quickly. Thinking back, the boys could only remember bits and pieces.

Patricia screaming, running to her husband and throwing her arms around him. Cindy's eyes growing huge, the sweet stench of the blood alerting her pregnant belly, and her immediately throwing up in the corner. Mr. Peterson yelling, "Oh my God, where's the phone?" and disappearing to call the police.

"Mark, Mark!" It was Patricia who was yelling, cradling her dead husband's head in her arms, not noticing the blood that was covering her skin, working its way into her blouse, a stain that would never come clean.

Mr. Peterson's startled voice could be heard from the kitchen, yelling at the police, telling them to hurry. Cindy was still puking in the corner, spit and the remnants of her lunch running down the corners of her mouth. Charlotte was in the opposite corner, shaking, wanting to help but not sure how, trying to figure out the powerful scents of blood and vomit that were filling her nostrils and putrefying the air.

On auto-pilot, the boy picked up the dropped gun from where it landed next to the desk, its presence on the floor seeming odd and out of place. It felt lighter than it had the day they had learned how to shoot, as if the bullets it had released had carried the burden of the gun's weight.

It must have taken about ten minutes for the police to arrive, or maybe it was ten seconds; when asked about it later, the boys simply could not be sure.

But one thing everyone could agree on was what happened as soon as the police arrived. One officer ran to Mark and squatted down on the floor, holding two fingers to his neck. The other officer ran to the boy who was quite literally holding the smoking gun. The cop realized the boy was in shock, and eased the gun out of his grasp.

"He's gone," the first officer said, shaking his head. Patricia screamed and burst into violent sobs.

"I've got this one," the second officer answered, taking the boy and cuffing his hands behind him. Then he started reading the boy his rights.

As he was being led out of the room, his hands heavy from the cuffs, but his heart heavier still, Nick turned and blinked away tears he didn't know he'd been holding.

Sam watched in silence as the police hauled his best friend away from the room that housed his dead father. Cindy wandered over, looking wretched, put her tiny hand over his.

***

When Sam and Nick were about seven or eight years old, Nick thought of a fabulous money-making scheme. They would collect worms.

The idea was simple; they would get up early, because of the saying about the bird and all that, dig a few inches into the soft dewy ground, and quickly collect hundreds of worms which they would then sell to fishermen in the nearby area. The fact that Stony Meadows was in the middle of Missouri, with not a lake or a pond or a fisherman to be seen for miles, was not a deterrent to the boys.

In fact, true to the saying, Sam had suggested a foolproof way to find the hiding place of the worms. They would watch where the birds were landing in the grass, then dig in the same spots. Let nature tell them where the worms were hiding just below the surface. Nick thought his friend was a genius and a true entrepreneur. They would be rich.

One morning during the summer the boys collected the tools of the trade (buckets and small gardening shovels they had grabbed from Nick's tool shed, along with several Pepsi's and a box of Whoppers) and set out.

It was early by any means, eight o'clock in the morning or so, which the boys assumed was just past the crack of dawn, by the time they got their gear in place and arrived at their destination. There was a house nearby that was empty, it had been on the market for several months now, and the front yard had been neglected and was getting overgrown. It seemed the perfect refuge for critters to thrive. As if to prove the theory, several birds were sharing the yard with them, some in flight, some just hopping around rather inefficiently on their skinny little legs.

"I can't believe we never thought of doing this before!" Nick said excitedly as he passed one of the tiny metal shovels to Sam. "We're going to make a fortune this summer!"

"Yeah, there's gotta be a ton of worms here. I feel like this is a good spot," Sam agreed, tentatively digging his shovel into the soft ground.

"And no overhead either!"

"What's 'overhead'?"

"I don't know, but when I told my dad what we were doing, he said, "that's good, no overhead costs". I think it means something about that the worms are already here, we just have to find them. Or like, they're in the ground as opposed to over our heads. "No middle man", my dad said. Or maybe he said that we were the middle men, I can't remember. But either way, it's good business."

Sam nodded his assent, digging his hole deeper into the muddy earth, chopping into the dirt carefully with the tip of the shovel so as not to injure any of the worms that would soon be on their way to death's door.

"How many have you found yet?" Nick asked as he sorted through his own clumps of dirt.

"None yet. You?"

"Same. Maybe they just live a little deeper. Do you want to take a candy break?"

"Totally."

With his fingers caked in mud, Nick opened the box of Whoppers and poured some into his hand, then popped them all into his mouth at once. He passed the box to Sam, who did the same thing. Even though it was early, the sun was already warming the day and the chocolates were starting to get gooey and soft.

They boys each opened a soda, enjoying their break from doing man's work for the last five minutes. Then it was back down to business.

For several more minutes the boys dug holes in various areas of the ground, until Nick yelled triumphantly, "I"VE GOT ONE!"

"Really? Lemme see." Sam peered into the bucket as Nick tossed the wiggling, slimy worm into it. It swirled around on the bottom of the plastic, seeming to do an intricate dance.

"Cool," Nick said, as both boys watched the worm slither around for several moments.

"Very cool."

"Now we just need to find a few hundred of his friends," Nick said, digging vigorously. "How much money do you think we should sell them for?"

"I don't know, maybe a dollar each? If you figure each one will bring a fisherman one fish, that's a pretty good deal. Only a dollar for a fish."

"Hmm," Nick answered, thinking hard on this. "A dollar for a whole fish seems pretty cheap. Maybe we should sell them for like five dollars each."

"I don't know, that seems expensive for one worm."

"I do want to get a reputation as fair businessmen. How about three dollars per worm?"

"Sounds good."

The boys each looked back into the bucket, in which they now saw three whole dollars slithering around.

With renewed energy, each began digging into different spots in the earth, poking through clods of dirt with their fingers, each lost in their own thoughts.

Nick was counting money in his head, Sam was counting how long it was going to be until he had to go back home for lunch.

Twenty minutes and three worms later, the boys were starting to get hot and sweaty. Their fingers were caked in mud and chocolate; it was hard to tell which was which, but the residue cracked as it dried and hardened over their knuckles.

"This blows," Nick said, wiping his grubby hand on his forehead, leaving a dirt mark smeared all the way across like one long, mean eyebrow. "I'm hot and we don't even have that many worms."

"Yeah, this really isn't as easy as I thought it would be," Sam agreed. "Let's go sell what we have."

"Okay."

The boys stood up, brushed themselves off, and looked into their bucket of four small slithering worms. Nick carried the bucket since it held their financial future, while Sam scooped up the shovels, candy carton and empty soda bottles.

He certainly didn't want to litter, even if it was in an empty yard. No one would buy the poor lonely house if it was surrounded by a mound of trash.

"So…" Nick said, as they set off in no particular direction. "Where do the fisherman around here live?"

"I have no idea," Sam answered, a flaw in this plan starting to become obvious.

"Well, I guess we just go door to door then and ask," Nick declared, undeterred.

"Um…"

"It will be fine; that's how the Girl Scouts sell cookies and it works for them. Let's just go up to this first house here."

"Okay," Sam answered, always agreeable.

Nick knocked, then rang the doorbell, then knocked again.

Eventually a tired-looking woman with two screaming children in the background came to the door.

"Hello, what can I do for you?" she asked in the voice of a mother who hasn't gotten enough sleep in the past three years.

"We're selling supplies; would you be interested?" Nick asked in his most grown up, professional voice.

The woman smiled at the two dirty little boys on her stoop, curious, and asked, "What sort of supplies?"

Thrilled to be asked for more information, Nick proudly held the bucket up to the poor woman's face, just under her nose. "Worms for fishing, only three dollars each."

The woman let out a surprised scream and cried, "What on earth are you trying to do, scare the daylights out of people?"

Sam thought that an odd expression.

"Buy three get one free?" Nick offered sincerely.

"Uh, no thanks. Please take your foul 'supplies' elsewhere," the woman scoffed, and practically shoved the door in their faces.

"Well, that was a very rude customer," Nick mused. "C'mon Sam, lets go to the next house."

Surprisingly, each house they went to, people had much the same reaction; disgust over a genuine business proposition. The closest they came to selling a worm was when a young boy of about four or five answered the door with his father, and upon seeing the wares, begged and pleaded for his father to purchase a worm as a 'pet'.

But alas, even with the help of a child's temper tantrum, no buyers were to be had.

"Man, this seriously sucks," Nick said, the wind finally knocked out of his sails. "I can't believe there isn't more of a call for worms around this neighborhood."

"Yeah, I thought this would work better," Sam admitted. "So what do we do with all the worms now?"

"I don't know." Nick heaved a dramatic sigh fit for a businessman who has wasted his entire morning on a venture that left him no gain. "Find some birds to feed them to?"

"I guess we can just put them back where we found them, and watch and maybe some birds will grab them up," Sam suggested, not sure why he felt a sudden sadness about the impending death of the worms, since that had already been the plan to start with.

"Cool."

The boys wandered back to the original yard, which Sam noted was at least free from trash. They sat down on the ground and emptied the bucket of worms between them, waiting for a flock of hungry and appreciative birds to show up, but none ever came.

Instead, the boys ended up watching as the worms burrowed their way back down into the dirt, deeper and deeper until they were completely out of sight. If he hadn't known better, Sam would have thought they had never been above ground at all, content to living in the safety of darkness, and never seeing the clear light of day. After all, the open air brought danger along with beauty, so perhaps the worms would have been better off to not know what they had been missing.

Nick was talking, saying something about a new business venture that was somehow related to people betting on how many Whoppers he would be able to fit in his mouth at once, but Sam wasn't paying attention. He was thinking about those poor worms living deep beneath the earth, feeling sad that they now knew what it was like to experience the warmth of the sun, but knowing it was too dangerous to ever return to the surface.

***

It usually takes years for a boy to turn into a man, starting at puberty, and continuing at a pace made by life events. For Sam and Nick, the moment they became men was instantaneous, and later on could be identified easily as the moment that gun went off. Gone were the days of happy childhood treehouses and testosterone-filled high school parties. Suddenly, in an instant, everything changed. The moment the first bullet left the chamber of the gun, the innocence left them behind and each boy became more of an adult than he ever dreamed of being. Because with being an adult comes the extra feelings that one doesn't necessarily want: overthinking and second guessing one's actions, grief and pity, gratitude and guilt. All the feelings that a person, or a man, could ever possibly feel were rolled up into one nameless feeling, one that started in the pit of your belly and worked its way up through the bile in your throat until it reached the anxiety of your head.

The police were confused when Sam showed up to the police station shortly after their arrival there with Nick. The police were even more confused when both Nick and Sam admitted in full to killing Mark Maver.

Each boy was taken into a separate interrogation room, where each signed full confessions and gave a story so similar to one another, except for who actually shot the gun, that it was eerie.

The police scratched their heads. They had been expecting these two young boys to be terrified (which they were) and perhaps each trying to blame the other one for the shooting (of which the opposite was happening). The cops questioned and re-questioned, rephrased and then questioned again. They conferred about Sam's ability to shoot a gun based on his missing fingers; Sam insisted quite indignantly that his body had adapted and he was able to do everything he could before the accident. His handwriting may be a little more messy, but he could most certainly pull a trigger, rest assured.

There were two boys in separate holding rooms, each being interviewed, sweating and begging for water, shaking with worry and adrenaline. There were two men in separate holding rooms, each being interviewed, and each trying to play the hero to protect the brother of which a single drop of blood was enough to mean family forever. And family protects one another; old promises made had finally been followed through with, and the two men each refused to change their stories.

The police shook their heads, baffled. The boys were both arrested, as they each insisted they should be. The cops decided to put them in the same room together, where they watched in fascination from the next room, anonymous behind the shroud of the darkened mirror.

"What in the hell are *you* doing here?" Nick asked, shocked, as Sam was brought into his holding room.

Sam could only stare at Nick in response. His friend, normally so comfortable in his own skin, was sunk low in the old metal folding chair, his body too lanky to find any comfort on the already cold and unforgiving surface. Nick's hair was unruly, the way it looked after he'd been running his hand through it one too many times, and there was a sheen of nervous sweat on his brow and above his lip, mixing with just the slightest trace of what Nick commonly and with hope referred to as his 'mustache'.

Sam bit his lower lip, his own nervous habit. The searing pain in his arm had been somehow sent to the far reaches of his mind, almost as if his body knew that there were more important things to be dealing with in this moment. Was that what people meant when they used the phrase 'adrenaline rush'? That you could have a debilitating pain in one part of your body... but manage to *forget* about it? He gaped at Nick, all the thoughts in his brain churning around, trying to grasp at anything that made sense.

"Dude. I *said*, what in the *hell* are you *doing* here?" Nick asked again, as if by enunciating different words he may be able to get his point across more clearly.

Sam glanced to his right at what he knew was a two-way mirror. He wanted to choose his words carefully, but his emotions were running so high that he feared his own voice. He turned back to the folding chair, to the cheap wooden table, to Nick's un-cuffed hands splayed on it, his fingers tapping back and forth over the lines of the wood. Nick didn't seem to realize his hands were moving, and he stared intently at Sam, furrowing his brow.

Sam took a deep breath and focused on the face of his best friend, on the face he knew almost better than he knew his own. "Um... I could ask you the same thing."

Nick threw back his head and laughed in a way that was entirely serious. "Are you fucking insane? Like, are you being serious right now?" He peered at Sam and said, more quietly, as if he was explaining something to a child, "I shot your dad."

Sam's eyes grew wider but his stance didn't change as he said, "No, I did."

"Ha." Nick looked down at the table and seemed to notice the frantic pace at which his own hands were moving along the surface. Letting his arms drop to his sides, he used a toe to tip back his chair, so that it was balancing on the back two legs. He looked so casual in that position, a gleam of the simple high school student that he was only yesterday, suddenly apparent. With a carefree wave of his hand, he scoffed, "No, dumbass, you didn't. I saw he was beating you, like, really bad. I thought he was gonna kill you or something. So I beat him to the punch. So to speak."

Sam opened and closed his mouth a few times without making a sound, like a fish. Nick didn't drop his gaze, watching his friend, trying to bait this fish into defying him. The air in the room hung heavy and still.

Sam swallowed and got ahold of himself, replying, "Nick, why are you doing this? We both know that I shot him."

"Sam, come on, I'm a big boy. That means that you don't have to protect me anymore the way that you always did when we were kids." Nick looked intently at Sam, and let his chair fall back onto all four legs with a metallic clang. "I know you always looked out for me. You didn't think I noticed, all those years, but I did. And today it was my turn to protect you."

Sam shook his head, trying to clear it. "No, no that's not the way it happened…" he shifted his gaze to his right, staring into the mirror, almost as if he was looking directly into the souls of the officers who were on the other side, and added, "it's *not*."

Sam's reflection stared back at him, but at that moment Sam couldn't see himself. It was as if the suffocating, stale air in the room had simply wrapped around him and swallowed him up whole. For some reason, Sam thought back to that day not that long ago when he had been walking to school in the fog. He had been there, for sure, but anyone who happened to be standing about ten feet away from him would never have guessed at his presence. At the time it had been a comforting feeling, that he was alone and free. Now he had a similar feeling, but instead of comforting, it just felt... wrong. He wasn't alone and free, he was simply alone.

Nick had watched enough crime shows to realize who his friend was directing his last remarks to. He stood up and walked over to the mirror, until he was standing mere inches away from it. "This is bullshit! I shot him. I swear it! Sam didn't do anything!" His breath fogged up the glass as he shouted at his own reflection.

Sam hurried over and stood next to Nick, yelling and trying to be heard over Nick, "No, no! I did it, I shot my father, and Nick is just trying to take the blame!"

The boys shoved each other, elbowing one another and both trying to get into the center of the mirror, yelling toward it the whole time, each insistent that they were the guilty party.

Officer Tony Etindoer, who had been the arresting officer at the scene, stood baffled. He glanced over at his partner, who simply shrugged in response. Tony turned his attention back to the scene that was playing out before his very eyes. It would have been funny, had it not been so completely and utterly *un*funny. Never in all his time on the force had he seen such a display of two young kids who both appeared so determined to be sent to prison, and therefore declared the 'winner'.

"Remarkable, isn't it?" said James, who had been his partner for more than ten years. "I've never seen two kids trying to stick up for each other like that. Or even two adults, for that matter."

"Yeah... stoic, perhaps. But not at all helpful," replied Tony. "I'm going to talk to Matt about this one."

James nodded his assent. Captain Matt Daniels would really love this one. And he had thought it was going to be a quiet week.

Meanwhile, Nick and Sam had tired themselves out, and were now just standing quietly in front of the mirror, each looking at their reflections. It was a bit unsettling for the staff on the other side, but for the boys it was an important moment in their young lives.

Nick looked at Sam, his best friend since forever, the person that was his 'person' for life. Sam was not a violent person, he was the type to actually catch spiders from the bathroom and let them go outside, rather than take the opportunity to stomp on them and watch the guts ooze out onto the linoleum. Nick turned his head to look directly at himself. He was most definitely the spider-stomping type. Hell, he *liked* hearing the satisfying 'pop' after his sneaker made contact, thought it was cool to see what had once made up a spider end up as simply a gooey and inconsequential mess on the floor.

Nick squinted his eyes, and watched as his reflection followed suit. Here he was, in freaking jail for goodness sake, and he's thinking about spiders.

Nick ran his fingers through his rumpled hair, a nervous habit, and saw that Sam was watching him intently as he did so. Nick met Sam's eyes in the mirror, so that they were standing side by side and not facing each other, yet starring right at one another.

"I made a promise, do you remember?" Nick asked the mirror. "I told you that one day I would kill him. And so I did."

Sam let out a deep breath and both boys watched as his shoulders slumped.

"All my life, I've felt that I haven't done enough to protect you," Nick continued, his gaze level. "Let me protect you today."

As the boys watched, their mirror images grew in that moment. Not in stature so much, not in any physical sense exactly. It was something in how they held themselves up, maybe a bit taller, their chests more puffed out? Perhaps it was something in their eyes, eyes that had seen too much, bodies that felt too much. Most definitely it was because the day's events had forever changed their worlds, because what constituted 'normal' yesterday would not be 'normal' tomorrow.

The boys were quickly let out on bail, thanks to the Lynch family. (Who knew each boy would use his one phone call to call the same house? The police shook their heads, astonished.)

Nick and Sam had woken up that morning as boys, but they walked out of the police station that day as men, their footsteps a little heavier, their worlds forever changed.

Lawyers were hired, tears were shed, both of hatred and of thankfulness. Since neither man was willing to change his story, it was the ballistics report that told the real story, for only one boy had gunshot residue on his arms.

During her interview with the police, Cindy had tearfully broken down and stated that Nick Lynch, and not Sam, was the father of her unborn baby. She was beside herself; had she stated the truth earlier, would Sam's dad still be alive? Was this her fault, starting with a small lie that turned into something too big for her to go back on? Something that had so drastically altered the course of so many lives? No, she didn't know who had pulled the trigger, she hadn't seen it, and she could hardly believe when the policed announced who was to blame. Could this make her go into labor early? She'd seen that happen to some woman on a TV show once. The woman had been in an overly stressful situation, and this certainly qualified as the same. Could she leave the police station now to go to the hospital, pretty please?

The interviews with Cindy's father and Sam's mother were less eventful, and each party was dumbfounded to learn the true father of Cindy's child. Mr. Peterson was left to forever second-guess his actions on that day. If he had never dragged his daughter over to that house, where that maniac lived, all to *blame the wrong boy...* well, it was a question that would remain unanswered, one that would haunt him for the rest of his days.

Patricia, for her part, grew oddly calm. After the devastation of that day, she seemed to recede inward, even more so than usual, and didn't talk much. She wouldn't speak to either boy, and she only answered questions that the police made her believe she had to answer (no, she didn't need a lawyer). She didn't know anything anyway, she had been outside during the shooting. No, she wasn't aware that Sam's ex-girlfriend had gotten pregnant by Sam's long-time friend. She hadn't in fact known that Sam was dating anyone. No, she wasn't sure if Nick was the jealous type; didn't know him well at all, in fact. Yes, she supposed her late husband was hard on Sam. Too hard? Probably. Violent? Well, that was harder to say, you see he had a temper...

In the end, the case never even went to trial. After conducting multiple interviews the police and the judge decided this was a clear cut case of self-defense, and both men were released in every sense of the word to live another day.

The sound of the bullet was deafening, much louder than the boys had remembered it being that day outside when they'd first learned to shoot. The noise throbbed in their ears, almost as though the sound was a tangible thing. The boy who pulled the trigger let the gun drop to the floor and raised his hands to cover his ears, trying to block the sound that seemed to be echoing in his brain, bouncing between his ears. He tried to block out the sight too; the dark red of the blood, more of a maroon really, as it gushed out of the wounds on Mr. Maver's chest. He watched as the man's shirt was taken over by shades of blood so dark they looked almost black by the eerie light of the lamp on the desk. They grew into bigger and bigger splotches, expanding outward as if the blood was a force that needed to grow in order to be understood and appreciated.

He tried to block out the lifelessness in the man's eyes. Where moments before there had a been a life, now there remained only a shell. The arms had fallen to his sides as he laid slumped against the wall, looking almost as though he were resting. The hands, at first, seemed calm until one looked harder and took notice that the fingers were still clenched with anger. But even if a person had looked at Mr. Maver, slumped as he was, and somehow missed the bullet wounds and the bloody mess that was soaking onto the floor (and really, how could anyone miss all of that!), one would still have realized right away that Mr. Maver was no longer among the land of the living. For as he stared out from his final resting place on the floor behind his desk, any passer-by could see that Mr. Maver was looking through eyes which had gone empty, and still. But if the eyes are the window to the soul, only a select few would realize that the father's soul, all that was good and fair and right in him, had died long before the bullet pierced his chest.

CHAPTER NINETEEN

It would have seemed like any ordinary day... except for the fact that there was nothing ordinary about it. On the day that Sam and Nick returned to school, they could feel the eyes boring into them. Some were judgmental, many were sympathetic, but above all else, those eyes were full of questions.

Students spoke in hushed tones as the boys walked past, busying themselves with tasks of sudden great import hidden in the depths of their lockers, their faces hidden. Once Sam and Nick walked on, the students would elbow one another, pointing and whispering as their backs were turned.

Sam, by nature, was more accustomed to the quiet, but Nick seemed haunted by it. He shuffled along down the hallway, not looking up, not wanting to accidently catch the eye of anyone he passed. He heaved his books protectively against his chest as his book back hung slack on over his shoulder, as though he'd forgotten its primary function.

The teachers doled out sad smiles and Sam's geometry teacher actually gave him a thumbs up and a pat on the back, which only drew attention to the situation. Sam returned the smile anyway before taking his seat. He cracked open his math notebook and turned to a fresh sheet, sharpened pencil at the ready, determined not to let his grades slip.

Sam wouldn't have a class with Nick again until the afternoon. He was hoping to run into him in the hallway between classes. Normally they saw one another as they passed, Sam on his way to English as Nick headed the opposite way to Spanish, which they thought was amusing. Sam liked to joke that Nick hadn't even mastered English yet, and Nick agreed, usually shouting something like, "No habla Espanol! No habla English, either!" Often he'd turn around and pretend to start walking with Sam, saying he was giving up on Spanish and that he'd like to give English another go. (Sam was enrolled in Spanish as well, but in a different class. However, he knew from tutoring his friend that Nick could really only ask "where's the bathroom?" with any sort of proficiency, and his only real goal was to convince Mr. Gonzalez to teach him how to use curse words in another language.)

The clock ticked by annoying slowly, but eventually the bell rang, signaling the end of class. Sam stood up and stretched, then tucked his books into his bag and hurried out of the room in just a few long strides, wanting to get out into the hallway as quickly as possible.

Sam felt his shoulders sag a bit when he got all the way from geometry to English without laying eyes on his friend. Perhaps Nick forgot something in his locker, or had to use 'el bano'.

Sam took his seat in English and took out his books. He found his pencil as well, its edge worn smooth from all the math he had jotted down in the last class, and he sharpened it again. Sam liked to have sharp pencils; it helped him to write more legibly, and what with his forced new handwriting technique, he figured he could use all the help he could get. There was also something satisfying about watching the little strip of waxy wood grow longer and longer as he spun the pencil into his plastic sharpener. He tried to turn the pencil gently, in an effort to get the wooden spiral to stretch as long as possible before it broke off. Sam also liked to see how much of the pencil shavings he could cram into the clear plastic holder before he was forced to empty the sharpener.

Nick liked newly sharpened pencils also, but mainly just because they worked better when you shot them straight into the air to lodge into the ceiling. Most of the desks where Nick sat had a pencil or two hanging from the cheap ceiling tiles above, threatening to rain down unexpectedly on the perpetrator that put them there in a supreme act of karma. Whereas Sam wore his pencils down until they were just a nub, barely longer than the nub left of his finger, Nick rarely kept a pencil for very long. Sam mused that the Lynch family probably spent quite a bit of money replacing Nick's pencils, and he wondered what excuse Nick offered up for the whereabouts of all the pencils he 'lost'.

Sam was so lost in thought that he was startled when the teacher called his name, but he was still able to answer the question when asked. Even though he had missed nearly two weeks of school, Sam had a knack for understanding his studies, and English had always been one of his better subjects. He felt his tense shoulders relax a little as the teacher nodded her approval before moving on to the next victim in grammar. Sam knew that he would get caught up on his work in no time, and he was pretty sure he'd be able to help Nick to do the same.

His thoughts back on his friend, Sam wondered what Nick was currently doing in his class. Was he dutifully conjugating Spanish verbs into his notebook? That was pretty doubtful. Perhaps he was tilting his chair back in an effort to get a better angle at shooting his pencils into the air? That was more like it. Sam just hoped Nick wasn't as sullen as he had been during the car ride to school that morning. He had greeted Sam with a smile, but had barely said a word during the drive to school, which was unusual to say the least.

By the time lunch finally rolled around, Sam was carefully balancing his tray so as not to allow his bread roll to do as its name suggested and escape from the tiny little plastic divider that was the only thing keeping the bread from the dingy cafeteria floor. He was so intent in his concentration that he didn't notice Dylan until they nearly bumped into each other.

"Hey there, man, good to see you back again!" his old friend said uncertainly. Sam noticed him hesitate, then relax as he broke out into a grin. "C'mon, sit with us."

Sam nodded and followed Dylan to a table near the center of the room, where he saw with relief that Nick was already sitting. A few other students, all popular, were sitting at the table as well, and they were laughing. Jessica laughed so hard that milk threatened to spill out of her mouth. Horrified, she clapped her hand over her mouth and squeezed her lips together, which forced the milk to shoot out of her nose instead.

This sent the group into peals of laughter, with the exception of Jessica, whose face had turned a dark shade of crimson.

"Here," Sam said to her, handing her his napkin as he carefully sat his tray across the table from Nick. She took it gratefully and began dabbing up the milk that had soared over her tray. The little divider holding her bread roll was now full of the liquid, leaving her soggy roll to resemble a lone island.

Nick grinned as Sam sat down between Jessica and Dylan. "Wow, Jess, I know my joke was funny, but you're really milking it!" Everyone at the table hooted at this show of wits, and even Jessica gave him a wry smile.

Sam looked across at Nick and managed to meet his eye, raising his eyebrows in a question. Nick answered with a half smile and a shrug. Sam nodded and grinned, and that was that.

***

Nick was beginning to enjoy his newly acquired celebrity status at school, but at home he tended to overthink. Thinking was something that Nick normally didn't enjoy, so overthinking was just downright annoying. Still, though, it was hard to control... which made him think about the fact that he was thinking too much. Then Nick would just end up confused, and would go turn on the TV instead.

When Nick had allowed his mind to wander in the past, it had always been about girls, or parties, or how he could convince his buddy Brian to score him more alcohol and how to convince Sam to drink it with him. His thoughts would drift to what television shows were hot, which would lead him to wonder about whether he was good looking enough to score a girl like Candace Cameron on Full House, and that thought would lead him to think about the girls in his class with the biggest boobs, and that would make him think about how to remove a girl's bra with more efficiency than he was doing now, and eventually he'd grow tired of thinking and would just retreat to his bedroom to jerk off.

Now, though, things were different. Now, everything was different.

Nick ran his fingers through his hair as he considered the events of the last several weeks, sighing as he leaned back on his the pillows he'd stacked up against the headboard. His room was dark, it was just past eleven o'clock at night after all, and Nick knew he should be sleeping. Why was it, when a person knew they needed to sleep the most, that it became virtually impossible to fall asleep?

Normally sleep never eluded him. His father often joked that as soon as Nick's head hit the pillow, he'd be dead to the world, no matter where he was.

Dead to the world.

Nick shifted his weight and made an attempt at fluffing up the pillows behind his head. He had asked Sam yesterday if he'd been having trouble resting as well, but Sam said that he'd actually been sleeping better lately than he had in years. That answer had surprised Nick, but Sam had responded quietly and with his eyes misting over just a bit, that he didn't have to 'sleep with one eye open' anymore. Sam had said that he could finally let himself relax, probably for the first time in forever.

Nick closed one of his eyes, and quickly decided that it would be impossible to actually sleep with one eye open. Whoever made up that saying must have been a complete idiot. He turned his one eye to the digital clock on his nightstand, then closed that eye and opened the other, watching the numbers as they changed in perception. No matter which eye he used, the clock still said 11:08. Eleven-oh-eight. Ate. Nick was hungry.

He kicked at his sheets until he managed to untangle them from his gangly legs, and threw his feet over the side of the bed. He squeezed his toes, feeling the carpet fibers tickle the soles of his feet, then stood up and quietly padded to the kitchen.

Nick opened the refrigerator and stared at its contents, hoping something appealing would magically position itself right up front so that he didn't have to root around digging for something decent to eat. Luckily, his mom had made some kind of dessert involving banana pudding and Cool Whip, and it was on the top shelf.

As quietly as possible, Nick reached for the glass bowl which was heavier than he expected, then grabbed a spoon from the silverware drawer, closing the drawer with a bump from his hip. He then took his find and went to sit down at the kitchen table. Not bothering with a bowl, he simply dipped the spoon into the creamy concoction and shoved a giant bite into his mouth.

"Hey there, what are you doing up?"

Nick jumped a little, startled as his father joined him in the kitchen, and shrugged.

"Hmm, leftover dessert. Nothing wrong with that." Pete grabbed a spoon for himself, then sat down at the table opposite his son and dug his spoon into the pudding as well.

Nick nodded, and the two ate in silence for a moment.

Pete chewed thoughtfully on a chunk of banana, then swallowed and said, "Have you been having some trouble getting to sleep tonight?"

"Yeah, I guess so."

"Hmm... just tonight, or for a while now?"

"A couple weeks, I guess."

"Ah. I figured as much." Pete took another spoonful of dessert, then added, "You know, your mom and I don't blame you for what happened, right? With any of it, I mean."

Nick had a mouthful of pudding in his mouth, and he swirled it around with his tongue, pushing it up against his teeth, then to the roof of his mouth, then into his cheeks. Then he swallowed the whole thing in one gulp and replied, "Yeah, I know. You told me."

"Yes... well..." Pete licked off his spoon and set it down on the table, then steepled his hands in front of him. "I know we discussed what happened with Sam's dad. You know, the court said that it was self-defense, something that couldn't be helped, and that neither of you boys were at fault."

When Nick nodded, Pete continued, "Honestly, I'd say that man got what was coming to him. Now, don't go telling your mother I said that, but that's what I believe. If someone isn't a good person, if someone intends to do harm to others, than that person really shouldn't be too surprised when harm comes right back to them."

Nick grinned at that and nodded more enthusiastically. He dug his spoon into the bowl, churning the contents around and watching as the layered ingredients mixed with one another into a spiraled pattern.

"How's Sam doing with everything?" Pete asked, his eyes on the bowl as his son continued to twirl the spoon around.

"He seems ok, really. He was pretty weirded out at first, ya know, but he seems more relaxed. Things are still really fucked up between him and his mom though." Nick jerked his head up, ready to be scolded for cursing, but his father just smiled and gestured for Nick to continue.

"His mom is talking to him a little now, I guess, but they've never really been close anyway. Sam said something about feeling 'at peace' with what happened, so I guess that's good, right?"

"Yes, I think so."

"But it's weird though. Like, I get that his dad was a dick. But he was still his dad, you know, and how can you be at peace with that?"

"I think it's a pretty complicated situation," Pete answered thoughtfully. "Sam probably loved his dad, at least at some level, but you and I both know what kind of a person that man was. So maybe now that he's gone, Sam can just think about the good times they had together, without having to worry about any more bad times in the future."

"That doesn't sound so complicated to me," Nick mused. "It seems pretty simple, actually."

"Yes, I suppose it does."

Nick heaped a massive amount of pudding on to his spoon and brought it to his mouth slowly so none of the sugary substance would fall victim to gravity.

"And the two of you seem to be getting on pretty well, right?"

"Yeah, we're good. Things are kind of weird cause of, well, you know. But it's good. I mean, considering."

Pete nodded and said, "You guys have been through so much in such a small amount of time. Between Mr. Maver, and everything else..."

"I know, things are weird with Cindy too. But she's being pretty cool about everything, and we're both excited for the baby to be born."

"Yes... but that's another worry I have about you, Nick. I know when we all sat down with Cindy and her parents, everyone agreed that it was the best decision for the baby to be put up for adoption. But I'm concerned about the effect that could have on you and Cindy."

"Nah, it's cool."

Pete smiled and said, "It's a pretty big deal, Nick. Not something you can just brush aside."

"Yeah, but we've already gone through all this. I've talked about it with Cindy, and you and Mom about talked my ear off over it, too. Remember, during the same conversation where you went on and on about condoms and safe sex and being responsible and all that. Plus I talked to Sam. Adoption is the best way. We're too young. We're not even boyfriend and girlfriend for goodness sake."

"Are you sure you're not just parroting back the things other people have said to you?"

"Da-ad, that's a stupid expression. Plus other people might have said stuff like that, but I've given it a lot of thought, believe it or not. And I happen to agree with all that stuff." Nick set his spoon down and looked directly at his father. "Honestly, Dad, I have thought about it. I'm not ready to be a dad. This baby deserves a dad as great as you are, and I just can't do that."

Pete smiled sadly at his son, sensing the maturity that Nick had only recently gained. "You know, I think you will make a really good dad. You know, one day."

Nick smiled back and nodded. "Yeah, for sure. One day."

Nick fingered his spoon where it sat on the table, giving it a little push with the tip of his finger, sliding it forward until it clanked when it made contact with the pudding bowl that sat in the center. His thoughts shifted gears, as they so often did, and he looked back up. "You were right though, Mr. Maver was a jerk who deserved to die."

Trying to keep up with the backtrack in conversation, Pete answered carefully, "I didn't say I thought he deserved to die."

"You didn't *say* it exactly... but did you *think* it?"

Pete started to answer, but then he looked into his son's eyes. Nick, who he had been so worried about, the boy who may never grow up, who was now wise beyond his years. For the first time, he gazed at his son as he might an equal, and said truthfully, "Yes, I thought that. Every day of my life."

If the comment surprised Nick, he didn't let on. Rather, he smiled knowingly, and replied, "Me, too."

The boys looked at each other, locking eyes. Both pairs were frantic, pupils dilated. One pair shed tears openly while the other pair were opened as wide as possible.

The boy who had so recently fired the gun now dropped it as if it were on fire. It fell to the ground with an unceremonious thud. He looked at his hands, empty now, as if they didn't belong to him. After all, guns were to be shot in TV or movies. Or in the woods where the bullets were aimed at makeshift targets, and no one could ever get hurt. Or it was something you heard about on the news, something that bad people did to other people. It didn't happen in the normal, everyday houses in mid-Missouri. It didn't happen in Stony Meadows. And it was certainly never the good *people that were doing the shooting. Was it?*

For a brief moment after the gun went off, there was silence. Then the other boy looked toward where the gun had dropped. Without thinking, simply allowing his body to respond, he rushed toward it. Not hesitating, he picked it up. The boy who had dropped the gun stared at his best friend, who now held the gun firmly in his grasp, his hand shaking slightly. The boy who had pulled the trigger, who had fired the bullets, who had dropped the gun, now shook his head back and forth, confused.

The boy now holding the gun stayed put. For reasons he didn't understand, he knew this was something he had to do. He owed it to his friend. For years now, he had owed him this.

Looking down at the weapon, the boy found it almost impossible that this inanimate object had the power to cause such damage, as could be seen in the heap piled against the wall of the study, the remains of what just a few moments ago had been a human being. He felt the weight of the gun in his hand as well as in his heart. This was what needed to be done. This was right.

The boy holding the gun glanced back at his friend, who was now shaking his head more vehemently as tears continued to streak down his face. Nick looked back down at the gun in his hands. He needed to do this for his friend. Sam was the innocent one. It should *have been Nick who killed Mr. Maver.*

He was simply righting a wrong, making the events go as the universe had always intended.

As a door opened and closed, and the sounds of people rushing through the house echoed into the study, the boys stared at one another in an eerie calm.

"Let me protect you," Nick whispered, clenching the gun tightly in his fist. It was as if the gun had become a part of him, a protrusion of his hand. He couldn't drop it. And he was still holding it a few minutes later when officer Tony Etindoer finally pulled it from his grasp.

CHAPTER TWENTY

"That's a good girl. C'mon now, bring it back!"

Dutifully, Charlotte clenched the stick in her teeth and trotted back to where the boys were sitting on the back porch, dropping it at their feet. Nick picked up the stick again and threw it, and the boys laughed as the dog bounded after it, hurling her body through mountains of fallen leaves.

The breeze picked up, gently tugging more leaves off the trees, sending them billowing down to join their already fallen brethren on the soft earth below. Sam wrapped his jacket a little tighter around his shoulders and Nick tugged his ball cap further down onto his brow.

Charlotte trotted back over and dropped the stick again, wagging her tail in anticipation. This time Sam picked it up and threw it across the yard, and the dog tore after it with a flourish.

"Man, I can't believe you're finally gonna get a car. It's about freakin' time," Nick said, leaning back to rest on his elbows.

"I know. I'm pretty excited. Between my savings and the extra money that Mom said she'd give me for my birthday, I should be able to find something pretty decent."

"Yeah, it's cool that you and your mom are getting on better now."

"I know, it's still weird but in a nice way. She is even planning on coming to watch me when the debate team competes next week."

Nick rolled his eyes. "Only you would find such a lame club to join. Who wants to sit there arguing with strangers, for fun?" Nick made air quotes with his fingers as he said the last few words.

Sam laughed. "It's challenging, and it really can be fun. I don't know, I think maybe I'd like to be a lawyer one day."

"Oh yeah? That would be pretty awesome. You'd get to, like, bang that little hammer and yell, silence in my court!'"

"Actually, it's the judge that does the whole gavel thing. But I think maybe I'd like to work with child advocates or something. I could help kids who don't have a good home life, do family law, stuff like that."

"Oh, wow. Yeah, that would be sweet! You'd be really good at that, Sam, seriously."

"I don't know, it's just a thought. But it's something I'm definitely interested in."

Nick nodded and tossed the stick again as it was dropped at his feet. "I don't know what I want to do with my life. Maybe be a professional football player. Or basketball. Or maybe baseball. I also think it would be cool to be a teacher."

Sam coughed back a laugh and said, "Really? But you hate school!"

"Yeah, when I'm forced to be there. But if I was the one who got to dole out the assignments, instead of the person having to *do* the assignments, then that might be okay."

Sam grinned, playfully nudging his shoulder into Nick's side. "Well, I think you have some time to figure it out. We won't even be seventeen for a couple weeks yet."

"True," Nick admonished. "Maybe by then I will have changed my mind. Like, I could probably be a really good porn star."

Sam threw back his head and laughed in earnest as Nick grinned and shoved him back.

Charlotte returned and climbed onto the porch, dropping her stick on the stairs. She came over behind where the boys were sitting, walked in two complete circles, then laid down behind them, her head butting up against Sam's back. He changed his position so that he could reach around and nuzzle the dog between her ears, and Charlotte let out a contented sigh.

"So anyway, are you gonna go to the homecoming dance this year?" Nick asked, glancing sideways at his friend. This could potentially be awkward territory.

Sam shrugged and replied, "Probably. I was thinking of asking Meagan. We've been getting to know each other more since we're both on the debate team now. She's really smart, and sweet."

Nick nodded his approval. "She's pretty cute. That would probably be okay."

"Gee, thanks for your permission," Sam quipped.

"Whatever, you know what I mean," Nick laughed. "Plus, I'll be busy with my own date."

"Yeah, that I'm sure of. I seriously can't believe you ended up with Sarah Connelly as your girlfriend. You used to hate her."

"What can I say? She started investing in miniskirts, and I started paying attention."

Sam grinned and stroked Charlotte gently on her back. Her eyes fluttered closed.

"Plus, I heard that Cindy will be there, too," Nick offered.

"Yeah, she told me. We've been talking quite a bit lately."

"Us too. I'm really happy she transferred back here for school."

"So am I. She was so quiet after everything, but once she returned to school after having the baby, she seemed better."

"Yep. Popping out a kid will do that to a person. 'Cause she was really fat, but now she's not," Nick said matter-of-factly.

"I don't really think that was all there was to it," Sam replied, grinning because he knew his friend was joking.

It had been rough there for a while, for all of them. Cindy re-enrolled in school, but had to miss several weeks because of the birth of the baby. Nick surprised everyone by dutifully bringing Cindy her assignments each and every day so that she wouldn't fall behind in her classes.

Cindy had had a son, and they had learned that the adoptive parents named him Bradley Grayson. Bradley was a healthy baby, and Mr. and Mrs. Agave seemed like truly amazing people. Nick was sure upon meeting them that they would make excellent parents, and they even agreed to let Nick and Cindy know how Bradley was doing from time to time. Cindy had mentioned during the whole adoption process that as soon as the young couple walked into the room, she 'had a good feeling' about them and knew these were the right people to raise the baby. Nick had agreed at once, adding, "Since this kiddo is lucky enough to let us choose his own parents, I'd say we found a good deal. And I don't even like shopping." Cindy had shaken her head.

"Have you heard anything from the Agave's lately?" Sam asked.

"Not lately, but they said they'd check in every six months or so. Cindy has Bradley's newborn picture tucked into the frame of the mirror in her room, I've seen it when I used to go by there with her homework. Do you think that's weird?"

"Huh," Sam replied, stroking Charlotte's fur. The dog let out a small snore. "I don't know, I would think that would be kind of a painful reminder."

"See, that's what I thought, too!" Nick said triumphantly. "But I asked her about it once, and she said that it doesn't make her sad, that it actually makes her happy. She said that she knows that she and I created this wonderful thing, and that now he has a good life."

"That makes sense, I suppose. I guess it's good to remember all the parts of your life, even the ones that didn't turn out the way you expected them to. It's what shapes the person you become."

"In that case, maybe I should put a condom in the frame of my mirror, you know, so I never forget about that particular part of my life."

Sam glanced at Nick, and both boys burst out laughing. Charlotte lazily opened her eyes, but upon seeing that her people were both smiling, she closed them again.

Still chuckling, Nick added, "Seriously, though, things are good with all that. Cindy still sees that counselor, the one both of our parents made us go to. She says she's working through everything but that she is doing really well, and she knows she made the right decision for her, but especially for Bradley."

"That's good, that's really good. And I'm glad all three of us can still talk and stuff. For a while there I was worried that it would be weird."

"Um, dude, it *is* weird," Nick responded, grinning mischievously. "But I know what you mean. It's weird, but it's okay-weird."

"Yeah, whatever *that* means."

"Yeah."

Sam leaned back, gently resting his head against Charlotte's back and inhaled deeply. It was late in September and the air smelled of cooler temperatures ahead. He held the breath in his lungs until he could take it no more, than let it out slowly through his mouth.

"Hey, I was wondering about something," Sam said. "About that first day we were back at school. You know, after everything."

"What about it?"

"I don't know, I was just thinking. That morning, you seemed really worried, and you were so quiet. Then by the time I saw you at lunch, it was like nothing had happened."

"So?"

"So... obviously something changed. What was it?"

"Oh, well..." Nick trailed off, then cleared his throat and continued. "I guess I was pretty worried, about what the other kids would think and stuff. Some people were looking at me like I had two heads or something."

"I know what you mean."

"At first I thought, 'this is going to mess everything up', like with our other friends and stuff. But then I decided that I was going to stick to my original plan."

"Which was...?"

"My plan of having a blast in high school."

Sam scoffed, "And just what does that mean? You decide things are going to be fine, so therefore they just are?"

Nick grinned and petted Charlotte down her back, making a big show of 'accidently' petting Sam's face since he was still laying on top of her. Sam swatted his hand away.

"I mean, basically, I guess, I had Spanish class with Dylan, you know, and he kept staring at me. So I said to him, 'well, we've been sitting next to each other for that last ten minutes, and I haven't managed to shoot anyone or knock anyone up, so I guess we're good here'."

Shocked, Sam sat up and glanced at Nick.

"Yeah, I said it kind of loud so that everyone could hear. What was that thing that my dad always used to say? Something about beating people to the punch? Well, I figured that if I said something it might, like, relieve the tension."

"Wow!" Sam exclaimed, somewhat astonished. "I can't believe you said that!"

"Well, it seemed to work. Dylan's mouth kind of fell open, then Mr. Gonzalez told me that that would be quite enough, then everyone started laughing. We were almost ready for summer break anyway by then, so everyone was probably more chill than usual. And after that it was just kind of... okay. I mean, okay-weird still, but basically just pretty okay."

"Huh. Yeah, I guess that wasn't a bad idea then."

"Yeah."

Sam rested his head back on the dog, who hadn't stirred, and stared out thoughtfully. From this vantage point he could see the top half of the tree house, which still hung suspended in the tree, seemingly suspended in time. Some of the boards were warping a bit, and the tree itself had ballooned out. What had been small branches were now large limbs, obstructing much of the tree house from view. But there it stood, a testament to what used to be. He let his thoughts wander.

After Sam had been cleared of any wrongdoing for shooting his father, the police actually started to focus on his mother instead. Something about being negligent. But Sam had actually come to his mother's defense. He knew better than anyone what she had been through, and he believed that she was as much a victim as he.

For her part, Patricia seemed to morph into another person. It didn't happen right away, of course. She had been furious when she learned that her own son had pulled the trigger that killed her husband. For the first couple of weeks, she barely spoke to him; she was simply too angry and she didn't know how to release that feeling. Little by little, though, the anger started to dissipate. It wafted out of her in drifts and waves like it was a heavy and tangible thing, draining out through her head and shoulders and leaving her feeling lighter.

Soon, she and Sam had a long conversation. They both apologized. They both cried. They both hugged. And then, most importantly, they forgave one another for their actions.

It was as if an invisible line in the sand that had separated mother and son for all those years had suddenly been erased. Patricia was starting to take more of an interest in Sam's life. She was starting to take more of an interest in *her* life as well. She now went for a walk every morning, and just the other day she had accepted May Lynch's invitation to have lunch and 'girl talk'.

They still had a long way to go, their relationship was by no means perfect, but it was improving and that was something. Both Patricia and Sam were feeling more comfortable in their own skin, and around one another. Sam didn't yet know it, but his mother and May had recently set up another lunch date, in which to plan a surprise birthday party for the boys. Patricia already had a car picked out, and she'd put a down payment on it a few days prior. She had gotten a little insurance money, and she'd decided she'd surprise Sam with the car. Let him keep his own savings; he could use the money to take out that sweet girl he'd told her about, Meagan-something-or-other. Sam had flushed a little when he admitted that this girl smelled like coconut, and that he thought it was the most refreshing smell in the world. That had made Patricia smile.

***

When Nick and Sam were about seven or eight or somewhere in between, they had a camping trip together. Well, not exactly, but it was close enough. Pete had set up a tent in the back yard and the boys had been given permission to sleep there for the entire night. They had spent the evening dragging out sleeping bags and pillows and blankets. May packed up lots of snacks, she even warmed some marshmallows to make S'mores, and placed them in Tupperware containers inside the tent. The boys had stated that they would not be entering the house all night, and therefore would need food inside their campsite. They were especially looking forward to peeing on the tree rather than using the bathroom, as Nick had suggested.

The boys had spent the better part of the night doing all the things that they believed campers did. They wandered around outside of the tent, admiring how different the back yard looked at night, and pointed at stars. They snuck up to the tree house until they got eaten alive by mosquitoes, then they retreated back to the tent, zipping themselves safely inside. They told one another ghost stories as they munched on their treats, gooey marshmallow sticking to their lips.

The tent had a little built-in flap up top. There were two layers, and the inner canvas layer of the tent had been pulled back and secured with Velcro. This meant that the upper screened-in layer remained open, shielding the boys from bugs while allowing them to peer up above them into the night sky. A calm summer breeze blew in from the screened flaps on either side of the tent, cooling the warm air inside.

The boys were laying on their backs, side by side on top of their sleeping bags. It was too warm to actually get inside them, but the bags were still required because that's what real campers always used, even if it was the middle of summer. The days were unbearably hot and the nights could often be humid and sticky as well, but the forecast had called for a slightly cooler evening tonight, and it was turning out to be correct. The boys took deep breaths, filling their lungs with the cool, fresh nighttime air.

"It's pretty rad that your parents let you hang out over here so much; it's practically like you live here," Nick was saying.

Sam hesitated a moment, then replied, "Yep, it's pretty great."

"You spend the night here so much, it's like we're actually brothers or something."

"For real. Like we're best friends *and* brothers."

"Totally. Hey, that reminds me of something!" Nick sat up and crossed his legs Indian-style, peering through the hazy darkness at his friend. "I've got such a good idea!"

Sam looked up with interest. His friend's ideas normally were pretty good.

His eyes gleaming even in the dark, Nick went on, "Yeah, my dad was talking about it the other day. He was talking about how good of friends you and I are. He said we reminded him of *his* best friend when *he* was little. He said one day they took a knife and each stuck it into the palm of their hand, so that some blood squirted out."

Sam scrunched up his face. So far, this wasn't sounding like one of Nick's better plans.

Nick poked Sam in the side and continued, "No, it's cool! So then what you do is, both people press their hands together and the blood gets all mixed up. So then you are both sharing the same blood, and you become for-real brothers. We should totally do that!"

Sam started to catch some of his friend's enthusiasm. "Then we would actually be brothers, right?"

"Yeah, for sure, that's how it works! We'll be brothers!" Nick laid back down on his sleeping bag, pleased with himself. "Let's definitely do that tomorrow when we wake up."

"Okay, cool!" Sam agreed, warming to the plan. Tonight they would go to sleep as best friends, but by this time tomorrow they would also be family. Sam didn't much get on with his own family, so this sounded like a good idea.

"This will be awesome for sure!" Nick cried in delight, and Sam nodded. He was excited about the idea, but it was getting pretty late, and his eyelids were growing heavy.

The boys were quiet, laying side by side and looking up into the night sky. The branches of the tree that held the tree house blew softly in the breeze, but through holes in the canopy they could just make out some of the stars. They appeared like tiny dots of light when the rest of the world was shrouded under the darkness of a nearly moonless sky.

Thrilled with the idea of having a brother, Sam smiled to himself and casually scooted his body closer to Nick's. Best friends and brothers, just as the universe intended. Moving closer still, the space between the boys grew smaller and smaller, until their shoulders touched.

Then the boys fell asleep, dreaming of what the future might hold.

CPSIA information can be obtained
at www.ICGtesting.com
Printed in the USA
LVHW030010280219
609005LV00001B/11/P